POTIONS AND PAJAMAS
MIDLIFE MAGIC IN MEMORIAM BOOK ONE

KEIRA BLACKWOOD

ALSO BY KEIRA BLACKWOOD

Midlife Magic in Marshmallow
Sweatpants and Spells
Scrapbooking the Supernatural
Wrinkles and Runes
Hijinks and Hot Flashes
Crosswords and Curses

Forbidden Shifters
(with Liza Street)
Claimed in Forbidden
Fated in Forbidden
Bound to Forbidden
Caught in Forbidden
Mated in Forbidden
Forever in Forbidden
Destined in Forbidden

Forbidden Fangs
(with Liza Street)
Fangs and Familiars
Billionaires and Bodybags
Exes and Exorcisms
Cowboys and Coffins

Alphas & Alchemy: Elemental Shifters
(with Eva Knight)

Once Upon a Wolf

Dragon Guardian of Land

Wolf Warrior of Land

Dragon Guardian of Water

Bear Warrior of Water

Werewolves of Sawtooth Peaks

Running to the Pack

Defending the Pack

Uniting the Pack

Howling with the Pack

Leaving the Pack

Werewolves of Greenville City

Bodyguard

Enemies

Heir

Warrior

Scoundrel

Brawler

Werebears of Riverwood

Grizzly Bait

Grizzly Mate

Grizzly Fate

Shifter Protectors Unlimited

Can't Prove Shift

Suave as Shift

In Deep Shift

Shifter Protectors Quick Bites

(with Eva Knight)

Midnight Wish

I Dream of Grizzly

The Ocean's Roar

To Catch a Werewolf

Outfoxed

Tactics and Tails

Vampires & Chocolate

Vampire Prince Exiled

Vampire Prince Hunted

Vampire King Dethroned

Spellbound Shifters: Dragons Entwined

(with Liza Street)

Dragon Forgotten

Dragon Shattered

Dragon Unbroken

Dragon Reborn

Dragon Ever After

Spellbound Shifters: Fates & Visions

(with Liza Street)

Oracle Defiant

Oracle Adored

Spellcaster Hidden

Spellcaster Embraced

Spellbound Shifters: Standalones

(with Liza Street)

Hope Reclaimed

Orphan Entangled

Copyright © 2022 Keira Blackwood

All rights reserved.

No part of this book may be reproduced in any form or by any electronic or mechanical means, including information storage and retrieval systems, without written permission from the author, except for the use of brief quotations in a book review.

This is a work of fiction. Any resemblance to any actual persons, places, or events is coincidental. All characters in this story are at least 18 years of age or older.

Edited by Liza Street

CHAPTER 1

"You're FaceTiming me *from a public toilet?*" Scott's tone suggested this was the absolute worst thing anyone had ever done in the history of anyone doing anything.

Feet shuffled in the stall next to mine.

I put my finger to my lips, hoping Scott could see me better than I could see him. He was weirdly shadowed, with a harsh light blocking out everything but the vague semicircle that was his head. Was he hiding out in his office's supply closet? Held against his will in a police interrogation room? Or even the lab of an alien spaceship? It was impossible to tell.

"Rosemary." Scott sighed, loudly.

Shoes strategically placed on the toilet seat, I hugged my knees tighter to my chest, so tight I could hardly breathe.

The lady in the stall beside me cleared her throat in an exaggerated manner, flushed, and left without washing her hands.

"Was that a toilet flushing? You're not alone in there?

Ugh. Disgusting," Scott said. "Is the meeting over yet? Tell me you didn't leave the meeting to call me."

I wished it was over. More than anything, I wanted to run, to be anywhere but the bathroom of a two-bit lawyer's office, stuck discussing my recently-deceased mother's belongings.

"I know that look," Scott said. "Only children run away, Rosemary."

Sometimes it was smart to run. Sometimes it was all a person could do, like when they were being chased by an alligator, or when the stress of a situation ballooned so much they had to flee or they'd explode into a thousand squishy pieces.

"Never FaceTime me from a bathroom again," Scott said.

"I promise." I nodded my agreement. "I wish you were here."

Tears welled in the corners of my eyes.

"Keep it together. Don't let the lawyer talk you into doing anything with the funds. You know how you can be. I have to go. See you tonight." He hung up.

The tears I'd been holding back streamed down my cheeks. I wiped them away with some toilet paper, climbed down off the toilet, and headed back out to face the meeting I'd excused myself from.

Mr. Gross, Attorney at Law, stared at me through dull eyes from across his desk. Those eyes had a perpetually sad turn to them that had either to do with unfortunate genetics, or his occupation of delivering perpetually bad news. His appearance was otherwise sedate and unremarkable, traits he shared with my first almost-husband.

The security guard behind Mr. Gross was far sharper, a cobra poised to strike. She flared her nostrils as she stared at me. What threatening act she expected me to commit, I had no idea.

"Let us proceed," Mr. Gross said.

I sat down. He started talking.

I tried to figure out what Scott thought Mr. Gross would talk me into doing. He wasn't even my lawyer. This day was too much.

"All remaining properties of the estate henceforth belong to Noodles McDoodles Butterbelly."

The lawyer's monotone voice buzzed in the back of my head, an emotionless yet aggressive swarm of bees stinging my brain. Remembering I needed to breathe, I filled my lungs. The offensively dry air burned its way from my nostrils through my chest.

My stomach in my throat, I stared at the rusted key on the desk in front of me. The plastic diamond tag attached to it may have once been a deep red or orange, though the color had faded to something akin to diarrhea. The key looked at home in the dated, brown office with its wood paneling and puke-green carpet.

"Mrs. DeLaCrux, are you listening?" Mr. Gross asked. His voice sounded distant even though he was sitting a mere six feet away.

"Ms." I glanced up and blinked away the glassy haze clouding my vision. DeLaCrux was my mother's last name. It did not belong to the father I didn't know, and certainly not to my non-existent husband.

"*Ms.* DeLaCrux," Mr. Gross said. "Did you hear what I said?"

"Yes, of course." My mother had left me the contents of a storage unit that she had never mentioned renting. And she had left everything else to someone else. "Are you certain this is the correct key? It doesn't look like it belongs to the type of establishment my mother frequents."

Frequented. She could no longer go anywhere because she was dead and had been for eight months.

"I assure you it is the correct key," Mr. Gross said.

"Okay. Thank you." I plucked the key from the desk. "Do you always have security in these types of meetings? It seems…unnecessary."

I rose from my seat.

Mr. Gross bolted to his feet at the same time. His security guard circled around the desk toward me. Her hands remained clasped to her belt, hovering above her taser and zip ties.

"You understand you are not to go to the property or attempt to contact Mr. Butterbelly in any way," Mr. Gross said. It was unclear whether it was meant to be a statement or a question. But, he'd completely ignored my question.

And *Mr. Butterbelly?* It took me a moment, but then I recalled him saying that name during our meeting, possibly more than once. What an unfortunate name. Unless, perhaps, this mystery beneficiary was employed as a circus clown.

"I don't know who Mr. Butterbelly is," I said. "Even if I wanted to, I'd have no way to contact him."

"Mr. Butterbelly was your mother's cat."

Cat? "She doesn't have a cat."

Didn't have.

I had to be missing something, clearly due to brain fog. That's why I'd wanted my fiancé Scott to come with me. He hadn't, of course. His job as a financial analyst left no room for time off. My best friend Wendy would have dropped everything and called out sick for work at the animal shelter to come along, which was why I hadn't asked her. I couldn't.

I swayed on my feet. "Is that everything?"

"You have to sign, promising you understand the terms of your mother's will," Mr. Gross said. He pushed a paper and pen across the desk.

Understand it? No. I absolutely did not understand how my mother could drown in the Caribbean. She was a strong

POTIONS AND PAJAMAS

swimmer, and she hated both beaches and vacations. I couldn't fathom why she would travel to a small island during peak hurricane season. Nor could I comprehend how she could leave all of her earthly belongings, save for a storage unit, to a cat instead of to her only daughter.

I signed the paper, squeezed the key in my palm, and left.

The security guard kept pace by my side, apparently tasked with accompanying me out of the building. We stepped into the elevator. She pushed the button for the ground level. The doors slid shut with a click.

Her gaze burrowed into my cheek. I kept my attention ahead.

The elevator lurched and hummed as it sprung into motion.

"Are you okay?" the guard asked, with a surprisingly soft tone. "I've never seen a reading so…cruel."

The key dug into my palm, the stab of pain a reminder of what I did have, a distraction from what I had lost.

"My mother didn't have a cat," I said. "She hates cats."

The guard licked her lips. "You asked why I was there. Mr. Gross has been on high alert. I didn't get the specifics, but I'm glad for the job. Do you have someone who can drive you home? Is there someone we could call for you?"

"I'm fine." I tried to offer a placating smile. The expression was so practiced it almost felt real.

"I shouldn't say this, but you could get your own lawyer, contest the will. I can't imagine anyone would actually—"

The door opened.

I stepped out, turned back to the guard and said, "You don't know my mother."

Fortunately the elevator doors closed before her frown of pity could sear itself too thoroughly in my brain. What I needed wasn't pity. What I needed was to go home.

I zipped up my coat and folded the collar up so I wouldn't

have to make eye contact with the receptionist as I hurried out the front door.

Outside, I hardly felt the cold. Blinding sunlight reflected off freshly-plowed snow banks, remnants of a freak winter storm in what should have been solidly spring in Piccadilly, Pennsylvania. The wildflowers that lined the small city's streets had been in bloom for weeks already. They'd recover. And so would I.

Emotionally exhausted, I tucked the storage unit key into my purse and cracked open the door to my '98 Camry. A globular, carrot-colored something skittered between my legs and into the car. I yelped in surprise.

Had a monster-sized rat taken a bath in mac and cheese? Was that rat looking for a warm spot to sleep off its pasta coma? Maybe the orange thing hadn't skittered at all. Maybe it had been a basketball, and it had bounced. It could go either way.

I did a quick look up and down the parking lot for any sign of more of whatever it was before opening the door the rest of the way.

Keeping my distance, I bent down to get a look inside.

On the floor by the passenger seat, in the cardboard box that had been empty, was a loaf of fur, more yam than orange. In the center of the loaf, a set of big beady eyes stared up at me. Over the left eye was a spot of white, like a checkmark, or even an eyebrow. It was adorable. I let out a long breath and a cackle.

"Hello, kitty," I said. Unlike my mother, I had always liked cats. "Unless you're planning on going for a ride with me to an unfamiliar street far from your home, you should take this opportunity to come back out now."

In answer, the cat made the most un-cat-like noise I'd ever heard. It was a scream, really, and so loud that it could easily convince any passerby that I was murdering some poor woman.

I tried to take a step back, but my foot slipped. Ice. Of course there was ice.

Down I went, so slowly I had time to realize what a foolish mistake I had made, so quickly there was nothing I could do but hit the pavement. I *tried* to catch myself, but getting my hands down under me only made the impact on my wrists as rough as that on my bum.

I let out a hiss at the crunching, reverberating pain.

The cat went silent.

"Look," I said, no longer endeared by the cat's cuteness. "You come out, or I'm pulling you out, box and all."

The cat watched from its loaf state, its irises dancing with predatory instinct or laughter, maybe both.

"All right then," I said. "The hard way it is."

I reached in toward the box.

Fast as a fiddle, the cat shot its paw out of the box and smacked my hand.

I recoiled, laughed, then reached a little lower.

Like a game of whack-a-mole, the cat smacked at the box, following my hand. I grabbed the bottom and pulled the box a little closer so I could get a good grip and lift it up over the seats.

At the jostle, the cat launched itself up out of the box and returned to a ball shape. It landed on my head, scratching my scalp a bit, before scurrying down my back and out of the car.

I could still feel the tiny spots on my head and back where its feet had landed as I climbed into my seat and shut the door. I turned the car key in the ignition. With a *chuck-chuck-sputter,* the old engine tried to turn over, but failed.

"Come on." I summoned my best coach pep talk voice. "Please. I know it's cold, but we'll both be happier at home for the evening, right? It'll only get colder once the sun's down. Turn over. You can do it."

I gave the dash an affectionate pat, even though I'd rather have given it a bash or two with my fist. Then I tried turning the key again.

The engine roared to life. I threw victory fists to the sky, well, as far up as I could without punching the roof, and then I drove home before the car could change its mind about getting me there.

Scott's Range Rover was in the driveway. He was supposed to be at work for another two hours at least. Had he come home early for me?

A small sense of relief hit me as I hurried to the front door.

"Scott?" I slipped off my shoes and coat and made my way inside.

He wasn't in the kitchen or living room.

I started up the stairs.

I could hear his voice, somewhat tense as he spoke. There had been no other car, and there was no other voice, so he had to be on the phone.

I stopped in the hall when I spotted him. He was pacing in the bedroom, phone clutched to his ear, knuckles white. His dark curly hair fell down over his face, and his sharp shoulders curved forward.

I knocked on the door frame to let him know I was home.

He whipped around. "I've got to go."

He hung up the phone. The stress lines on his face faded, and he smiled.

"Hey," I said.

He tossed the phone on the bed. Little lines formed on the sides of his eyes as he approached me with open arms. "You're home."

"Yes," I said. "And so are you. I'm glad."

He pulled me in for a hug, and I leaned my head against his chest. But he pushed back so quick I almost got whiplash. Holding my shoulders he looked over my face as if there were some kind of amazing secret he was expecting me to share.

"How much are we getting?" he asked.

The *we* was interesting, as *we* were not yet married and every time I tried to discuss anything financial with him, he'd squirmed out of the conversation.

"Zero," I told him.

"I find it difficult to believe Lenore had no liquid assets." He let go of my shoulders and waved his hand at me. "But that's all right. The house is worth at least a million, low end."

"I'm not getting the house," I said.

Scott scoffed. "There has to be some kind of mistake."

"No," I said. Lenore DeLaCrux believed devotion to the all-mighty dollar was the only path to self-worth. Raised in poverty, she'd earned everything she owned through hard work. Likely she'd given away her fortune so I would follow in her footsteps. It wasn't surprising, but it did leave a small ache in my chest. I wasn't, and never had been, like her. I didn't want to be.

Scott was waiting for me to elaborate.

I said, "She left everything to a cat."

"I thought you said your mother hated cats. It was the one relatable thing about the awful woman."

I didn't find it particularly relatable. I liked cats. Also, she wasn't awful. She was a lot of things, but never awful.

"She did hate cats," I said.

Scott let out a long, slow breath and ran his hands through his hair. His curls diffused, leaving messy waves. When he spoke again, his voice was lower and despondent. "This is not what I wanted to hear, Rosemary."

My mother was dead. None of this was what I wanted either.

"I know," I said. I didn't have the energy to argue. "I'd like to take a bath."

Something flashed across Scott's face. I wasn't quite sure how to read his expression. And I was too tired to care.

He said, "You do that. I'll get you a glass of wine."

"That would be lovely, thank you."

He left the room. I started the water and poured in chamomile and lavender soap. Relaxing floral scents filled the bathroom as I gathered my towel and washcloth.

I was just about to get undressed when Scott returned with a glass flute and handed it to me. On the stem was a charm I'd made out of an antique ring and handcrafted beads ages ago, when I used to somehow find time for hobbies. The metal on the ring was dull, and one of the beads had a crack down the center.

I raised the glass to my lips and took a sip—white wine. Scott liked white. I preferred red.

I said, "Thank you."

He sat on the edge of the tub and crossed his legs. He stared at my lips, almost like he wanted to kiss me. But not quite. Was he waiting for me to say something else?

The sound of flowing water echoed off the tile. Steam filled the air.

I reached to set my glass on the counter so I could get undressed.

"Drink up," Scott said, stopping me.

I took another sip.

He rose from his seat, tipped the glass to my lips and smiled as I took a long swig.

The white wine was palatable, but I was looking for relaxation, not forced drunkenness. Of course that was a bit dramatic for a single glass of wine. Also, it was nice that he was showing an interest in my well-being. He'd worked so much lately, we felt more like two strangers passing in the night than a pair of lovebirds preparing for marriage.

I pulled the glass away and smiled back at him.

He tilted the glass up.

"There you go," he said as I finished the last of it. Then he took the glass and headed for the door. He turned back and said, "Everything will work out. One way or another."

My head swam. My pulse pounded. My vision swirled.

Something was wrong. Something was very wrong.

My balance faltered. I reached for the edge of the tub.

And my world went black.

CHAPTER 2

My head throbbed. I hadn't drunk *that* much wine, had I?

Everything was dark, too dark to see, which meant I must have been passed out for hours. After the emotional toll of the day, I must have crashed.

I lifted my hands to rub my temples, but they smacked into something hard. Had I somehow managed to crawl under a table?

I squinted, straining my eyes to see. Even in the dead of night, there was always at least a little light. But my eyes weren't adjusting.

"Scott?"

The air had a damp quality, and an earthy smell. Like my best friend Wendy's garden.

That didn't make any sense. A sickening sensation twisted my gut.

"Scott?"

I felt around since there was nothing to see. The surface above me was rough, unpolished wood.

There was hardly any room to move. Wooden walls surrounded me on every side. I was in a box. I blinked and strained my eyes for some clue as to what had happened.

"Scott? *Where are you?*"

A sudden wave of panic struck me. Had someone broken into the house, knocked us out, and put us in boxes?

"Help!" I screamed. "Someone, please!"

I banged and kicked and pounded on the box, thrashing and screaming as loudly as I could.

I clawed at the wood above me, desperate for something to grab onto, something to break. Small clumps of dirt fell through the cracks and landed on my face.

I was underground, in a wooden box.

I'd been buried alive.

My chest grew tighter by the moment. There was only so much air in this box. Already it was becoming difficult to breathe. How long had I been trapped and unconscious? How much air had I already lost? Too much, probably.

Had robbers really broken into our modest house, snuck up to the second floor and knocked us both out before we noticed them, then toted us into wooden boxes, carried us into the yard, and buried us? That was a heck of a lot of effort for little reward.

And extremely unlikely.

Scott had fervently insisted I drink the wine he'd poured me. He'd practically poured it down my throat. Then I'd passed out.

Scott wasn't here.

I was in the ground alone, left for dead by the man I'd intended to marry.

Scott had buried me alive.

Almost certainly.

My body shook. Anxious breaths burst in and out of my chest.

Unbidden thoughts filled my head, of the eulogy someone would inevitably have to write. One thing was certain—that someone wouldn't be Scott.

Rosemary Annetha DeLaCrux, moderately overweight, died alone after an unremarkable forty-three-year life. Her daughter was saddened by her passing, as was her best friend. No one else particularly cared.

I flailed and screamed. My lungs seized up. I was making zero progress at prying open the wooden box. The most important thing I could do was be loud, attract attention, because time was running out.

I gasped for air, kicking, fighting.

Rosemary Annetha DeLaCrux wanted what she considered very little from life—a warm and quiet existence, filled with love.

She would never receive that warmth or even approval from her mother before her mother perished. She would never have the chance to tell her daughter that she didn't mean to smother her. Even if her affection was too much at times, she couldn't help it. She needed her daughter to know just how much she loved her.

And she would never marry a decent man, even though she'd tried, three times.

The edge of my voice faded from a fierce wail to a pathetic whimper.

Rosemary Annetha DeLaCrux trusted too much. She was too desperate for love.

It killed her.

A knocking came from above my head.

I craned my neck and tried to speak. My voice wouldn't work. My lungs were too tight. There wasn't enough air.

I raised a weak fist and hit the wood, knocking back.

The wood behind my head ripped away. The splintering was so loud, so abrupt. Light peeked in, so bright, too bright.

I gasped for breath, wheezing. I fought to fill my lungs, but they didn't seem to be working.

"I knew it." The voice was male, deep and unfamiliar.

The stranger slipped his large hands under my arms. He pulled me toward him, out of the box and into a dirt hole as deep as he was tall. His flashlight fell into the box, abandoned.

The shadowy shape of his head moved between me and the moon.

A small light flicked over one of my eyes and then the other.

I flinched, or some semblance of it. I could hardly move. I still couldn't breathe correctly.

I should have felt relieved. I was alive, or at least I probably was. Maybe this was a dream, the last hopes of my oxygen-deprived brain tricking me into a lull before the end. No, if it was a dream, I'd have picked Scott to save me. He'd explain how all of this was some horrible misunderstanding.

"Mm-hmm, mm-hmm. Mostly dead," the stranger said.

I tried to say something. No words came.

"There will definitely be brain damage *if* you survive on your own. Big if," he said. "There's another option, should you be so inclined."

Brain damage didn't sound so great.

"You'll have to tell me, though. This is a big decision, and I'm big on consent." He said some more words, but I missed them.

I gasped for air. The light faded though my eyes were open. Either it was getting darker, or I was losing consciousness.

"Decide now, love. You're fading fast. Thumbs up for the potion."

Potion? I tried to ask what potion he was talking about. A weak *mmm* was all I produced. I didn't want to die. Whatever the alternative was, it had to be better than that. I tried to form a thumbs up with my right hand.

I couldn't say if I was successful or not, because everything went black and numb and distant. Again.

CHAPTER 3

I stretched my arms and let the natural light hitting my closed eyes heat my skin. The term cold-blooded never deserved a negative connotation. As a child, not knowing who my father was or anything about him, I'd imagined he was a magical lizard, a tyrannosaurus, or even better, a dragon. Like me, his temperature would always run a little cold, and like me, he felt the most himself when he'd lie in the sun and soak in its warmth.

The thought was a pleasant one, especially after I'd had the absolute worst nightmare—waking up in a coffin after my soon-to-be husband had tried to murder me. Pre-wedding jitters plus stress from my mother's passing explained the bad dream. But I was awake now, and everything was fine.

I opened my eyes. I woke in a bed that was a lot larger than mine, in a room that was also a lot larger than mine.

This was not my bed.

Did that mean my nightmare was not really a nightmare? It was too terrible to be real. Except if it *was* real…everything was very much not fine. I'd suffered the ultimate betrayal.

Reality smacked me hard, with a stick.

Suddenly cold, I rubbed my arms. They were shaking. I squeezed my eyes shut, hoping beyond reason, I could still wake to a world where none of this was true. When I opened my eyes, I was still in a room that wasn't mine. I pinched myself. It hurt, and I didn't wake. This was reality.

Scott had tried to kill me. I was in a stranger's bed. *The* stranger's bed?

I tried to recall details about the man who had pulled me from my premature grave, but the only thing I remembered was his voice—deep, comforting, touched by an accent I didn't recognize. Was this his bed?

I couldn't remember anything after he broke me out.

The entirety of the past twenty-four hours had been surreal, a sequence of unbelievable events that felt foggy and fake. It felt make believe, a story that had happened to someone else.

Had it even been twenty-four hours? I wasn't sure.

I took a quick peek down under the sheets, and found I was still wearing the slacks and blouse I had worn to the lawyer's office. Dirt stained the white satin of my shirt. There was no evidence the man who had put me here had done anything inappropriate to me. Still, I didn't love the fact that I was in an unfamiliar bed.

I pushed off the mattress, my feet landing on cold hardwood. I did a quick look around for my shoes before remembering I hadn't been wearing any when Scott had drugged me.

The man I had intended to spend my life with had tried to kill me. *Tried* was the important point to cling to, right? Because I was alive, and fine. Weirdly fine. I'd process my loss later.

I flattened myself against the wall by the open bedroom door and listened for signs of the stranger. He was probably a perfectly good person, having saved my life and all, but given what I'd been through, I didn't feel particularly trusting at the moment.

My ears met silence.

I did a quick look around the bedroom for something I could use to defend myself. The room was frustratingly empty—lifted bed with no drawers under it, no nightstand, and a small, black dresser with nothing on top of it. There were no lamps, no picture frames, no baseball bats, and no anything else I could use.

The correct term for this aesthetic was probably along the lines of modern minimalism or something of the sort. It was nice, I guessed. Sterile in a fancy way, more expensive hotel vibe than hospital. But I preferred my cozy Victorian with its rich colors, cracks, and charm. At home, there was a lamp or decorative bowl within arm's reach everywhere in the house.

What kind of man didn't have a lamp by his bed? One who didn't read. *Shiver.* One who liked the dark. That went right along with the sterile space. One who was a serial murderer who took women back to his murder room to murder them.

Reason suggested he wouldn't bother saving my life just to kill me later. But clearly my survival instincts were nonexistent.

Even without a weapon, at some point here I was going to have to risk leaving the room.

I sucked in a deep breath and tiptoed out into the living room. Based on the set-up, it seemed I was in an apartment, and oh—spotting the wall of windows—high up in a tall building. I hurried over to the glass and peered down at cars whizzing past on a busy street. I was downtown, a good twenty minutes from my house.

I took a more thorough look around the spartan living

room and spartan kitchen areas, and found no one. But I did spot a framed photograph and a fruit bowl on the counter.

With a rumble, tumble, and churn, my stomach cried out at the prospect of a meal. Apparently I was absolutely starving.

I ran over, abandoning any worry, and grabbed an apple in each hand—one golden and one red. Choosing to go with the golden one first, I took a huge bite.

My teeth clanked into a too-hard-to be-food surface. A metallic taste filled my mouth. Something small and sharp scraped against my tongue. I opened my mouth and fished out the tiny shard covered in red gloss.

The shard was hard and white-ish, like porcelain. A sinking feeling fell over me. I slowly ran my tongue over my teeth and *ouch*. A sharp sting accompanied a fresh gush of warmth in my mouth and down my throat. I'd chipped a tooth.

My stomach growled so loud the entire city would likely hear it.

I was *famished*.

I ripped open the fridge, grabbed the first thing I could—a bottle of orange juice. I tore off the lid and poured the contents down my throat. The cold liquid tasted like nothing on my tongue. But *wow* did the acid smart against my new cut. The bottle empty, my hunger unsatisfied, I tossed aside the empty container and opened a Chinese takeout box. I dug my face in and sucked up the noodles, remotely aware that this was not at all what I should have been doing. They felt wet, but had zero flavor.

My behavior was disgusting. It was inappropriate. It was…unstoppable.

Compelled, fevered to devour more, I tossed the empty paper box on the floor and grabbed the next item, a bottle of sriracha.

I'd never been able to tolerate spice. I should have replaced the bottle on the shelf, but instead, I found myself unscrewing the cap and dumping the contents into my mouth.

The sauce was cold and hot at the same time, burning the cut on my tongue like hellfire. In terms of flavor, it was…not bad. It almost had some, like adding a dash of black pepper to newspaper. In terms of pain, it was writhe-on-the-floor level misery. And I couldn't seem to stop myself. Spicy tears rolling down my cheeks, I finished the sauce and dropped the empty bottle on the floor. The fire continued to burn my tongue. Still, my hunger was not satiated.

Only one package remained. I could see it through the front of one of the fridge's drawers. Sad that the man who lived here didn't have more to eat. Even before my ravaging of his supply, he'd really needed to go to the store.

I opened the drawer, grabbed the paper-wrapped package, and was struck by the scent. I paused and inhaled. Metallic, fresh, and fatty—it smelled divine.

I folded back the paper and found a raw steak.

In the recesses of my brain, alerts sounded. This had gone too far already. I needed to clean up all of the mess at my feet, regain some sense of self-control, and get the heck out of here. I wasn't acting like myself, or even any semblance of a human being.

But that smell.

One closer sniff wouldn't hurt. I lowered my nose toward the steak, closed my eyes, and breathed it in. So freakin' good. When I opened my eyes, I had no control. Hunger tore at my insides like furious claws. That hunger took the wheel, pushing sanity into the passenger seat.

I could only watch.

My teeth were already tearing into the meat.

I was a beast—ravenous, rabid.

My tastebuds lit up with the salty, savory notes. So, so freaking good.

Only when the feeding frenzy was over did I start to feel like myself again.

I looked over the carnage. Packages littered the floor. Blood stained my shirt and hands. Acid roiled in my gut. I searched the cabinets for a trashcan. When I found none—what kind of psychopath doesn't have a trashcan in their kitchen???—I ran around in search of a restroom.

I found it.

Just in time for my stomach churn to turn into full dry heaves.

I leaned over the toilet and waited for the entire kitchen to burst through my lips. Other than a few chest-crushing coughs, nothing came out.

I sucked in a deep breath and tried to rationalize what I had done. Near death experiences could cause weird behaviors. That was all this was, some kind of trauma response. Everything would be fine once I…what…went home? *To Scott?* Ha. No.

My next move, whatever it was, needed to be determined when I was somewhere safe. I couldn't be near someone who would try and fix his mistake by killing me correctly the next time.

Absolutely not going home.

I checked the floor and under-sink cabinet for a trash can. There wasn't one. Of course.

I turned on the sink, washed my hands, then cupped some water and splashed it on my face. I held the towel over my eyes, then lowered it and looked in the mirror, a little nervous to see what a mess I had become.

Only it wasn't a mirror. Instead there was a glass covered picture that looked like a mirror, I guessed.

I wasn't there. I looked over my shoulder to the apartment that did seem to be reflected. That was weird. No weirder than anything else, I guessed. The dude who spends his time hanging out in graveyards, possibly for graverobbing purposes, and maybe for worse, had a picture of the reflection of his apartment in his bathroom where the mirror should have been. Whatever. I needed to get out of here.

But even if the guy could be a psychopath, I couldn't leave a mess. It was bad enough I had eaten everything in the fridge. I couldn't leave the trash behind on the floor. I scooped up the containers into my arms, because there was no trash can to put them in, the only reasonable solution was to take the trash with me.

When I spotted the framed photograph on the counter, I paused. Curious, I leaned in for a better look. Bright light reflected off the river surface, but the smiles were even brighter. Two people stood together, thigh-deep in the indigo current, both wearing flannel and holding long fishing poles, both beaming at the camera. The man was particularly tall, or the grandmotherly woman beside him was so short he appeared that way by comparison.

With broad shoulders, thick biceps, and a short but full beard, I pegged the man as a lumberjack—the kind women fantasized about carrying them off into the woods to a secluded cabin when they happened to find themselves lost with a twisted ankle. The kind who would be tender yet firm as he wrapped her injury and nursed her back to health.

He looked to be about my age, but he wore it better. His lips were full, too pretty to match his square jaw and rugged look. Lips perfect to kiss and make everything better.

A monstrous roar broke the apartment's silence. Startled, I jolted upright.

Had the stranger been here all along? Was he about to exact his revenge for my kitchen-destroying binge fest?

Heart in my throat, I scuttled across the floor, arms full of garbage, and looked back toward the window, toward the sound.

It was only the radiator.

I'd had more than enough of being here. I hurried out the door, down the elevator, with my garbage in my hands, and no shoes on my feet.

Later, I'd make up for this. I'd pay the stranger for his groceries once I had my purse. I'd thank him for saving my life. And I'd ask him the billion questions I needed to ask but hadn't thought of yet.

Everything will work out. One way or another. Those were the last words my fiancé had said to me.

I would make sure everything worked out all right. Only, not in the way he'd intended.

CHAPTER 4

Cement was basically rough sandpaper, and it was exceptionally unpleasant to walk on in bare feet. With every hurried step, I expected the pain to dull, for numbness to finally take over and for my poor soles to stop hurting, but that wasn't in the cards.

Still, I hustled away from the condo as quickly as I could, for fear of running into the guy who'd dug me out of the ground. I wasn't ready to talk to him yet, just like I wasn't ready to confront Scott yet.

I turned a corner and took a moment to give my feet a rest and compose my thoughts. I leaned against a brick building that looked like another apartment complex, less fancy than the one I'd run from.

A single car turned off the main road down the side street where I stood. The only other person around was a woman heading up the sidewalk from the other direction. I stared down at my feet, from the red skin spattered in dirt, to my chipped nail polish on my right big toe.

The small surge of confidence and righteous anger I'd

managed to muster had already begun to fade. I wanted to go home, crash in my own bed, and not be bothered for a week. But if I didn't work out how exactly to handle Scott, I'd definitely screw up my chance to ambush him correctly. If I strolled in unprepared, he'd tell me how all of this was my fault, and if I wasn't feeling stronger, I might actually believe him. Ugh.

No, for strength of body and spirit, there was only one place I could go—my best friend Wendy's house. Her reassurance would ground me, and she'd keep me from going back to deal with Scott unprepared. She'd help me come up with a plan.

The snow that had lined the streets was completely melted, even in shady nooks. Either it had been a searingly hot morning, or more likely, multiple days had passed instead of one.

I turned to the woman walking toward me on the sidewalk. She was about ten feet or so away.

"Excuse me," I said, with what I hoped would be interpreted as a friendly wave. Moving my hands wasn't easy with copious amounts of garbage in my arms. "What day is it?"

She looked up from her phone and froze mid-step. Her eyes went wide.

Probably she was afraid because I was carrying food trash, because I had no shoes, and because I was covered in dirt and blood. I mean, just a guess.

"I've had the worst night," I said. "I woke up in the dirt."

The woman looked to one side then the other. Her lips twisted and her feet spread in a defensive stance. "Uhhh…."

She was afraid of me.

"I assure you I'm not dangerous, the opposite even. I'm quite nice. This isn't human blood on my hands." Some of the blood on the shirt might be, though, from when I broke my tooth. I didn't have to tell her that.

She spun on her heel and ran, glancing over her shoulder to make sure I wasn't chasing her. She raised her phone to her ear, likely calling the police.

I couldn't blame her. I had to look like a wreck.

Without my purse, I had no way to make any calls. But I also definitely couldn't stay here. So, I got back to walking.

Wendy lived five blocks away in the basement apartment of her aunt and uncle's rancher. Even though the distance wasn't absurdly far, every barefoot step hurt. And the sleepy cul-de-sac felt worlds away, due to the quiet nature of the mostly retired neighborhood.

The afternoon sun hung heavy in the sky, casting shadows that broke the day's moderate heat and would soon lead to a cool evening. Forest flanked large backyards, dulling the noise of city traffic. Front gardens were in full spring bloom, with blossoms of red and white and yellow and pink.

Everyone seemed to have figured out the key to spring tulips, something I had yet to master. They were supposed to be easy, plant them and they come back every year, sometimes twice a year. I'd finally managed to get a single tulip to bloom in my own front yard. It was the Tiny Tim of tulips—small and bent, and likely to keel over at any moment. I was fiercely proud of its shriveled pink pedals, and dreaded the day a slight wind would put it out of its misery.

I kept my thoughts as much as possible on flowers as I walked. Flowers were a safe, happy subject. The distraction mostly worked, and I made it to the cul-de-sac without having another breakdown.

When I reached Wendy's place, I shuffled the garbage in my arms and awkwardly lifted my fist to knock.

Before my knuckles could make contact, the door flew open.

Worry lined my best friend's forehead. Wrinkles carried

down over her clothes, which when paired with her frazzled auburn and silver hair, made her look like she'd just climbed out of bed. She was a mess, and given the crazed look in her hazel eyes, it was because of me.

Wendy launched herself at me. Startled, I stumbled back as she squeezed me hard. The large resin stone on the bracelet I'd made for her back in college stabbed into my shoulder blade. The trash in my arms crunched between us, and relief filled my heart. This was exactly where I needed to be.

"You're okay," she said, then again an octave lower, "You *are* okay, right?"

She pulled back, put her hands on my arms and squinted as she looked me over. I put on what I hoped was a reassuring smile. It would be better if I could get in the door before I made her worry too much more than I already had.

"You are clearly *not* okay," she said. "Scott did this, didn't he? He's gone from gaslighting to physical abuse. I've been journaling everything for the cops and the lawyers. I have dates, details, everything. You're keeping your house, and if the world truly is just, he's getting the chair."

I opened my mouth, shut it again, and hugged my best friend, dropping all of the garbage onto our feet.

"Thank you," I said.

"I haven't done anything *yet*," she said with an inflection that implied she definitely planned to do something more violent than journaling.

"I'm okay," I said.

She scoffed, shook her head, took my hand, and led me inside. "You, Rose, are many things. Okay is not one of them."

"It's not as bad as it looks," I said.

"Well that's a low bar," she said. "You look like you fell over the railing into a gorilla cage."

"Thanks," I said dryly.

"I mean it with love," Wendy said.

"I know."

Everything Wendy did was with love, from her gardens to her relationships to her work at the animal shelter. She was warm and caring and would do anything for the people she loved. We'd been friends for twenty years, give or take, and I only wished any of the men in my life were half as Wendy as Wendy was.

She brought me to the sofa. "Where are you bleeding? We should get you checked out, bandaged, stitched."

"It's not my blood," I said. *Mostly.*

"All right," she said, too calmly for my proclamation. "Let me get my journal, make you some tea, and you can tell me everything."

"Don't you want to know whose blood it is?" I called after her as she headed to the kitchen of her studio apartment.

"Tea first."

The cool leather sofa sucked me in, lifting my feet from the floor, and offering immediate relief.

Twenty feet away, Wendy busied herself setting up a pot on the stove.

She came back and sat down next to me with a notebook and pen in hand. Then she snapped a picture with her phone, blinding me with the flash.

"We're going to need the evidence later. Maybe keep the clothes, too."

I looked down to my stained blouse. Wendy assumed the crusty blood would be evidence in my favor, and I loved her for it.

"If you need a shower, we can do that," she added. "You know you can borrow anything of mine that you want."

"I'm all right, really."

Wendy took my hands in hers with a look that said she didn't believe me. I didn't believe me either.

She popped back up and hustled into the kitchen. The tea pot whistled just as she got there, as if she knew exactly when it would. She poured a cup, put in a splash of oat milk and honey for me, and returned to the sofa. I didn't love oat milk, but that's what she had, so when I was here, that's how I took it.

I graciously accepted the cup and took a small sip. The herbal scent and warmth of the cup eased my stiff muscles. The tea washed across my tongue and relaxed my nerves. I couldn't taste it, but it didn't even burn my cut.

This was just what I'd needed.

Wendy put her phone right up in my face and snapped another shot. "When you're ready, tell me how he broke your tooth exactly. In great detail."

"Scott didn't break my tooth," I said.

She narrowed her eyes like she didn't believe me.

"*I* broke it."

"You know that's him talking, right? Just because he says something is your fault—"

"Really," I said. "I broke it on a piece of fake fruit."

The concern lining her face eased a little and her lips perked up on one side. She chuckled softly. "What?"

"I was in this guy's house," I said, and swallowed a big sip of tea to give me time to think. "I thought the fruit was real."

"Whose house?" she asked. "What does *this guy* look like?"

"I have no idea." Well, I hadn't actually seen him, so I couldn't say for sure. If he was the guy in the photograph though, he looked like a sexy lumberjack.

"You've been M.I.A. for three days, Rose. You're covered in blood. You don't know what the man you've been staying with looks like. I'm going to need you to back this story up a few steps and start at the beginning."

Three days?

Also, Wendy had made fair points. Better not to mention that after I woke up in his bed and chipped my tooth on his fake fruit, I tore into his raw steak like a starved coyote. Or at least not without some context. Starting at the beginning of my tale didn't seem like such a bad idea.

"I came home from the lawyer's," I said.

"On Wednesday," Wendy said.

I nodded. "When I got home, Scott—"

"You went to see the lawyer alone, didn't you?" Wendy asked. "I would have gone. You shouldn't have had to—" She pressed her lips together. "Sorry. Please go on."

It was nice that she cared. She was probably right, too. If I'd have asked her along, maybe none of this would have happened. Or maybe it would have happened later. Maybe it would have gone worse.

I took a moment, then continued. "Scott poured me a glass of wine."

Wendy's gaze sharpened. "He drugged you."

"Yes."

She smacked her fist down on the sofa. "I'm going to kill him."

"No," I said. I cleared my throat, and barreled on before Wendy could suggest other bodily harm. "I woke up in a box."

She put her fingers to her lips, and watched me, waiting for what would come next.

My throat felt tight. I said, "Underground."

Tears welled in the corners of her eyes. My eyes blurred as I looked at her. If she cried, I'd cry. I closed my eyes and said the rest in a rush. "A man saved me, somehow. He poured something in my mouth. I woke up in his bed." Before she could ask, I added, *"with my clothes on.* He wasn't there. Apparently I lost three days. I ravaged his fridge, broke my tooth, and came straight here."

I peeked through one eye first to gauge Wendy's reaction. She inhaled a slow breath, puffing out her chest and wafting the air with her hand.

"First things first, you should kill Scott," she said. "And I'll help."

CHAPTER 5

In theory, part of me liked the sound of murder. I mean, Scott deserved it. The man had tried to kill me. I felt guilty indulging in the fantasy though, even half-heartedly, even for a second. Because in reality, murder was definitely a no-go.

Wendy rubbed her hands together as she talked herself further and further into exactly how satisfying it would be to end him. Her face lit up in demented delight.

"Before we shoot him, we have to read off his list of crimes, make sure there's no question as to why he's going to die," she said.

"Neither of us have a gun," I said.

Wendy was generally a gentle soul, but fiercely loyal, so she was *probably* not serious.

"Aunt Petunia does," she said.

Okay, she may have been a sliver serious.

Wendy went on to explain, "She uses it on groundhogs, a remnant of her farm days. If a horse steps in one of their holes and breaks its leg, it costs more than the horse is worth to try and fix it. They put the horses down, Rose. It's just awful."

"But there aren't any horses here."

"You don't have to tell me that," Wendy said. "I've told her that people won't break their legs back here, and that life is precious, and that groundhogs are actually adorable, but she won't listen. That's why I hid her shotgun from her. No animals will die on my watch."

"Scott is a living being, too," I said. I couldn't go from love to wishing he was dead in the snap of my fingers, even if I should.

"Eh." Wendy waved a dismissive hand. "I guess. Groundhogs are better."

I couldn't argue with that.

"Even if we don't kill him, you deserve revenge, Rose. He can't try to kill you and get away with it. We should *at the very least* call the police."

"Not yet."

What *I* wanted wasn't revenge, even some kind of nonviolent revenge. Listening to Wendy scheme made that clear to me in a way it hadn't been before. If I could wave a magic wand and give him syphilis, I wouldn't even do it. And I wasn't ready to have him arrested, either.

What I really and truly wanted was a clean break from Scott, and also answers. I really needed to know *why* he had tried to kill me. A knot formed in my chest. I attempted to rub it away, but it persisted.

Wendy patted my hand. "Take your time. I'm here no matter what you decide."

"Let's not talk about it anymore," I said, my throat tight. The knot in my chest grew.

"You got it," she said. "Want to binge my college VHS collection instead? Stay up late like we used to and—"

"Drink cheap wine coolers?" I finished for her.

She nodded.

It was what we'd done forever ago, in college, when we'd shared a tiny apartment and one of us had suffered a particularly rough breakup or failed an exam or when I needed to unwind after a particularly brutal visit with my mother.

"It's perfect." I leaned my head on her shoulder and thanked the stars that no matter what the world threw at me, at least I had Wendy.

* * *

By morning, the stiff feeling in my chest had unwound a bit. I suffered all manner of other stiffness, though. Some things hadn't changed since college, but others certainly had. My muscles and joints cried at having slept on Wendy's sofa instead of in a proper bed.

I borrowed one of Wendy's many flowy dresses and a set of her sandals. And I politely passed when she offered me breakfast. While I knew her oatmeal flax bars were good for health food, the idea of consuming anything made my stomach churn. If I had to guess, I'd say it was a combination of stress and food poisoning due to my digestion of raw meat.

I tried to forget about that. I failed.

"You're sure you're ready?" Wendy asked, for the fiftieth time since I'd rolled off the sofa.

"I have to be," I said again.

She made the disapproving noises she did when she was trying to keep her thoughts to herself the whole drive back to my place.

Yes, I probably needed to talk to the police. Yes, I knew that the conversation I was about to have with my soon-to-be-ex fiancé would be one of the worst interactions of my life. And yes, I had to go home and get this over with now.

Putting off the inevitable would only cause me to stress about it more. I was already at anxiety level eleven out of ten.

Wendy parked in the driveway behind Scott's Range Rover.

"Thank you so much for everything," I told her. She'd given me all the support I'd needed, as she always did. Without her company last night, I would have come home covered in meat juice and dirt, and who knows what would have happened. Now I had the benefit of a few hours of sleep at least, and the pretense of a somewhat sane person.

"You can thank me after this is over, and Scott's sorry hide is behind bars. I'm recording everything he says."

Scott had never liked Wendy. That should have been enough of a red flag to send me running early in our year-long relationship. But I'd ignored it, just as I'd ignored all of Scott's other questionable behaviors. He was too smitten too fast. And I was eager to finally find true love, my happily ever after, so I didn't question it when he proposed we move in together after only three weeks. Worse, the man poured ketchup on everything, including pancakes. *Ketchup.*

I told Wendy, "Scott will not be happy that I'm not alone."

But I shouldn't have been considering what would make Scott comfortable. It shouldn't have mattered at all to me anymore. I told myself it didn't, and hoped I could prove that true.

"Rose, the man tried to kill you. Under no circumstances do his feelings count for anything."

Wendy reached into her purse and pulled out a taser.

My jaw dropped open. "When did you get *that?*"

"The same time I got the bear spray. The internet is filled with marvelous things."

"Weapons you won't actually use on the bear who's stalking you," I said.

"Bears can't stalk people. But this isn't about Teddy,"

Wendy said, using a cuddly name to refer to the terrifying bear who had taken up residence in the forest behind her house. "It's about Scott."

"You can't tase Scott," I said.

"No promises. You should be happy," she said as she climbed out and headed for the front door. "I'm leaving the shotgun in the trunk."

I laughed and headed up beside her.

I was really glad she was here.

"Do you know how to use that thing?" I asked at the door.

"Point. Pull the trigger," she said. "It's not that complicated."

I was not reassured. But, it didn't hurt that she had a weapon. What if Scott tried to kill me again? No, he wouldn't make a move with Wendy here to witness.

I put my key in the lock, but the door opened without resistance. It was unlocked. Scott never left it unlocked.

"Something's amiss," I whispered to Wendy. Was Scott wallowing in regret? Had he lost his usual cool, even demeanor? Did he miss me? Was he sorry?

Wendy followed me into the living room and shut the door behind us.

From the foyer, a woman's voice carried through the house. Muffled and low in pitch, her words were impossible to decipher. Scott must have had the news running on the TV in the bedroom.

"It's your name on the house. One call to the police is all it takes to get rid of him. And no matter what happens," Wendy said, "I've got your back."

I bumped her shoulder with mine and shot her a smile that I hoped said everything I should have said out loud—I know, thank you, you're the only reason I haven't fallen completely to pieces.

Different scenarios played out in my head. In one, Scott

was drunk, lying on the bed, completely disheveled. My thinking he'd tried to kill me was a misunderstanding. It hadn't been him who had buried me. He'd simply left me to my bath, and when he'd come back, I was gone. Someone else had dug that hole and put me in it.

The next scenario started the same way, with Scott beside himself in grief. Sure, he had tried to kill me, but it was the greatest mistake of his life, and it was tearing him apart.

I started up the stairs.

Like the others, the next scenario began with a distraught Scott. Only this time, I had wandered off in a crazed state after my meeting with the lawyer. Confused and out of my head, I'd fallen into a hole…into an open box…and somehow I wasn't seen when the hole was filled. All of this was an unfortunate accident. Was that possible? Part of me wanted to believe it was.

I needed to find Scott as upset as I felt.

But when I reached the top of the stairs, I didn't hear Scott wailing in sorrow. I heard the woman's voice distinctly.

"If that's not true, I'm going to enjoy taking my time with you," she said.

There was no background music. It didn't sound like TV. There was a real woman here, in my bedroom, with my fiancé.

I rushed through the hall and stopped in the open doorway to our bedroom. Scott's back was up against my dresser. A woman with golden hair and a head-to-toe leather getup pinned him there. She splayed her hand across his chest and leaned over him.

All the air whooshed out of my chest, replaced by a strangling sensation that clawed at my throat, my lungs, my heart.

He wasn't grieving. He wasn't worried. He knew exactly what he'd done to me, and those crimes didn't weigh on him a single bit. After everything, I was about to deliver the surprise of his life. What a shock it would be to see me alive. Let it give him a freaking heart attack.

"Hello, Scott," I said.

Without looking, I could feel Wendy standing beside me. I drew from her strength, and fortified my own.

The woman let go of Scott and turned toward me. She was pretty in a sharp way, like a bird of prey. Her boobs were perky, her face taught with youth and the pull of the tight ponytail on the top of her head. A whip hung coiled on the side of her belt.

"Who are you?" she asked, her voice as pointed as her cheekbones.

It was me who should have been asking her that.

"I'm Scott's *fiancée*," I said. "This is *my* bedroom. *My house.*"

Scott peeked out from behind her. He wore his favorite short-sleeved shirt with the collar and the ketchup bottle pattern. The color drained from his face. "Rosemary? How did you…."

That's right, jerkhole. Take it all in. Realize exactly what this means. You failed to murder me, and now I am the one in control.

I put my fists on my hips and tilted my chin up to punctuate my point.

Before I could respond to him, his dominatrix turned back to him. *"Your fiancée?"*

It seemed he hadn't told her about me.

"I was." I straightened my fingers and pulled on the engagement ring. The ring didn't budge. "After the attempted murder, I'd say we're done."

My hands were damp with sweat, but that seemed to be working against me instead of helping. My fingers slipped on the ring as I tried to pull. It wouldn't budge, likely due to the fact that I'd put on extra weight since my mother had died.

"I can explain," Scott said.

"All you spew is lies," Wendy said.

I twisted and fought with the ring, until finally it slipped off my finger. I chucked the ring across the room at him.

It hit Scott's mistress in the shoulder and fell to the floor.

She swung her whole body with the motion of her arm, straight toward Scott's face. Her fingers formed a fist. It wasn't a slap that followed, but a cartilage-crunching knuckles-to-nose impact.

A small thrill zipped up my spine. This woman was not my enemy. She was Scott's victim, same as me.

The metallic scent of blood tinged the air.

Scowling, the mistress charged toward me. She slowed and gave me a curt nod. I stepped aside and let her pass.

"Should I zap her?" Wendy asked from behind me.

The mistress was already halfway down the hall. She laughed at Wendy's words, and didn't stop walking.

"Let her go," I said. She didn't matter. She was not the problem here. Scott was.

He leaned against the dresser, hands cupping his face, tears rolling down his cheeks. He sniffled, then snarled. Shock and anger filled his voice as he said, "She broke my nose."

"Let's break his balls next," Wendy said.

It wasn't a bad idea. Adrenaline pumped through my veins—I was in this to win this. I wasn't going anywhere. My fingers trembled. Maintaining my power pose—chin up, fists on hips, elbows out—I took up as much space as possible and reminded myself that I was in control.

"Tell me why," I said to Scott. For good measure, I kicked his ankle.

"Ouch." He dropped his hands and bared his teeth. Quickly his anger morphed to something more dangerous, something that had always held more sway over me. His brows dropped in disapproval. It was a look that said I was in the wrong. It was a familiar expression, one he used on me often. "You *kicked* me."

The scent of blood seemed to grow stronger. I stared at Scott's stupid face. I watched the stream of red pour down from his mangled nose over his lips.

My stomach growled.

I kicked him again. It felt good.

"Ow. Rosemary, this is completely unacceptable behavior. What has gotten into you? It's your *friend,* isn't it?" He practically spat in Wendy's direction.

Suddenly I was so hungry I practically drooled on myself.

My pulse pounded in my ears. Was that my pulse? Or was I hearing Scott's?

I approached the man who was supposed to love me until death do us part, to the man I'd been prepared to devote the rest of my life to, to the man who had tried to kill me.

With a calmness I didn't feel, I said, "You buried me alive."

Fury flooded my veins. I wanted answers, yes, but seeing his smug face, I realized it didn't really matter what his reasons were. What he had done to me was unforgivable and inexcusable.

"I wouldn't have had to if you hadn't made me," he said. "If you had only—"

No. His words were poison, and I was done letting him speak.

I lunged at him. It wasn't a conscious decision. It just happened, and happened fast.

I pulled his shoulder and chin in opposite directions, exposing the vulnerable expanse of his neck. The smell of his cologne clouded my brain with emotion, with memories. I *hated* this man.

He swung wildly at me. He hit my shoulder, kicked my

knee. I lost my balance and he knocked me back. We fell onto the bed, him on top of me, pinning me down.

No. This was not how this was going to go. I was supposed to be the one putting him in his place. He couldn't do this. I couldn't let him.

"Oh my—" Wendy gasped. "Turn him this way. I'll get him."

Her words felt distant. I hardly heard them.

Any pretense of charm or disappointment left Scott's expression. He was raw, unveiled anger. In his brown eyes I couldn't see anything I had once thought had been there—no love, no humor, no devotion.

I was the one who deserved to be angry, not him.

"You stupid wench," he said. "I left you buried in a graveyard. Why couldn't you just die?"

He wrapped his hands around my throat and pressed down, squeezing so my breath should have been cut off. I felt fine. If anything, I felt more alive than I ever had.

The veins in his neck bulged as he put everything he had into choking me.

I smashed my fist into his elbow. His arm buckled. He lurched downward, close enough.

I tore those bulging neck veins open.

With my teeth.

I pulled him in and held him still as he screamed.

A buzz and snap sounded—Wendy's taser going off.

Scott howled.

My body convulsed. I lost control of my limbs as sharp pain rippled through my nerves. The weight on my chest lifted. The taste of hot metal tinged my tongue.

Scott fell off of me.

"Oh my gosh, Rose, I am *so sorry.*" Wendy appeared over me.

I lay still a moment, unable to move. My brain went all hazy, or hazier than it already was, I guessed.

What was happening to me?

Wendy offered me her hand. Her eyes were wild, so was her hair.

"Are you okay?" she asked, panic raising her voice two octaves. Then she shook her head. "Tell me he didn't crush your windpipe. Tell me I didn't make it worse."

"I'm okay." I took her outstretched hand.

She lifted me upright to a sitting position.

Then she squeezed me into a hug. When she pulled back, there was red all over her shirt.

"You're bleeding," I said, though I knew that didn't make any sense. She hadn't been in the fight, had she? Had Scott somehow hurt her? I'd kill him if he had.

Wendy laughed in a strange, slightly psychotic way. "It's not my blood."

My brain kicked on, working faster to catch up. Somehow everything had gone terribly wrong. My stomach churned.

Hesitant to hear the answer, I asked, "Where's Scott?"

Wendy pointed to the floor, to where my almost-husband lay, unmoving. Blood spilled out of his neck and pooled around him. His skin was pale.

I looked down at my borrowed dress. Right. I'd bitten Scott in the neck. I'd ruined Wendy's clothes.

"You look—" Wendy pulled me to my feet. "Come see."

We stepped over Scott and stood in front of my bedroom mirror. Except there was only one reflection staring back at us: Wendy's. Not mine.

CHAPTER 6

"Well, this is unexpected," Wendy said.

I stared through myself in the mirror to the bedroom I knew so well. This wasn't my life. These weren't my problems. No reflection, *assault*—it felt like it was happening to someone else.

Wendy flashed her phone in my face and clicked a photo. "Don't worry, I'll delete this one right away. We don't want any evidence of…." She trailed off, frowned, and looked at her phone. Her expression brightened. "There you are."

She turned the phone and showed me the screen.

The woman in the picture had crazed brown eyes, deathly-pale skin, and blood all over her face. She looked like a monster. Although it was horrifying, I knew that woman was me.

"Your mirror must be defective," Wendy said, like that was actually a thing.

"I didn't have a reflection at the stranger's house, either," I said. "I'm broken."

"Never," Wendy said. "You're wonderful, just the way you are."

"You saw that picture." I swirled my finger in front of my face. "You're looking at this mess right now. How can you say that with a straight face?"

"Because I believe it one hundred forty-three percent. Now what are we going to do with Scott? We have to call an ambulance." She reached down and touched his neck. "Or maybe not."

I pushed her out of the way and checked his pulse. I couldn't find one.

This was bad.

Really, really bad.

I hadn't just bitten Scott. *I'd murdered him.* I should feel something—panic, devastation, sadness, and, at the very least, regret. Instead, I felt numb.

I looked down at his lifeless body. "We have to call for help."

Wendy frowned. "Maybe that's not the best idea."

"When someone is hurt, you call nine-one-one," I said. "We have to."

Wendy pulled her lips in and gave me a kind smile. She was trying not to tell me that I should have done that before coming here, trying not to say I told you so. She was definitely holding back that I was screwed because I'd screwed up.

"It's not like there's any saving *that.*" Wendy pointed down at Scott's body and shivered. "Scott's dead. We call for help, they come and arrest you. No, we think about our options first."

"I killed him."

Wendy grabbed my shoulders, pulling my attention back up to her. "He already tried to kill you once," she said. "He just tried again. It wasn't murder. It was self-defense, Rose. You did what you had to do, and the world is a better place for it. You hear me?"

I wasn't entirely sure that I agreed, but I nodded anyway.

"Your freezer," Wendy said. "We stash him there while we figure out what to do next."

I nodded again, going through the motions of being an actual living, breathing person.

Wendy went to his shoulders, lifted one arm, then the other. Scott's head fell backward.

Wendy gagged. "Eww. He's looking at me."

"Let me." I took over for her.

She went around to the legs.

We carried him downstairs to the basement and stuck him in the chest freezer. Then we returned upstairs and scrubbed the carpet for hours in silence.

Eventually, Wendy said, "You go take a shower. I'll finish this up."

I thanked her, shed my clothes in the bathroom and stepped into the hot water. Steam filled the room. The water burned hot against my skin. I leaned into it, and against the shower wall. And I cried. Tears burst out of me in a flood, pouring down my cheeks.

I stayed there, just like that, until I felt like a person again, no matter how hollow. Then I got dressed and headed out to meet Wendy. She wasn't in the bedroom, so I went downstairs. She waved at me to join her on the couch, so I sat down next to her and accepted the cup of tea she offered me.

We sat in silence for a while. She was waiting for me to speak first.

"There's something wrong with me," I told her. "Ever since that man dragged me out of the ground."

"Since your would-be-husband buried you alive."

"That, too."

"You need time. That's quite the trauma."

"It's not just that," I said. "I don't have a reflection. I'm ravenous for meat. At the stranger's place, I tore into his fridge like an animal. I licked his steak."

She squished her lips together, stopping a grin.

"It's not sexy," I told her.

"I didn't say anything."

"It was raw, a slab of uncooked cow, nothing to do with the man's penis. He wasn't even there."

"Okay," Wendy said. "Maybe you need some iron. When I get my spontaneously irregular period, the only things that can tame my beastly hormones are steak or burgers."

"And my reflection? Is that supposed to be part of the big change into infertility, like mood swings and hot flashes?"

"Societally, maybe. Women of a certain age are often treated like they're invisible. But no, I don't have an answer for that. But you know who might—"

"Don't say it. I can't go back and—"

"Your stranger."

"We need to figure out what to do about my dead fiancé. The last thing I need is another man in my life."

"I don't know," Wendy said. "Maybe it's exactly what you need, if he's a decent person. It's even better if he's good in bed. But my question is, how did this guy find you? You were buried underground, right? Maybe he has the answers you're looking for."

I grumbled into my tea and ignored her sound advice. The stranger did know more than I did about what had happened to me. My memories of what he'd said to me, and certainly of what liquid he'd given me, were fuzzy. I remembered something about consent…and something about brain damage.

"As for Scott," Wendy said, "there's not much else we can do yet. I mean, maybe we can dump him in the forest…or a river somewhere. But I don't feel confident he'll stay hidden like that. What if a bear drags him out into the open? Then there's his mistress. I'm not convinced she's completely out of the picture. We'll need to move him before she comes back or calls the cops and *they* come here looking for him. No matter what, we'll have to wait until dark to try and move him or someone will see. For the record, I didn't actually mean it when I said we should kill him. I don't have any of this thought out."

"I know," I said. My stomach churned. "I don't love the sound of any of that."

"I don't think I have the stomach to break him into pieces."

"Ugh. Why would you even suggest that?"

"It seems like the thing to do," Wendy said. "I take it back."

"We should call nine-one-one," I said. "All of this other stuff, it's crazy."

"Maybe you're right."

A loud thump sound echoed through the house. Wendy and I held our breath and looked at each other.

"You heard that right?" I asked.

Wendy nodded. "Sounds like it came from the basement."

CHAPTER 7

The banging grew louder as we made our way toward the basement. It wasn't an even sound, like machinery, but more erratic like someone trying to beat their way in through the basement door. I grabbed the poker from the fireplace. Wendy grabbed the little broom.

"Do you think Scott's girlfriend is back?" Wendy asked.

Why would she be? Had she witnessed our altercation through the window?

"I don't know," I said. "But why wouldn't she come to the front door?"

Wendy shrugged, just as lost as I was.

"What if it's the police?" I said.

"I think they'd also come to the front door," Wendy said.

We crept down the steps, holding onto our weapons and to each other. I should have called nine-one-one right away after I'd bitten him. I should have listened to Wendy in the first place and called the police to tell them Scott had buried me alive. I never should have come here.

The noise stopped as we reached the bottom of the steps.

The basement was dark, just like we'd left it. Instead of

being reassuring because it concealed my crime, the darkness felt like it hid danger instead. Every shadow was some unknown foe about to spring into an attack.

Through the window on the basement door, I didn't see anyone. I peered through the glass, practically smashing my nose to it to see where whoever had knocked had gone. There was no sign of anyone.

The freezer hummed away, off to the side. I shuddered, imagining Scott in there in his ketchup-print shirt with little ice crystals forming on his nostril hairs.

"I don't see anybody," I said.

Wendy pulled the string that hung from the ceiling in the center of the room. The bright bulb flashed on, sending all the shadows into hiding.

No one was here.

"Maybe it was…a rat?" Wendy looked under the staircase.

"To make all of that noise, it must have been a really big rat." I glanced again out the window.

"Like the ones in the forest in *The Princess Bride*. Remember when one jumped at Cary Elwes and he had to wrestle it."

"Of course," I said, a smile pulling gently at my cheeks. It was a great movie. "It was a bit like the way that Scott and I wrestled on the bed before you tased us. *I* bit *him*, though, so I guess that makes me the rat."

Wendy's expression fell. "Aww, no, you—"

With a bang, the freezer burst open.

A bare arm flung straight upward, its manicured fingers curled at unnatural angles. The hair on the arm was so thick, if I squinted, I'd think it was clad in a black sweater. With as much manscaping as Scott had done, I'd never understood why he hadn't waxed his arms.

More importantly, *Scott was alive.*

A fresh storm of emotions rolled over me—relief, hurt, vengeful bitterness. If he was alive, I hadn't murdered him. That was good. Still, I hated him too much to want him to be alive.

The arm dropped and sagged out the side of the freezer.

"He's supposed to be dead," I said.

"He had no pulse," Wendy said, her face as white as the freezer. "One hundred eleven percent. We both checked. He. Had. No. Pulse."

"Maybe it was just faint, too faint for us to notice."

Wendy wrinkled her nose and narrowed her eyes. "Maybe."

Scott flipped one leg up over the lip of the freezer. Then he flopped down to the floor as gracefully as a crash test dummy. His shoulder hit first, before the rest of him crumpled to the floor, accordion style.

My certainty that Scott was dead evaporated. He'd survived my mauling. I mean, what other explanation was there for him to move? The freezer had come to life and spit him out?

My hands began shaking. What was I supposed to do now? What could I possibly say to him? "Scott?"

I pushed down the urge to say I was sorry. I wasn't sorry, and I had no reason to be.

"Hey, dirtbag, why'd you try to kill Rose? Keep it nice this time, or you'll end up back in the freezer." Wendy lifted her broom up into the air like she was about to hit a homerun. "And this time, you won't crawl back out."

He wasn't moving.

I turned to Wendy. "He doesn't seem to be in the mood to talk. Maybe he's dead for real this time."

She shook her head. "He's too stubborn."

We walked across the floor and stopped a few feet away. Scott's head was turned so we couldn't see his face.

I swapped tools with Wendy, reached down, and poked Scott in the side with the broom. He didn't move.

"You should have used the poker," Wendy said. "I'll try."

I shouldn't have given her the poker.

"Don't," I said. I had to fix things, do the right thing. I needed to call an ambulance. "If he's still breathing—"

I caught a flash of movement out the corner of my eye. I looked down just in time to see Scott whip his body over. He opened his mouth with a gargling sound, and sank his teeth into the top of my bare foot.

Stinging, stabbing pain pierced my skin.

I screamed.

Wendy screamed.

Scott latched on.

We both smacked him in the back with the fireplace tools. I needed him off.

He didn't let go. He grabbed onto my ankle with both hands and shook his head as he dug his teeth deeper into my flesh.

He was rabid, a wild animal.

I hit him harder. *"Let me go!"*

Wendy whacked him in the side of the head.

Finally, he released me and snapped his jaw at the poker.

"Whoa," Wendy said, pulling back.

But Scott bit down on the metal before she could get away. He pulled with his teeth, making growling sounds.

I stumbled back, my steps faltering as soon as I tried to put weight on my injured foot.

I pulled off my shirt and wrapped it around my foot like a fat bandage to stymie the bleeding.

"What is *wrong* with you?" Wendy squealed, and kicked Scott in the side.

He relaxed his jaw and let go of the poker. His eyes rolled back. He put his head gently onto the floor and stilled.

With a slow rise of his chest and subsequent fall, a loud snore belted out of his slack jaw.

"He's asleep?" Wendy asked, her wild eyes landing on me like I had some kind of answer.

"I don't know."

"What do we do now?"

"Call for that ambulance?" I suggested, again.

We looked back to Scott. His chest was moving, so he was breathing. That was good, I guessed. The swirl of overwhelming emotion boiling up my chest wasn't entirely sure.

Scott, still looking half-dead, half-asleep, smacked his hand around like he was reaching for something.

"I don't think this is the behavior of a human person in need of help," Wendy said. "He's possessed."

"Possessed by what? Brain damage?"

Wendy narrowed her eyes. "Vampirism."

"Like possession, that's not real," I said.

She ticked off on her fingers. "No reflection. Craving blood."

She wasn't talking about Scott anymore. She was talking about me.

"I don't crave blood," I said, perhaps too defensively.

She cocked her head and shot me a look that said she knew better. "You chomped his artery."

I crossed my arms and fought to keep my tone even. "I was defending myself."

"I'm not arguing with that," she said. "Scott deserved it, one thousand percent. But that doesn't mean you aren't a vampire."

I considered this particular brand of lunacy for half a second, which was half a second too long. "It's not possible."

"Why not?"

"Aside from the obvious reality of vampires being fake," I said, "I can walk around in daylight."

She nodded and twisted her lips. "Zombies. On a scale of ten to ten, how much do you crave brains right now?"

Scott smacked the concrete and flipped his head in our direction. Both of his eyes opened. One was pointed toward the ceiling instead of at us. In an extra throaty voice he said, "Br…ain…s."

"Scott agrees with me," Wendy said. "Zombies."

"Head injury," I corrected.

"Okay, try this," Wendy said. "Put your fingers to your neck. Feel for a pulse."

To humor her, I did as she said. It was totally ridiculous.

I didn't find my pulse, which didn't mean anything. I tried my wrist. And I still couldn't find it.

"It's probably the stress. I'm not doing it right." I shook my head, then reached out my hand to her. "You try."

She pressed down on my wrist, held her hand there a minute, then let out a long breath. She plastered on a grave expression. "Sorry. It's zombies."

I searched my brain for any other explanation, but I couldn't find one. At least not right away. Of course there was some reasonable answer to all of this, I just didn't know what it was.

"What did that strange man who dug you up *do* to you?" Wendy asked.

Actually, that was a really good question.

I said, "I wish I knew."

A smile crept over Wendy's face. "You could ask him. I'll come for moral support."

"Tomorrow," I said. "After work."

And after I got some help for Scott.

"It's a date," Wendy said.

Scott slapped the floor, snapping our attention back to him. "Brrr…ai…nsss."

CHAPTER 8

"I maintain that Scott belongs in the freezer," Wendy said. "It's safer."

She held Scott's feet, while I held onto his arms. It was only fair that I take the bitey end, since this was my problem.

"I can't," I said. "He's a living, breathing person."

We carried him up to the living room and dropped him onto the floor. I dug through the junk drawer in the kitchen and retrieved the duct tape.

"First, are we sure he's breathing?" Wendy countered. "Second, he gave up all rights to empathy when *he tried to kill you.*"

Scott crawled across the floor by his hands, dragging his legs for some reason. I couldn't think of any reason why he couldn't get up onto his feet and walk, but it was probably better for us at the moment if he didn't.

He followed me into the kitchen. Wendy didn't.

Her voice sounded farther away than the living room when she said, "You don't owe that dirtbag anything. You gave him everything, and this is what you get in return? No. Let him be someone else's problem for a change."

"Braaaiiinnnns," Scott said, his weird eye rolling back and forth in his head, the iris a pendulum.

I shivered. With a satisfying *ziiip*, I pulled a sufficient length of tape and ripped it from the roll.

I bent down toward Scott's face. He snapped at my fingers. Moving just in time, I smacked the tape over his mouth.

"Bwwaay...bwaay." Scott's muffled sounds were indecipherable behind the tape.

Better still, as he smashed the front of his face against my ankle, his teeth couldn't get through.

"You're done biting, mister," I told him.

"Bwww."

"Are you listening to me?" Wendy popped her head around the corner, then joined us in the kitchen. She carried an armful of bandages and creams.

"I'm listening. What's the first aid for?" I glanced down at Scott's neck to where I'd bitten him. "He doesn't seem to be bleeding anymore."

"It's for you, dummy. Your foot, remember?"

I looked down at my foot, wrapped in my shirt. Right. That had happened. It seemed it wasn't as bad as it had looked and felt at first, or I wouldn't have been able to forget. Or maybe I'd just lost all feeling.

"Thanks," I said.

Wendy handed me a shirt.

"And for this. Thank you for *everything*," I told her.

"You're welcome. Now put on that shirt and let me take a look at your foot."

Scott continued to bump his taped mouth into my calf.

"Um." Wendy frowned at him. "Let's go to the living room first."

I did as she suggested, put on my fresh shirt, and sat on the sofa. Wendy unwrapped my foot, dumped the entire tube of antibiotic cream on the wound, then wrapped me in gauze.

"You need to get this looked at," she said. "Talking to a doctor about the after effects of being buried alive wouldn't be such a bad idea either."

Wendy's phone rang in her pocket. She frowned.

"It could be the shelter," I said. Since Wendy's recently-inherited animal shelter was in disrepair and perpetually short on funds and staff, emergencies happened often. "You should check."

She pulled out her phone and answered. Her face went pale. "I'll be there as soon as I can. Yeah. Thanks. Bye."

"It was the shelter?" I asked once she hung up.

She nodded. "Toast broke the door on his kennel. There was a fire. I have to go. I'm so sorry."

"It's okay, Wendy," I said.

She wiped her hands on her thighs and squeezed her fingers into the fabric of her dress. "Let's...get Scott in the freezer, and then I'll drop you at the hospital, and then—"

No way was I going to let her waste time worrying about me. This was an emergency. She had to go.

"I'm okay. Go."

Indecision warred on her features.

"Please," I said. "We'll check in."

"And confront your mystery rescuer tomorrow. Together, right?"

I put on my best I'm-totally-fine smile. "Absolutely."

She shot one last look at Scott, who sat on the floor by the edge of the living room. She groaned in dismay before hugging me. "Don't let him do anything to you. Don't trust him for a second."

"I won't."

Wendy went past both of us and grabbed the tape, then she wound it around one of Scott's hands and then the other, binding them together. "That's better. Okay. I'm going."

"Okay," I told her. "Good luck."

"You, too."

With that, she left, and it was just me and Scott. I decided then that the best move, my only move, was to take Wendy's advice. I needed medical help. Scott did, too. He needed it even more than I did, clearly.

A passing thought occurred to me—what if Wendy was right and the pair of us didn't have pulses? I mean, I certainly couldn't find them. What would the hospital do then—experimental testing? Quarantine and call in the CDC?

Everyone had a pulse. Ours were just faint, really *really* faint…that was all.

So, I gathered my things. By the time I was ready, he'd gotten to his feet on his own, which was great, because dragging my fiancé out of the house with his hands and face taped up was not a great look. Better if no one called the cops, at least until we arrived at the hospital.

I did a quick look around before we stepped out of the house, and another once we were safely in the vehicle. With just-in-case duct tape in my purse, I ushered Scott into the cargo area so he couldn't attack me while I drove. It was a kindness to take his Land Rover, because there was a lot more space in the back than there was in the trunk of my Camry.

As soon as the engine started, Scott settled in.

Along the road, at the corners of my vision, I could swear there was a strange shadow. It was shaped like a man, only when I turned my head to actually see it, there wasn't anything to see. There was no shadow.

After a weird but quiet drive, I pulled into the hospital lot and parked in the nearest open space. The lot was quite full, so we had a ways to walk.

I pushed the button on Scott's key fob and popped open the back. The cargo door lifted. Before it could even open halfway, Scott shoved his feet straight out at me, kicking me in the stomach. I stumbled back.

Don't fall. Please don't fall.

My heel caught on the curb. It felt like it was happening in slow motion. Cue the sad piano music, or maybe silly accordion instead, just before the inevitable womp-womp up landing. My body twisted as I fell. My foot somehow caught, wrenching my ankle in an unnatural direction. I flailed my arms to try to cushion myself, to try not to land on my face.

My shoe slipped off my foot.

The cement came for my face, fast and sure.

I closed my eyes automatically just before impact.

My hands caught, scraping against the rough surface, immense pressure followed, the weight of my arms buckling. But my face didn't hit the ground.

I opened my eyes to the sight of the cement a foot from my face.

A laugh boiled up through my chest and echoed into the lot.

I turned over onto my butt.

An elderly couple was standing at the other end of the sidewalk watching me. I was a mess. I was certain that fact radiated off me in waves, from my shirt to my tumble. Anyone in a fifty-mile radius had to be able to sense it.

Heat carried up my neck and settled in my cheeks.

"Are you all right?" the woman called over to me.

A quick flash of movement was my only warning before Scott launched himself at me, knocking me down onto my back.

The tape dangled halfway off his mouth.

"Bwwaainnns," Scott said through the hole in the tape.

The elderly man whisked his lady friend toward their car.

I waved as I fought Scott off with one arm. The fact that his hands were still taped together worked in my favor. I said, "We're fine. No need to get anyone to help or anything. Totally normal things happening here."

Too tired and overwhelmed to think, I wasn't sure if I was being sarcastic or not anymore.

Scott shoved his pink tongue out of the hole and licked my fingers.

"Eww." I karate chopped him in the throat. When that didn't faze him, I kneed him between the legs.

He stopped fighting. He completely stilled. Then his body went limp. He groaned, "Ugghhh."

No matter what else happened, it seemed I could still count on a good knee to the nuts.

I struggled to my feet, retrieved my shoe, and glanced back toward the couple. They were already gone, as was their car.

I looked in the cargo area and snatched Scott's hockey mask. Then I taped it to his face.

"Let's see you try and get that off," I said to Scott. Then I helped him to his feet.

He didn't say anything or make any moves as we headed up to the hospital. He slumped his shoulders and let his head droop, but he let me lead him.

The emergency room was packed. There weren't even any open seats in the waiting area. One woman sat with an icepack held to a nasty looking wound on her head, with blood all over her face.

We joined the line waiting to speak to reception, but I wasn't feeling particularly optimistic.

A large bald man writhed on the floor by the waiting area, moaning and holding his stomach.

The line moved up one. Two more people stood in front

of us. We waited. I kept half my attention on Scott, half-expecting him to attack someone at any moment.

Finally it was our turn.

Dark circles surrounded the eyes of the woman behind the desk. She shoved a clipboard up at me, hardly seeing me at all.

"Hi," I said.

"Fill out the pertinent information and return the clipboard when you're done," she said.

"We're having an emergency," I said. "This man—"

"This is the emergency room. Everyone is having an emergency. Fill out the pertinent information and return the clipboard when you're finished."

"I got that," I said. "But he has a head injury. He's been biting people, and I can't find his pulse."

"Fill out the—"

"I heard you," I said, "But—"

"Look, you can fill it out, or not. I don't care. There aren't any beds, anyway. You're looking at a six-hour wait, minimum, and that's even to get through intake. If this is an actual emergency, you might want to consider driving to the regional center in Holbrook."

"Holbrook's three hours away," I said, clenching the clipboard in my fists.

The wood snapped in two.

I clenched my jaw so hard I thought that might snap, too.

"Fill out the pertinent information if...." The woman kept talking but I stopped listening.

I reached for Scott's arm to lead him out of the way of the line. But he whipped his bound hands toward me, and bashed me right in the face.

My nose crunched.

Metallic liquid trickled down my throat.

"That's it. I'm done." I dropped the clipboard and threw

my hands up into the air. It was an announcement to the receptionist, to Scott, to the whole freaking universe. "This man has a head injury that's turned him into a raging cannibal. Don't let him bite you. And good freaking luck."

I spun on my heel and walked out the door. Adrenaline swelled through my chest, and a smile pulled at my cheeks. I couldn't believe I'd done that. I'd left him, and I didn't regret it even a little. Scott could be someone else's problem.

My stomach growled. I gave it a pat. I knew exactly what to do next—burger binge at the Snackthrough Station.

Life was a heck of a lot more pleasant when I finally decided to put myself first.

CHAPTER 9

Acutely I was aware that I was face down, asleep, and that my cheek was plastered to a cold surface. That awareness was easy to ignore as the vision of myself running through a dark forest overwhelmed the rest of my senses.

I was dreaming.

The cool, damp leaves of the forest floor crinkled under my bare feet. Icy air stung my bare arms and legs. My heart thudded in my throat.

Something else was here, a fleeting shadow, not quite man, not quite something else either. The heat of its breath on my neck threatened that if I slowed, it would catch me. If it caught me, I would die.

I needed to wake up.

Wake up.

My fingers flexed, not in the dream, but in reality. It wasn't enough to pull me from my nightmare.

My chest tight, my lungs leaden, I ran as hard and as fast as I could. But the shadow man was still there, still just as close. I couldn't escape.

I had to keep trying. I had to—

The melodic ringing of my phone grounded me to my body. I pried my eyes open. Harsh morning light flooded through the slits, forcing my eyes to shut once more.

A groan crept up out of my throat, and I rolled over, peeling my wet cheek from the couch cushion. My cheek stung and left a layer of skin behind. Why was I in the living room?

A soft set of pokes on my chest made it clear someone else was here.

I opened my eyes fully, adjusting to the morning light, and turned my head to see.

A cat stood on my chest, all orange fur and purring defiance. Every cat I'd ever met seemed to think he was king over all he could see. This one seemed to be no different with the lazy yet regal tilt of his head and knitting of my shirt.

Scowling at it, I said, "Who are you and how did you get in here?"

The cat reached a paw slowly toward my face. It batted my cheek.

I lifted an arm to block its claws, and laughed at the absurdity of the situation. I said, "Hey."

The cat jumped down.

My phone rang again.

I scrambled upright and spotted my phone by my keys on the coffee table.

The picture on the screen was of my daughter, her nose squinched up, her thick-lashed eyes crinkled, her voluminous black curls falling down over the right half of her face and covering half of her smile.

I couldn't answer fast enough. "Heather, hi."

"Hi, Mom. Are you all right?"

"Uh-huh, of course," I said, ignoring all evidence to the contrary. "How are you? It's nice to hear from you."

It was always me calling her, not the other way around.

After growing up with my mother always away, always putting her work over everything else, including me, I had to be a different kind of mom—present and loving, no matter what.

"You didn't call yesterday," she said, ignoring my question.

Yesterday…what was yesterday? Realization struck, a sledgehammer to the gut. "Your show at the gallery. I'm so sorry I didn't call. How was it? Did you sell any paintings? I am so proud of you, you know that, right?"

"It was fine. I sold two pieces," she said.

"That's great," I told her. "Did Carlos come?"

"I'm not seeing Carlos anymore," she said. "Remember?"

I did remember. He was a sweet boy, though, and perfect for her. They'd been friends through college, and had finally started dating when it had been clear for years that he'd absolutely adored her. I wanted her to have everything I didn't, including a partner who would support her no matter what.

I said, "Of course."

"What's up with you?" she asked. "I'm worried."

"I'm all right," I said, rising to my feet.

I looked around the floor for the cat who had somehow snuck into the house. As far as I knew, none of my neighbors had an orange cat.

"Uh-huh," Heather said, clearly not believing me. "How did it go at the lawyer's office?"

"It was quick," I said. "Granny left everything substantial to a cat."

Come to think of it, the cat that had snuck into my car at the lawyer's office was similar in color to the one who was in my house now. It couldn't be the same cat, though. That was ridiculous.

A throbbing pain manifested in the center of my forehead.

Heather said, "But Granny hated cats."

"I know. That's what I said." I rubbed the knot between my eyes. "She left me the key to a storage unit, so hopefully I'll get the photo albums. Maybe my grandmother's quilts. Sentiment means more than money."

"Granny was all about her money," Heather said. "She wanted to make and leave you enough that you never had to worry, like she had to when she was younger."

"If that's what she told you, she lied. Clearly," I said. "Her focus was on money, that's true at least."

"I don't believe for a second she would give it away to someone else," Heather said.

"Well, she did."

"Whose cat is it? It sounds like a scheme to me. Someone manipulated her into changing her will. Whoever owns that cat is the villain. I'd bet money on it."

I sighed. "There's no mystery villain. It's a lesson. She wanted me to know that I need to be like her and put building wealth above all else. It's fine. I should have expected this."

Heather sighed. "I don't believe that."

"You shouldn't worry about it," I said. "It's fine."

"Well I hope you're right about the albums, at least."

"I'll let you know," I told her. I spotted the time on the wall clock and cringed. I needed to hustle or I'd be late for work. "I really am sorry I didn't call."

"Mom. It's fine. You're here for me *all the time.* I'm not hurt. I've been worried about you is all. Did something happen with Scott?"

Scott tried to kill me twice, and I almost killed him in return. The wedding is off. I couldn't say any of that, not yet, or I'd make her worry.

"I'm all right. I do have to get to work though," I said. "I'm glad you called. Love you."

"I love you, too."

I raced around the house to get ready in the seven minutes left before I had to leave for the office. It didn't occur to me until I was in my bedroom that Scott wasn't here. Good. Hopefully he was at the hospital getting the help he needed. I shouldn't have thought about him at all. He wasn't my problem anymore.

I also found no sign of the kitty. My bedroom window was open, though, so I left it when I headed out, hoping the cat would find its way back out on its own.

It was a short drive to my job at the Lincoln building. I'd worked in data entry for the same company for the past twenty years. Yes, there had been opportunities to move up to different positions, but I'd never applied. The job I had offered everything I needed—financial stability, medical insurance, retirement, and flexible time off to be available for Heather. When she was growing up I never missed a field trip or school project. Now that she'd grown up and moved away, she didn't need me so much, but I could be there if she called.

I parked at the far end of the lot, like always, and raced inside. I sat down at my desk and dug into the mountain of papers piled before me. Only then did it occur to me that while I had been unconscious for days, I had missed work Thursday and Friday.

There was something about being in the office that made life feel normal. Maybe it was the sounds of the copy machine buzzing, the scents of freshly opened paper and faint industrial cleaners, or the harsh yellow lights. Probably it was the combination, plus the sound and feel of my fingers clicking away on my keyboard that soothed away any tension I brought from home.

Somewhere between files, a finger poked the crook between my shoulder and neck.

I stopped typing, flinched, and turned around to find a man half my age standing behind me. Colby Jackson, my boss.

The man's name was basically a type of cheese. Worse, he smelled like cheese, and not a pleasant variety.

I flexed my fingers on my slacks and attempted to hide my disdain from him. I plastered on a fake smile and hoped this wasn't about me missing work. Maybe he hadn't noticed. "Yes?"

"Mrs. Cruise, you look pale. Are you sick?"

Ms. DeLaCrux.

"No," I said. "I'm not sick."

I also couldn't use a mirror anymore, having no reflection, so if my lipstick was a bit off, it was the best that I could do.

"You've been with the company since I was in diapers." He chuckled.

I bit my lip so as not to snarl. I didn't know why exactly my mood had soured so fast. Sure, I didn't like Colby, but that wasn't a new revelation.

My stomach growled. Ah, I definitely should have made time to eat breakfast. That was the problem.

After this interaction concluded, I'd grab a doughnut from the breakroom, and hope my tastebuds were behaving today. They had to return to normal at some point, like after fighting a snotty cold with nasal drip.

"I'm going to reward your loyalty," Colby said. "I know your generation thinks it's worth something," he said, this time laughing outright. "We're scrubbing your entire department."

I felt the blood drain from my head. A wave of dizziness struck. "What?"

"Everything's easier, cheaper, going remote," he said.

My mouth went dry. I licked my lips. "But you're sparing me?"

Please spare me.

"Kind of. You'll have to work from home," he said. "And you'll get half the hours."

"What about my benefits?" I asked.

"They've been scrubbed, too. I'll let you in on a little secret." He leaned in too close. The scent of menthol mixed with the mint of his breath and the Limburger of his pits and pores. "Shop companies. Leverage your experience for better pay. There's a new guy starting at ten times what you're making."

"How does that save the company money?" I asked.

He shrugged. "Clean out your desk. New files will all come to your work email. The company uses a digital babysitter program, so you don't need to punch in or anything. You'll get paid for the time you work, up to twenty hours per week that is. Best of luck to you."

Twenty hours per week meant half the pay. Plus, the company was taking away my benefits. How was I going to pay my bills? How did they expect me to survive?

The company didn't care what happened to me.

Colby dropped an empty box on my desk, spun on his heel, and walked to the next cubicle over. "Mr. Barberger," he said to my next-door work neighbor Mrs. Burberry.

He gave her the same spiel, pretending like he was doing her a favor instead of decimating her livelihood. I wanted to crush something in my fists, preferably Colby's smug face, but that wouldn't help anything.

I zoned out and focused on the task I needed to complete. I picked up my personal effects—a framed photo of Heather at her first big gallery show, another of her when she was three with the fingerpaint mural she painted on her bedroom wall, my favorite pen, and the mug Wendy had gifted me from her pottery period. And I left.

My ears rang, high pitched. It was almost like I was underwater. This wasn't my life.

I sat in my car, leaned my head against the wheel, and closed my eyes.

Everything was fine.

Who needed medical insurance anyway? Not zombies. Wouldn't it be funny if Wendy were right about that nonsense? Wouldn't it be easier? Of course none of that was true. Indulging in fantasy wasn't helpful.

I rubbed my palms over my eyes and found tears prickling at the corners. Crying wouldn't help, either. I'd figure something out, some way to pay the mortgage, Heather's school loans, everything.

A dark figure moved behind the bushes in front of my car. The little hairs on my skin prickled alert. When I looked fully in that direction, I didn't see anyone.

But I could feel a set of eyes watching. Like the shadow man in my dreams.

Skin crawling, I threw my car in reverse, hustled out of my parking spot, and then booked it out of there. As soon as I left, the creepy feeling dissipated. It was so quick that I felt silly for feeling that way at all.

I couldn't be at work, Wendy would still be busy at the shelter for hours, and the idea of going home left a sour taste in my mouth. So, I pulled my inheritance—a rusty key—from my purse.

I put the faded address into my maps app and drove to my mother's storage unit.

The gates opened for me without having to prove in any way that I belonged. I parked, glanced around for someone to ask for assistance, but found no one.

A cracked cement path ran between two long buildings.

Massive trees from beyond the lot blocked out most of the sunlight, making the area feel ten degrees cooler. My footsteps echoed off the metal doors, even in open air. I watched the numbers count down—one-fifteen, one-thirteen—until I reached one-zero-one, the number on my key.

I tried it in the lock, but it didn't budge, likely from the rust on the lock. I wiggled the key a bit, and it turned.

The door popped open. It clanged as I lifted it up over my head.

The unit was small, and packed floor to ceiling with cardboard boxes. The cardboard was another detail that didn't sit right with me. My mother hated places like this, and she never would have stored any of her belongings in anything but the same black plastic totes she'd used my whole life. *Cardboard attracts bugs, Rosemary.* I could practically hear her voice in my head, see the way she grimaced at the very suggestion. As I scanned the unit, no bugs appeared.

I pulled out a box, sat on the ground, and opened the lid to examine the contents.

A mess of silk scarves tangled together. Why would she have packed up her scarves? Why would they be tangled? If nothing else, Lenore DeLaCrux was tidy in everything she did, and in everything she kept.

I dug a hand through to see if there was anything else, but the box only contained the knotted bundle of scarves. Perhaps Heather would want some, if any of them were in good enough condition to keep. I focused on the cool air and the warm sun, and I slowly worked to untangle the scarves. When each was neatly folded the way Mom had always kept them in her drawer, I put the lid back on the box and pulled out another.

The second box was full of bras, and a bikini. Why would she pack up her bras? Or go on a vacation to the Caribbean without her bathing suit? I wouldn't be caught dead in something like the pearl-hued crocheted number she wore to the pool. But she loved it. Even at seventy years old, she'd never been ashamed to show off her figure.

I smiled at the memory of her tending her vegetable garden one year on Easter morning when we arrived. She had worn shorts and her bikini top. Heather was little at the time. Fred, my first almost-husband, had been mortified when he spotted her. He'd covered Heather's eyes. She'd pushed him off and run to her granny.

My mother had been a lot of things. Modest wasn't one of them. I wished I had her strength. She was a force of nature, so sure she was right about everything. It had driven me crazy in the past, but in hindsight, it was a strength, never having to worry or second guess herself. She was self-assured, and self-sufficient.

Under the bras, at the bottom of the box, was a photograph. The corners curled, one bent up and torn. In the picture was Heather and my mom in matching dresses on a boat.

At least she'd bonded with Heather.

"Excuse me." It was a woman's voice.

I startled in response. I picked myself up to my feet, set the photo back in its box, and tried to wipe the dirt from the back of my pants without taking my eyes off the stranger.

She looked like she had just stepped out of a fifties diner with her hoop skirt, cherry lipstick, and red hair curled on top of her head. She held herself tall with confidence, and looked like she belonged at a place like this as much as my mother would have, which was to say not at all.

"Hi," I said. "If you're looking for someone who works here, I haven't seen anyone."

"I'm not," she said with an easy smile. "I'm here to speak with you."

"Do I know you?"

"Not yet." She offered me her hand. "Lily Fernsby, librarian."

The addition of her job title was particularly peculiar.

I accepted her hand and we shook, short and firm, professional. "Rosemary DeLaCrux," I said. "Not-quite-unemployed."

Lily's lips twisted like she wasn't quite sure what to make of that. I wasn't quite sure, either.

"There we go," Lily said, her smile returning. "Now we are officially acquainted."

"Sure," I said. "Why exactly are you here looking for me? Don't tell me you're here from the lawyer's office. I haven't gone near my mother's home."

"Not at all," Lily said. "I'm here to discuss your supernatural nature. What manner of death defiance have you employed?"

Supernatural nature?

The blood drained from my head. A knot formed in my stomach. "I don't know what you're—"

"There's no need to play coy," she said. "The library is well-versed in all manner of magic, alchemy, horoscopy, divination, curses, omens, and everything else. The library knows everything about everything and everything about everyone."

"If you know everything about me, then why bother asking me anything? Why not find out at your library." Either I'd been using libraries incorrectly my whole life, or this woman was in need of a psychiatric ward.

Pink settled into her cheeks. "That option…is not available to me at this time."

I placed the box back where it belonged, and held my hand over my phone. I asked, "What do you want with me?"

"Only to know why the reaper is stalking you," she said, tilting her chin up.

"I don't know what you're talking about."

"Don't you, though?" she asked. "Even if you haven't seen him, you have to have felt him. He eyes you like it's a sweltering day in July and you're a scoop of mint chocolate chip."

She could see this guy now? Some kind of stalker? I glanced around and saw no one but Lily.

"I prefer cookies and cream," I told her.

She gaped at me, but quickly recovered. "Your poor taste in dessert aside, you do know what I'm talking about. You'll have felt an icy chill at times when you're alone. Maybe you don't realize yet that you're supposed to be dead. But you do know something happened, something you shouldn't have survived."

A wave of dizziness hit me. My stomach heaved.

"There it is," Lily said. "My confirmation."

She produced a card in her hand out of nowhere, like a magician with a quarter.

"Do give me a call when you're ready to talk. We can do it over ice cream at Udderly Ice Dream. Once you've tried their mint chocolate chip, you'll see the light."

I took the card and watched her walk away. I didn't want to believe anything that she'd said. A *reaper?*

But I had dreamed of a shadowy man, and I could have sworn I'd seen one, too. Was it possible that's what she was talking about? And there was no denying that I'd escaped death after being buried alive.

A shiver carried up my spine, and I didn't wait to see if the shadow man was there, too, before I booked it the heck out of there.

CHAPTER 10

When I needed help, Wendy was always the one I turned to. Instinctively, since I had never needed more help in my life, I drove straight to her house. When I arrived, her car wasn't there, which if I'd have thought about it, I would have remembered that she was still at work and would be for another hour. Still, as soon as I turned onto her street, my nerves settled a bit.

Even if nothing was right yet, it would be. It could be.

I parked in the driveway, reclined my seat, and closed my eyes.

Was it possible I was supposed to be dead? That the grim reaper was skulking about following me around, trying to claim his prize? Of course not.

And what about what Heather had said about the cat who inherited my mother's house? Who did the cat belong to? Even if my mother wanted me to learn the value of being just like her, if she didn't want me to have her money and her house, why wouldn't she give it to Heather? She adored Heather. *And she hated cats.*

Nothing in the past few days made any sense at all.

There was a perfectly reasonable answer, at least to the cat mystery, and all it would take was a phone call to get it. I pulled out my phone and dialed the lawyer's office.

A woman answered straight away. "Bueford Gross's office, please hold."

Before I could respond, there was a click followed by crackly elevator music.

A moment later, someone picked up the line. Shuffling noises and muffled whispers came through.

"Hello?" I said.

"No, yeah, I've got it," a man said away from the receiver. "Louise, I said I've got it." More shuffling. Then he said clearly, "Hello. This is Bueford Gross, Attorney at Law. What legal needs may I assist you with?"

What was this guy's deal? Maybe his assistant was new, and that was all. Or maybe Heather was right and whoever had orchestrated the farce of a will had chosen Bueford Gross exactly because he was incompetent.

"Hi," I said. "This is Rosemary DeLaCrux. I was in your office on—"

Mr. Gross sucked in a sharp breath, and flew into a coughing fit. Seconds turned into minutes. Finally, in a rough and strained voice he said, "I know who you are, Ms. DeLaCrux."

"...Great. Now that I've had time to think over my mother's will, I have questions."

"Hmm," he said.

"When was this will created? Who was there when my mother signed? Did you personally see her in your office for its creation?"

He coughed again. "That's proprietary."

My suspicion grew by the second. Why hadn't I thought to ask more at the original meeting? Right, because I was out of sorts, reeling over my loss. I should have brought someone with me, if not Wendy then Heather. If I'd have asked, would Heather have come? I hadn't wanted to bother her, not with her art show on the horizon. I'd made a mistake.

"These are reasonable questions," I said. "I'd like to see a copy of the will, along with signatures of any witnesses, and most of all, the signature of my mother."

What if she hadn't signed this thing at all?

"It's proprietary," Mr. Gross said.

"That's ridiculous. Who owns the cat? Certainly it wasn't my mother."

"It's pr—"

"I know, *it's proprietary.*" I leaned my head on the wheel. "Shady things are clearly happening here. I'll get to the bottom of it. If you don't tell me the truth now, I'm getting legal counsel. This is your one chance to tell me what's going on. Tell me who owns the cat."

"That's...*eeep.*"

Click.

"Mr. Gross?" I pulled the phone from my ear and looked at the screen. The call had ended. He'd hung up on me.

I'd expected him to say something like maybe that I shouldn't make threats, maybe that there was a simple explanation. I hadn't expected him to hang up on me. I'd been a little suspicious before, but now I was certain that something fishy was going on. I closed my eyes and tried to unjumble the mess in my brain.

Tap tap tap.

I peeked through one eye and turned my head toward the sound. Wendy's Aunt Petunia stood beside the driver's side window, bent down so her face was an inch from the glass. Her glasses rested at the end of her nose. The beaded chain dangling from the ends of the glasses was the one I'd made for her a few years ago. Her dark eyes crinkled in concern, and her white hair puffed around her head a little more wildly than usual.

"Hi, Petunia," I said.

She smiled, waved at me, and said something about cookies and berries and almonds. The glass muffled the sound so I only caught a few words.

I rolled down the window a bit. "I'm okay here. I could use a nap."

"A nap at this hour? You're supposed to be at work, aren't you, Rosie? Is everything all right?"

"Mmm," I said with a nod, to all of her questions and to none in particular.

"Come now, you know I can't leave you here in this metal box in the sun. Join me for one of those cookies I was telling you about. You can put some meat on those bones while you wait for Wendy."

I was anything but boney.

She reached through the open window, unlocked the door, and pulled the handle. The door opened, and she ushered me out, offering me no choice but to follow.

The tension in my shoulders released despite my desire to stay put. I'd always adored Wendy's family. They were warm people. Pushy, sure, but that extra interest showed they cared.

I followed Petunia toward the kitchen. On the way, I spotted her husband, Ralph, snoring open-mouthed on the couch.

I took a seat at the kitchen table across from Petunia. She lifted the head off the cat-shaped cookie jar and pushed the jar across the table at me.

"Ralph is allowed to nap but I'm not?" I pulled a cookie out of the jar. It was firm and covered in powdered sugar, with a few lumps of dried blueberry sticking out of the boomerangish shape. Likely it was a variation of Ralph's family's Greek butter cookie recipe. Knowing him, he wouldn't appreciate the addition of the berries or any other change to "how they were meant to be".

"Ralph isn't out in the sun." She leaned in closer, mischief playing in her eyes. "Plus, when he's asleep it gives me a quiet reprieve."

"Ahh, now we get to the truth of the matter."

She nodded. "Tell me about your problems. There's nothing a good cookie and conversation can't help."

I couldn't help but smile. Also, there was no way I was taking a bite of the cookie without a drink to go with it. Even though I hadn't tried this particular variety, I knew the type. They were delicious, and gently sweet, but deathly dry to the point that they could be used as weapons. Feed two to your enemies. They gladly accept because who doesn't love a good cookie. Then they die of dehydration, their bodies shriveling to husks.

"Eat," Petunia said. She poured us each a cup of tea, for which I was grateful.

Once I had the tea at hand, I took a bite. It was as dutifully dry as expected. Sadly, my tastebuds were still on the fritz. I couldn't taste anything but ash.

"It's good," I told her. If I could taste, I was sure it would be.

She nodded, knowing I would say so. "Of course."

"I hear you have a bear problem," I said, turning the conversation away from me as quickly as possible.

"I wouldn't call it a problem as of yet," Petunia said.

"Wendy calls it Teddy."

Petunia smiled. "That girl fears nothing."

To Petunia, no matter how old we were, Wendy and I would always be children.

"Tell me about it," I said. "Did you know she's carrying a taser around, acting as if it's not dangerous?"

"Weapons are tools, only dangerous if you don't know how to handle them."

Right, I'd nearly forgotten Petunia was the one with a shotgun.

"The closest the bear has come to the yard is the tomato planters," she said.

"So about halfway in?"

"About halfway, sure. It only comes by when Wendy's home."

"It ventures over in the evenings," I said. "Like it sleeps all day."

"Not just evenings. Weekends too. Almost as if it's drawn to her specifically. Just in case, I keep my gun ready when I go out alone. But it hasn't bothered me. Or Ralph for that matter, either. He's always out there banging up a storm."

"When he's not napping," I said.

She chuckled. "When he's not napping."

At the sound of the door, Ralph stopped snoring.

"Stealing my best friend, Aunt Peti?" Wendy walked into the kitchen.

"I was trying, and it was working until you showed up," Petunia said, with a twinkle in her eye.

Wendy joined us and gave her aunt a grin and a hug. When she let go, she poked my arm. "Let me change my shoes and I'm ready to go."

We were supposed to go see the guy who had rescued me from my premature grave. In everything else, I'd nearly forgotten.

I glanced down at Wendy's feet. The pointed toes with kitty cats on them made this pair work shoes. Her usual flats were rounded in the front, and more worn in.

"It was nice catching up, dear," Petunia said.

"Likewise," I told her with a smile.

"Even if you don't want to talk with me about your job, be

sure to talk to Wendy. It's not healthy to hold things in," Petunia said.

"Come on." Wendy grabbed my arm and led me outside and around the house to her basement apartment. The sun hid behind the forest, slowly drifting away for the night. Wendy let me go by the back door and switched out her shoes just inside. "I didn't expect you to be off work before me. Is everything all right?"

Everyone kept asking me that.

"I got…demoted?" I said. I wasn't sure exactly what it was called when the company took everything away while leaving my title and expecting me to do the same job.

"That's ridiculous. It's the stupidest thing I've ever heard. They're stupid. You're the best data enterer they have. Why would they take that away?"

I said, "They're switching to contractors, I think."

"Of course, so they don't have to pay benefits."

"Exactly."

"What are you going to do?"

"Well, technically I still have my job," I said. "Only I have to work from home. And I can only clock half the hours."

"That's not good enough. You deserve better."

"It's what it is," I said. "I don't know. I've hardly processed it at all."

"Well you shouldn't settle, not for a job that treats you poorly. And not in other areas of your life, either."

I knew she meant Scott.

"I took your advice," I said.

We headed back out and into my car. I drove out of the driveway and toward the stranger's building.

"What advice?"

"I let Scott be someone else's problem. I dropped him at the hospital and I'm not picking him back up. He can call his…."

"You don't know his family," Wendy said. "Or his friends."

"He's always been really vague about his family. They don't live around here. He doesn't like to talk about them."

"That man isn't just full of red flags. He *is* a red flag. Only a monster puts ketchup on pancakes. You're better off without him."

She was right.

She went on, "You know at some point, if he's not eating the brains of everyone in the hospital right this moment, he's going to come back and try to manipulate you into letting him into your life."

"We're done," I said. And I finally felt firm about it. "I'm done looking, too. No more men. I accept that love is just not in the cards for me."

Wendy gave me a questioning look. Her gaze sharpened, and with it, a devious grin overtook her face. "Spinsters for life."

When I stopped at a stoplight, Wendy put out her fist. I bumped it with mine. Cool air blew through the open windows, fueling me with a fresh rush of energy.

"We'll have to learn to knit and collect cats."

"I know how to knit," she said.

"Okay, so you'll have to teach me."

"Of course," she said. "I also know where we can find cats. The shelter has twenty-three of them right at this moment."

"I woke up to one in my house this morning," I said. "It must have gotten in through my bedroom window."

"Upstairs? How did it manage that?"

"No idea." I pulled into the only open spot by the curb. We were across the street and about a block from the stranger's building, but it was as close as we were going to get at this hour.

"Whose cat is it?" Wendy asked.

"I don't know that, either."

"Weird."

"I guess I'm already on my way to the perfect life—ditching my would-be-husband, attracting cats."

"Maybe being alone after forty is like catnip. They can't help but flock to us. Except instead of cats, my pores emit bear-nip."

I laughed. "Maybe."

Wendy looked past me through the side window. Her eyes went wide.

A deep voice practically purred right beside me. "I was wondering how long it would take for you to return."

"Ah!" I whipped around.

The stranger was there, leaning on my open window. He was the man from the picture next to the fruit bowl, his square jaw covered in thick brown hair. Both his beard and the hair on his head were sprinkled with strands of white that reflected sunlight like the river where he had fished.

There was so much more to him than I'd seen in that photograph—for starters, he wore a tailored suit instead of flannel. He wasn't a lumberjack at all, but a businessman, or maybe a sexy chameleon who could easily slip into any role he chose.

And that mouth. He wasn't smiling. He wasn't saying or doing anything with those lips, but there was something about them that drew my attention and I couldn't look away.

Wendy grabbed my hand and squeezed. "Is this him? Tell me this is him."

"It's him," I said.

"Hello," the stranger said with a small smile for Wendy.

That smile was too charming for words, too delicious to be legal.

"Swoon," Wendy whispered. "Forget spinsterhood."

"Andrew Jensen." He offered his hand to me.

I stared at his long fingers. He'd touched me with them

before, pulled me out of the ground. I hadn't remembered before, but seeing him now, I remembered him popping open a bottle, lifting the glass to my lips. What had he given me? Water? No, it had tasted like something…like grass and hot garbage.

"I'm Wendy. My friend here is Rosemary," Wendy said. "It's nice to meet you, Mr. Jensen. Now what exactly are you? Sun-loving vampire or high-functioning zombie?"

His smile grew, and he withdrew his hand. "Nice to meet you, too. Call me Andrew. I'd invite you both inside, but perhaps a public setting would be more comfortable?" He turned his gaze on me.

"Okay," I said, forcing my attention away from his mouth.

"So you are not going to answer my question?" Wendy asked.

"I'm neither," he said. "We can walk down to the sports bar on the corner if that works for you."

"Sure," I said.

"So a more traditional, sun-hating vampire?" Wendy asked.

"No," he said gently to Wendy before turning his full attention back to me. He opened my door for me. "I'm a mortal man."

Although he appeared mildly amused, he didn't seem thrown by Wendy's questions. He was suave, smooth, used to hearing the absurd but not making people feel strange about it? Maybe?

"Hmm." Wendy frowned, unconvinced.

I was unconvinced, too. I hadn't seriously considered supernatural possibilities, no matter how many times Wendy mentioned them. I wanted Andrew's denials to put me at ease.

But my non-existent pulse picked up anyway. If anything, I was focusing on my new flavor of weird.

No reflection? No problem. There's a reasonable explanation of some sort. All the mirrors are broken. No pulse? Insanely low blood pressure, totally normal. Wacky tastebuds? Middle age can initiate all kinds of changes.

Everything was fine.

My brain told me I could trust him. He had saved my life, after all. But my gut—it was all twisted and confused. My skin flushed with a wash of heat. I had no reason to feel anything about this man, so why did I feel so flipping off balance?

CHAPTER 11

On the walk over, Andrew and Wendy put me in between them. Andrew looked ahead, his hands casually in his pockets, his stance completely at ease. Wendy peeked around me, watching him like he would turn into a bat and fly away at any moment.

Completely stiff and all too aware of how close Andrew was to me, I kept my arms tucked in at my sides, as if accidentally bumping his arm would be a world-ending disaster. I felt like a child—no, a hormone-crazy, socially inept, and completely irrational teenager.

Inside the bar, we settled into a corner booth that was both secluded enough for privacy, and near enough to yelling sports fans that our conversation would not be easily overheard. Wendy and I sat together across from Andrew.

We ordered drinks. They were surprisingly quickly delivered.

Andrew took off his suit jacket, pulled his tie loose, and unbuttoned the top button of his shirt. It took concentrated effort not to stare as he worked his long, nimble fingers. It took effort not to stare at him in general. I affixed my attention to a nice, neutral location—my drink. I spun the stem of the wine glass between thumb and forefinger.

Wendy was talking. I cared about what she had to say, so why couldn't I focus and listen?

"*You* must have questions, Rosemary," Andrew said.

I did. So many questions.

What had happened to me? How had he found me underground? Had he seen Scott burying me? If so, why hadn't he stopped him before Scott finished the job?

There was more to ask, I was sure, but my mind was spinning and no words came out of my mouth.

"She has no reflection," Wendy said. "Why doesn't she? You definitely know more than you're saying. Easy when you're not saying anything at all. Plus you show up just after sunset, before we can get out of the car, even though you shouldn't have known we were coming. I don't believe for a second that you're not some kind of vampire."

Those were all good points, except for the whole vampire thing.

Andrew flourished his fingers in a circle, as if he was tickling a tambourine or playing an invisible spherical piano. A small bottle of green liquid appeared in his hand. It was the size of a golf ball. Had he slid it out of his sleeve in a magician-worthy sleight of hand?

The glass shattered.

The green liquid burst into a cloud of green gas.

Wendy said, "What the—"

The smoke dissipated.

The world stilled. The roaring of the sports fans cut out in an instant. The game still played on the televisions around the room, but none of the people in the bar were making any noise. None of them were moving.

Neither was Wendy.

The only ones able to move, spared by whatever was

happening, were me and Andrew, and I certainly hadn't done this.

Shocked, horrified, frustrated, I grabbed onto Wendy's unmoving arm and kicked Andrew in the leg. *"What did you do?"*

This was a mistake. We never should have come here. Andrew Jensen wasn't a chameleon, he was a snake.

He leaned forward across the table. "Tell me now, how much do you trust your friend?"

"What? Fix her." Anger, confusion, panic. "Please undo this."

"It's momentary," he said. "She will be fine. *Do. You. Trust. Her?*"

His eyes weren't cruel, only insistent. If this whatever was happening was meant to be harmful, why did his gray eyes almost appear gentle?

I leveled my gaze at him. "With my life."

He lifted a brow. "All right. But do you trust her with your secrets?"

I was taken aback. "I don't have any secrets."

He drummed his fingers on the table, checked his watch.

Okay, maybe I didn't used to have any secrets. The last few days had been a lot.

"I trust Wendy. Now please—"

Before I could finish my sentence, he snapped his fingers.

"—heck are you doing?" Wendy finished her sentence.

Conversations around the bar picked up. Everything picked back up exactly where it had left off.

Wendy's expression fell when she looked over my face. "You're pale. What happened?" She turned to Andrew. "I have no problem stabbing vampires."

"He didn't..." I patted her hand, thankful for the support. "I'm okay."

"All right then." She sat back and took another sip of her chocolate martini.

Andrew was watching me, waiting for me to speak. He was waiting for me to ask my questions, I guessed. It was hard to focus after he'd just frozen the whole freaking bar. In that moment I'd learned something about him beyond the surface. He was dangerous in a way I didn't understand.

But I did have questions. I decided the best place to start was at the beginning.

"How did you find me the other night?" I asked.

"Ah, good question," he said. "I was gathering flowers when I heard you scream."

"Gathering flowers at night…in a graveyard," Wendy said. "And you expect us to believe you're not a vampire?"

"They're for my alchemy," he said, like it was the most normal thing in the world.

It was weird, and deserved more questions, but I was stuck on the other detail. "How did you hear me? I was buried six feet under."

"I have sharp hearing from my father's side," he said.

"Your ears look pretty normal from here," Wendy said.

"What did you pour in my mouth?" I asked Andrew.

"A potion," he said, "to heal your failing systems. It was the only way to save your life."

The next part was the scariest. Had he actually healed me with his mystery potion? But the healing only partially worked? I wasn't sure. Something was definitely still off.

"Why don't I have a pulse?" I asked.

"You're no longer alive in the traditional sense," he said.

Wendy leaned in closer, looking from me to Andrew and back again.

"If I'm not *traditionally alive—*" I tried to swallow the lump in my throat. "Then what am I?"

"You are a revenant," Andrew said. "It's why you wrecked my kitchen when you woke."

"Sorry about that," I whispered.

"Don't be," he said. "Hunger is as natural to a revenant as breathing is to the rest of us."

Wendy leaned forward and whispered, "She doesn't need to breathe?"

"No," Andrew said.

"Great. Just great." I shoved myself to my feet, chest tight. I needed space. I couldn't breathe. My head went fuzzy, dizzy. No, *I no longer needed to breathe.* The thought was suffocating.

I couldn't bring myself to look at Andrew or Wendy. I couldn't speak. I felt people turning in their chairs to stare at me as I grabbed my throat and gasped for air I couldn't breathe.

I needed to leave. Now.

I ran for the door, out into the night. I ran for my car.

Tears streamed down my cheeks. I didn't want to cry. I didn't want to run. I didn't want any of this.

People walked down the sidewalks. Some stopped and pointed or tried to talk to me. Just like inside the bar, they stared.

I didn't stop running until I reached my car. I climbed inside, locked the doors, and closed my eyes.

What did it mean that I was a revenant? It meant I wasn't human anymore. I had no idea what else it meant, because I'd run away. Andrew had more answers for me, certainly, but the idea of going back right now made me sick.

A small knock came from the passenger side window.

I looked up and saw Wendy. She gave me a concerned smile and a wave.

I unlocked the door, and she climbed in.

"Hey," she said.

"Hey." I flexed my fingers. "Sorry about that. I shouldn't have left you."

"Totally fine," she said.

"I'd like to go home now," I said.

"Want me to drive?" she asked.

"Yes, please."

We switched seats and Wendy drove me back to my house. The farther we went from the bar, the more *me* I felt. By the time we got home, the shock had worn off and I was ready to talk.

I glanced at Wendy as I unlocked the door and turned on the light. "Did he say anything after I left?"

"Yeah." She pulled a business card out of her pocket and handed it to me. "He asked me to tell you to eat a lot of meat. He said it's really important. And he'll be available to chat whenever you're ready."

I looked over his name and number on the card. His occupation was listed as alchemist. How was that a real job?

Lots of meat, huh? That fit with my recent cravings.

I said, "Available when I'm ready? That's nice."

"He seems quite nice," she said. "And hot. And devoted to you."

"Devoted?" I shook my head. "He doesn't even know me."

"But he still made the effort to dig you out of the ground when your fiancé tried to murder you," she said.

"If you heard someone buried alive, you'd help them right?"

"Sure. Unless they were making zombie sounds. But I wouldn't have heard. And that's all hypothetical. Andrew actually saved you."

"He turned me into a revenant," I said. "Whatever that means."

"And he's offering non-pushy support now, to tell you

exactly what it does mean. You'd be dead if he hadn't helped you, right?"

That part at least I was sure about. "Yes."

"I'm not saying marry him or anything, but what would it hurt to hear him out? When you're ready, of course."

Probably nothing. Yet again, possibly everything. I said, "I'll stick to the shrew life, thanks. Andrew froze time, Wendy. *He froze you.*"

"I'm all right," Wendy said. "Two hundred percent."

I frowned at her. "What about Scott? I must have turned him into a revenant like me when I bit him. Does that mean he's out there turning the whole city into revenants? What does that mean if we're the same? Will the city survive the epidemic of undead-ism I've unleashed upon us?"

"You're not licking your lips when you look at me and groaning about wanting to eat my brains," Wendy said. "You are *not* the same as Scott."

"Maybe I would be if I hadn't eaten enough," I said. The shiver that crossed my skin settled into my bones.

"Maybe," Wendy said with skepticism dripping from her tone. She pulled her phone out of her pocket. "It looks like 'revenant' is a broad term used for people who come back from the dead. Sometimes it's used for ghosts, sometimes vampires, or sometimes just people who die and then get brought back."

"So it could mean anything, basically," I said.

The small curve of Wendy's lips told me she was suppressing the desire to tell me that *Andrew* knew what it meant.

A ding came from the coffee table.

"That sounds like a text," Wendy said.

I snatched the phone that was sitting on the table. I recognized the camouflage case and the giant sticker on it—a bottle of ketchup. It was Scott's. Had his phone been sitting there all this time? I hadn't noticed, but I had been distracted.

Andrew may know about the new, revenant part of my life, but Scott's phone could hold answers to the events that had led me to this point. I could learn who his girlfriend was, maybe even why he'd tried to kill me.

I told myself I didn't care. I didn't want to, but I still cared.

I touched the screen. The numbers popped up, waiting for me to type in the correct combination.

"I don't know his passcode," I said.

"Try his birthday," Wendy said.

I punched in the numbers. It didn't work. I said, "Nope."

"What about all ones or all zeroes?"

I tried those, too. And our house number. I shook my head. "If I keep getting it wrong, it's going to lock me out for good."

Wendy twisted her lips and looked up at the ceiling, her focus inward as she searched for an answer neither of us possessed. "Maybe he kept a secret diary?"

"Dear diary, here's my phone passcode?"

Wendy chuckled. "Okay, maybe not. But I keep passwords in my Rolodex for banking and everything. He could have something like that."

If so, he didn't keep it here. Apparently I didn't know as much about Scott as I'd thought, though, so anything was possible.

Crash.

Wendy and I exchanged a look.

It sounded like someone had broken glass. It sounded like it came from the basement. And the scuffling that followed made it sound like that someone was inside my house.

CHAPTER 12

As we tiptoed down the steps, a feeling of déjà vu crept up over me. This was just like Sunday, when we'd searched the shadowy basement for intruders with our fireplace tools. This time the tools were already down here, abandoned on the floor. This time, the light was already on.

It was quiet except for the sounds of our footsteps on the creaking wood.

At the bottom of the stairs, Wendy bolted for Scott's old hockey stick from when he'd decided he'd take up hockey, and the lasso from when he'd considered becoming a cowboy. Neither hobby had stuck more than a week. A box of my untouched clay sat on the same shelf, so I didn't have room to talk.

Shards of broken glass lay scattered on the floor. The tiny curtains on the back door waved in the fresh air that flowed through the broken window.

Wendy poked my hip with the end of the hockey stick and nodded toward the freezer. I looked over.

The lid was open but down, resting on someone's back.

Two legs dangled out the back, not supporting the person's weight. If I had to guess, it was a man.

"Is it Scott?" Wendy mouthed at me.

I shrugged, unsure. It could be him. Scott wore jeans and loafers, like this guy did. But I couldn't be sure. Scott had a key. He had no reason to break in. But if he was a crazed, starved revenant, maybe reason wasn't in play.

"Scott?" I whispered.

He didn't move. He didn't make a sound.

I grabbed a folding chair from the corner, and some duct tape from the tool box. We could secure him here if we needed to. If it was Scott. If it wasn't, I wasn't sure what our plan would be.

"You going to tape his mouth shut?" Wendy whispered. "We could toss him in the freezer and tape that shut, too."

"He'd freeze," I said.

"We'll give him a blanket."

"He'd suffocate.

"We'll put a little straw in the seal for air to get in. Then we'll tape it shut."

I frowned at her.

She shrugged. "Do you have a better plan?"

"I wish I did."

"Don't shove him in," I said.

"Not unless we have to," she said.

I shook my head. "Ready?"

She lifted the hockey stick over her head. "Ready."

If I'd had breath in my lungs to hold, I would have held it. We crept closer, tiptoeing across the basement floor. I threw open the freezer lid.

And found Scott.

His usually tan skin was drained of color. His eyes were shut. He wasn't moving, just dangling halfway in and halfway out of the freezer.

"Is he dead?" I whispered. "Did I kill him?" I expected my heart to hurt at that thought, but it didn't. I was out of emotional energy. I was numb.

"First, if he is dead, it's his own fault," Wendy said. "And I'm not sure. Let's poke him and see." Wendy stabbed his arm with the end of the hockey stick.

As soon as plastic met elbow, Scott burst upright—leaving layers of skin on the packages beneath him. Half his face was missing. He hissed and swiped at us.

"Ahh!" Wendy tossed the lasso at me.

She smacked him with the hockey stick as I caught the lasso and spun it.

Scott grabbed Wendy's hair. *"Blaaaa."* His noises trailed off into a hiss and fizzle.

I dropped the loop down over Scott's head and shoulders, and pulled. The lasso tightened and pinned his arms to his sides.

Wendy was forced down to her knees, her hair caught in his hand. Quickly she freed herself and scooted away.

Scott tried to follow, but only one of his legs moved. I pulled back against him, the lasso slipped down his chest to his waist.

Wendy put all her strength behind the hockey stick, and swung, hitting Scott in the back of the knees. He went down. Hard.

His face crunched against the cement floor. He groaned and twitched but didn't try to get up.

"Now's our chance." Wendy snatched the duct tape from my hand and tied Scott's ankles together. Then she did the same to his wrists.

Scott turned his head and looked up at us. He chomped his teeth and wiggled on the floor, a bound worm, unable to free itself.

This was the man I had planned to marry. This is what I'd

done to him. He'd tried to kill me, and because he'd failed, I'd made him a monster. What a difference a week could make.

I stepped way around him and peeked into the freezer. I tried to ignore the chunk of skin inside and took stock of the peas, carrots, and roasts.

"I don't think he ate anything," I said.

"Maybe zombies don't like frozen meat," Wendy said.

She was right, whether it was the technical term or not, the best way to describe Scott in his current state was to call him a zombie. Could he be healed? Would this have been my fate, too, had I not binged on Andrew's fridge when I'd first woken up a revenant? Could this still be my fate if I screwed up now?

"There's sirloin in the fridge upstairs," I said. "Maybe we can fix him."

Wendy's tight expression suggested she didn't think so. She said, "Doesn't hurt to try."

I didn't want to risk Scott hurting Wendy. It was better if I watched him. I was already infected. "Do you mind getting it?"

"Not at all. But quick thought. Scott's phone—does he have the fingerprint unlock set up? We could take it."

"That's not a bad idea."

"Huh." Wendy leaned against the shelf, and looked down at her nails. "I thought you'd be opposed to the whole maiming thing."

"Wait. You don't mean take his fingerprint, use it against the screen…you mean *take his finger?*"

"He tried to kill you," she said with a frown. "He kinda succeeded. He owes you."

"He doesn't owe me his finger," I said.

"Okay, we can borrow it. We'll leave him with all his digits and just make him touch the screen. I'll be upstairs cooking for your murderous ex, ready to help if you change your mind. Don't chop off any of his bits without me."

"I promise to control the urge."

She smiled, handed me the hockey stick, and hurried up the stairs. A few minutes later, she came back, opened the package, and tossed the raw steak on top of Scott's head.

"Now we wait," she said.

"Or—" I pulled his phone out of my pocket. "We take advantage of the situation as it is."

I tapped the screen. The words *Face ID* ran across the screen before the keypad came up. I had to admit it was kind of better that it wasn't a finger scan after all the talk of chopping one off. Using the hockey stick, I peeled the steak off of Scott's face and placed it on the floor where he could still reach it. I held the screen close enough that I hoped the camera would recognize him.

His tongue darted out and lapped at the meat.

"It's working." Wendy clapped her hands together. "He likes it. And he didn't even have to drown it in ketchup first."

I chuckled. "I hadn't thought about adding ketchup."

The phone unlocked. Thank goodness.

"The face scan worked, too!"

"Here, let me see."

I handed the phone to Wendy. She pushed some buttons and handed it back.

She said, "Now you can use it without his face. The passcode is all ones."

"Thank you." I slipped it back into my pocket for later. I did still want to know if there was evidence of his affair on it, and if there was any explanation as to why he'd tried to kill me. But I was tired, emotionally and physically, and there were more pressing matters—like Scott writhing on the floor as he licked and nibbled on the raw meat.

"Ugh," I said. "I must have looked just like that in Andrew's kitchen when I first woke up."

"No way, babe. You have a whole face." Wendy smiled at me.

I smiled back.

Which was worse—this working and Scott returning to himself, or this being the end? I wasn't sure. If he never woke up from this zombie state, he would never lie to me again. He'd never try to convince me that everything he'd done to me was somehow my fault. And I'd have peace. A zombie to deal with, but peace.

Scott's phone dinged again in my pocket.

"Whoever is trying to reach him is going to start worrying that he's not answering," Wendy said. "Should we try and respond?"

I wasn't sure.

"To make them think we're Scott, we just have to sound as nasty as possible, uptight, self-righteous, conceited, cruel—"

"I get the picture," I said.

"What do you think?"

"That's not something I'm ready to do yet," I said. "He could be himself once he finishes eating."

Wendy shrugged.

We waited there, watching until Scott finished the steak. He rolled onto his back and burped.

Wendy laughed. I just stared.

"Scott?" I said.

"Murrrrrdurrrr," he said.

"I think that means he's ready to go in the freezer," Wendy said.

"Let's give him more time. He could still be more himself once the food kicks in."

He opened his mouth, closed his eyes, and started snoring.

"Maybe not tonight," Wendy said.

We taped him to the chair. Then we taped the chair to the shelf so there was no chance he could escape in the night. And when we were certain he was good and secure, we taped him some more.

We went upstairs and washed up. I dug a bag of jerky out of the back of the pantry.

"If he stays like that, we're going to have to figure out something to do with him at some point," Wendy said.

"I know."

"And when people notice he's been gone too long, like his girlfriend, they'll come looking."

I nodded. "I may have just the place to stash him." I flashed her the key to my storage unit. "Storage. My mom left it to me. But I'll have to make space first."

"I'll help." She yawned. "Tomorrow, after work."

I pulled her into a hug and squeezed. "Thank you for everything."

"You're my best friend. I'd do anything for you. Now get some sleep, and call if you need anything. Oh, and *don't forget to eat.*"

How could I forget? I could be one missed meal from turning into the brainless zombie in the basement. I shook my bag of jerky at Wendy. "I'll eat right now, promise."

CHAPTER 13

I spent the night tossing and turning. Rest was an elusive beast. My eyelids were heavy, my hands twitchy. Every time I tried to clear my brain and focus on my breath, I remembered I didn't need to breathe. Counting sheep didn't work out any better. When I imagined their fluffy little sheep bodies, their animal faces kept changing… into Scott's. It was all I could do to keep myself in bed instead of going down to check on the stupid jerk every five minutes.

Eventually I gave up on sleep and went down. He was still snoring. I sprinkled some jerky on his shoulder for him to eat when he woke.

I put in a few hours of work on my computer before the sun rose. Then I got dressed and went to the store.

It felt a little strange going to the grocery store first thing on a Tuesday morning. Routine required I be in the office, but my routine had been booted so far out the window, it had launched into space and exploded.

It felt stranger still pushing a cart brimming with meat.

I passed by the vegetables I would usually try to fill up on, and tossed a few in the cart even though I knew I wouldn't be able to enjoy them. Everything but meat tasted at best like nothing in my mouth, at worst like ash. Did revenants need the same vitamins and minerals normal humans did?

Before heading to the checkout, I took stock of my finds. Two hundred seventy-three dollars' worth of steak. One bag of carrots. One bag of celery. I whirled back around and returned three quarters of the steaks. Given I was barely employed, I needed to consider the repercussions of draining my entire bank account in one stop.

At the checkout counter, the cashier watched me load my steaks onto the belt.

A quick prick of pain on my jaw surprised me. I ran a finger over the spot, and found a droplet of blood. That was weird.

The cashier said, "Holding a barbeque, big party? Friends must be bringing the sides, right?"

"There'll be a party in my mouth," I said.

"This much red meat…all for you? You know it's bad for your heart, right?"

"I'm anemic," I told her. "And allergic to advice."

I chalked my snappy tone up to my lack of sleep, and also stress. I'd been under a crazy amount of stress. I was losing my patience. My stomach grumbled. None of this was the cashier's fault. I tried to smile and not snarl.

She gave me a confused, awkward half-smile and read off the total. I paid, grabbed my bags, and left.

I needed to eat. I needed to nap. I needed my whole freaking life to not be so crazy and return to what it had been a year ago, before my mother had died, before I'd died (mostly). Time-traveling Rosemary of the past wouldn't make the same mistakes. She'd kick Scott to the curb before he could screw her over. She'd tell her mom not to go to the Caribbean. She'd set herself up financially to securely quit her job before she was demoted. She'd have everything figured out.

Present Rosemary, *I,* still didn't have that last part worked out at all. If I could do anything, without worrying that I might eat people if I'm not properly fed, without worrying that I won't be able to afford the mortgage payment, what would I do?

Too bad jewelry couldn't be my job. Sure, technically people could make a career out of anything. But other people had skills I didn't possess, like marketing experience and business know-how. I'd have no idea where to start. I also needed a dependable paycheck.

When I pulled into the driveway, an orange cat stood in the middle of the pavement where I needed to park. I gave the horn a soft toot and waited for the cat to move. He didn't run off as far as I could tell, which meant he could have moved right in front of my tires.

I put my car in park, opened the door, and peeked under the frame. I couldn't see any movement or orange fur. I turned off the car and walked around front.

This had to be the same cat who had weaseled its way into my bedroom window yesterday. Which neighbor did he belong to? I guessed I should be happy he wasn't in my house anymore, but the driveway wasn't much better.

"Here, kitty kitty."

My stomach grumbled. My head throbbed. Not sleeping hadn't just thrown my mood. It had messed up my insides. With the twists in my gut, I couldn't tell if I was really hungry or about to be sick.

The cat wasn't by the tires. I crouched down and searched everywhere under my car. I couldn't see him.

"Where did you go?"

With a groan and a bit of soreness in my lower back, I rose to my feet. It seemed becoming a revenant hadn't spared me the aches and pains of aging. It also hadn't spared me from making involuntary elderly moans. Too bad.

Back on my feet, I scanned the street and then my yard.

I spotted the cat.

He was standing in the middle of my flower bed, over the single bloom—my Tiny Tim tulip. He looked me straight in the eye, lifted his little leg like a dog, and peed.

"No! Shoo!" I flapped my arms and ran toward the little jerk. "Get out of here."

He lifted the tip of his cat nose and turned his leg, swinging the stream right onto my shoe.

Warm heat soaked into the cushion of my shoe and sloshed between my toes.

Furious, I scooped the cat off the ground.

He stopped peeing. His beady black eyes turned into globes. My fingers brushed across something cold and hard—a collar? No, a strand of pearls.

The cat's pulse fluttered against my palm, so fast, so alive.

The hunger hit me hard. I was ravenous. It was an entity of its own, a force of will I had no control over. I watched in horror as my hands lifted the cat toward my face.

Hungry, so, so hungry.

He wasn't a typical orange in this light, but more saturated, almost orange-red. The white spot above his left eye—almost an eyebrow in shape was so distinct, I realized with certainty this was the cat from the lawyer's office.

Unable to stop myself, I pressed him to my face. His soft fur brushed my lips.

Saliva filled my mouth. My stomach quaked with feral need.

I was going to eat him.

I *had* to eat him.

I needed meat. *Now.*

Something snapped in my head, my conscious brain

retaking control. I cried out, freaked beyond words by what I was doing. I let go.

The cat scrambled and flipped and landed on its feet.

I caught a glimpse of the tag on its pearl necklace.

Noodles McDoodles Butterbelly.

Too horrified to comprehend anything about the situation, I raced back to my car for my steaks, then ran inside the house.

I started a cast iron pan on the stove, hands shaking.

I ripped open one of the packages in my bags, a ribeye, tossed it on the stove, and tried to keep my hands at my sides as I waited for it to sear.

It was taking too long. It was taking forever.

"Come on, come on. *Cook.*"

The meat sizzled, filling the air with delicious scents.

I couldn't wait any longer or I might explode. I reached into the pan, snatched the mostly-raw meat and devoured it. The sear burned the roof of my mouth, but I didn't care. The juices dripped down my chin as much as my throat. I didn't care about that, either. It was delicious and soothed the wild monster inside of me. It made me sane again.

When the steak was gone, my belly was full. I felt like myself, or as much like myself as I could, given the circumstances.

I'd almost eaten a cat.

I'd almost eaten the *cat.*

Noodles McDoodles Butterbelly, the cat who had inherited my mother's estate, had climbed into my car at the lawyer's office. He'd crawled into my bedroom window. And he'd peed on my prized tulip.

I'd tried to eat him.

Was I mistaken about the cat's identity? Had I imagined the pearls or the text on the golden name tag? No, it was all real.

Why was he here? And again, who did that cat freaking belong to?

I pulled out another steak and placed it in the pan, this time waiting until it was actually cooked, and then I ate it like a civilized human, with a knife and fork. With my stomach so full my pants dug into my skin, I took my time putting away the rest of my groceries and cleaning the dishes.

I checked on Tiny Tim Tulip. Three of its four pink petals had fallen to the ground. The one that remained was already shriveled, making it clear the cat's pee had been pure poison.

"I'm sorry, Tim," I told the flower. "We'll try again next year."

Defeated, I headed back inside. I took a rough, scrubbing shower.

I had nowhere to be, no one to see—at least, until Wendy got off of work. We'd made vague plans to possibly get together in the evening, though it wouldn't surprise me if she ended up held late at the shelter again.

I made a wild choice and put on my pajamas. I hadn't worn comfy clothes in the daytime since college, and it felt weirdly good. I sat down in front of my laptop, set an alarm for six hours, and dug into my work. Sure, I didn't have the usual sound of humming copiers for background noise, but I also didn't have to socialize either. No looking at pictures of Susan's granddaughter by the watercooler, or having to hide from Greg in accounting so he couldn't "accidentally" honk my butt again. I could get used to this.

Before long, I'd completed all of the files in my inbox. It was only eleven, so I scavenged through my craft drawers before remembering the clay in the basement. Over the years I'd collected block upon block of FIMO, snatching up every pretty color of modeling clay I could find for some future project that I never managed to make time for.

Eventually the clay would dry out so much I'd have to toss it.

The time to use what I had was now.

I looked over my rainbow of clay and chose shades of kelly green, lavender, royal blue, and canary yellow. I worked the clay in my hands, kneading and softening the hard blocks, then rolled out thin, equal, six-inch long strands of each. I placed them together just so, rolled them smooth into a precise cylinder, and baked the product in the oven. I wouldn't know how well the pattern turned out until I sliced through it, which was part of the fun.

With the first batch in the oven, I used the same colors to create a different shape in the next, and then a third.

When they were all done baking and cooled, I trimmed the edges, and got my first glimpse of the finished product. On the edge of two of the cylinders were flowers, a pattern that would carry well through the entire piece. Each was slightly different than I'd intended, each interesting and unique. The third cylinder went wonky. The color edges weren't crisp enough, the placement slightly off. That was fine.

I'd need to slice the two good ones thick enough to be able to create a hole for stringing the beads, but thin enough that the beads weren't clunky.

My alarm went off.

Six hours had gone by and it had felt like twenty minutes. Correct that—my *work* work had taken about forty-five minutes that felt like forty-five minutes. My jewelry crafting hours had felt like no time at all.

I was only going to get paid for forty-five minutes. This work babysitter business sucked. I'd have spent more time if there had been more tasks to complete. Tomorrow I'd need to force myself to slow down, creep through the tasks at a sloth's pace.

I tucked away my supplies, stretched, then went downstairs to check on Scott. I brought a cup of water with a long straw so I could offer him a drink without getting bit, along with the remaining beef jerky.

When I got downstairs, I noted the still-broken window. I needed to get that fixed, or at the very least tape it up.

Scott watched me, finally awake. His face looked better, less raw from where he'd lost skin to the freezer.

"Good afternoon," I told him, though it was four already, and before long it would be evening.

I grabbed the duct tape from the shelf and plastered the curtain against the open window, which would have to do for now.

Scott cleared his throat, sounding almost normal.

Some but not all of the jerky was on the floor, leading me to believe he'd been able to eat at least a portion of it.

"I hope you're feeling more yourself. Did you enjoy the jerky I left for you?"

He said nothing.

I approached with caution, though he hadn't and couldn't really move much while taped to the chair. I offered him the end of a sippy straw. He snapped at it, caught it between his teeth, and slurped down the cup's contents.

"How did you sleep?" I asked.

He didn't answer.

I almost felt bad for him being trapped in this state. Almost. "This is all your fault, you know," I told him. "If you hadn't tried to kill me, I wouldn't be a revenant. I wouldn't have bitten you. And you wouldn't be reduced to…this."

He continued to suck on his straw, making loud sounds since his water was apparently all gone.

"I'm going through your phone today," I told him. "I hate to do it, invading privacy and all, but you've left me no choice. That is, unless you want to tell me what happened.

What led us here, Scott? How could you bury me like that? Don't you have a heart at all?"

I pulled the straw from his lips. He chomped his jaw and stared blankly into the middle distance, his eyes glossed over.

He couldn't tell me anything. He was broken. The meat wasn't helping.

I turned to go.

"Ro…mary," he said.

I clenched the fabric of my shirt over my heart.

He hadn't said anything meaningful to me since he'd turned. Was it possible he *was* actually improving? I wasn't sure how I felt about that. It would be good, I guessed. Then I could get my answers and kick him out, guilt free. I turned back. "Yes, Scott?"

"Brains."

"Yeah, okay. I'll be back to check in later. Bye." I headed back upstairs, not really disappointed at all. I should have been, sure, but I wasn't.

Whether or not it made me a terrible person, I didn't want the old Scott back. I didn't want to be the cause of him lingering in this state, either, but even if he did get better, he could go live in a dumpster for all I cared.

If I was being brutally honest with myself, we were probably done a long time ago, if he'd ever really loved me at all. I'd gone from fiancé one to fiancé two thinking if I only tried harder, if I only gave more, everything would work out.

I was alone now, and no one was relying on me to take care of them. No one was waiting for me to put their needs before my own. It was liberating. I could work in my pajamas, make jewelry in my pajamas, and lounge in my pajamas on a Tuesday afternoon with no one judging me.

I popped in my DVD copy of *The Princess Bride,* grabbed Scott's phone from the coffee table, and settled in on the couch.

I listened as Buttercup made demands of Wesley, and Wesley showed his devotion, time and again, to the woman he loved. They didn't have to say the words. They both knew that true love existed and that they were lucky enough to have found it in each other.

If only life really worked like that.

With a series of ones, I unlocked Scott's phone.

The most surprising thing about the start of his text messages was that I didn't recognize any of the names. I figured his drinking buddies would be at the top of his list, wondering why he hadn't shown up to fantasy football last night.

But I didn't see the names he'd mentioned to me at all, not that he'd ever provided more than the bare minimum of details.

Had he even been going out with them at all in recent months like he'd told me he had? Did those people even exist? Was it all lies to cover for his affair?

There were messages about boxes at the office from someone named Paul, who Scott had never mentioned. But almost everything exchanged was with a person named Sam, a name that could belong to a woman or a man. Most texts were simply times and dates sent by this Sam person.

> Scott: *Give me more time, please. I'll talk to her, I promise.*
>
> Scott: *It's been over with Rosemary since it began. I have nothing but hate for her. It's not easy to start with something like this.*
>
> Scott: *I just need a little more time. She's so stupid, it'll be easy.*
>
> Scott: *It's done.*

I put my hand over my mouth so I wouldn't puke. The date was Wednesday, the time—ten forty-seven p.m.—the night he'd tried to kill me.

Sam: *Sunday. Nine a.m.*

Sunday was the morning I'd found them together in my bedroom. Sam was the other woman. *I have nothing but hate for her.* The messages went back for weeks at least.

He was supposed to love me. Scott was supposed to be my shot at a happily-ever-after, or at least my content-and-not-alone partner. How could I have been so foolish? *She's so stupid.*

I'd seen enough.

I chucked the phone across the room and fell to my knees. My chest contracted, and I dry heaved. My head pounded.

Why was I feeding him still? Why hadn't I thrust him out the door when he returned, instead of trying to help him? Scott was the scum of the earth. I would never trust a man again. I was better off alone.

My chest felt like an elephant was sitting on it.

I had to get out of the house, as far away from Scott as I could.

I climbed into my car. Something rustled in the bushes, probably the cat back for another round of pee-stravaganza. Let him do whatever damage his little heart desired. I didn't care.

I left.

I didn't realize I was heading to the storage unit until I arrived. No matter how strained our relationship had been, I missed my mom. Since she was gone, I went in and surrounded myself with her stuff.

"Hi, Mom," I said to the packed remnants of her life. "Remember how you told me I had a skewed world view? I believe your exact words were that my eyes are made of frosted glass? Well, I've been thinking about it a lot since you died. And you're right. Scott's a major turd, and I didn't notice. Also, I think I'm stuck in the denial phase of grief."

I opened one of the cardboard boxes. Inside were kids toys, ones I'd thought long donated. I found a bag of wooden blocks I'd built towers with when I was a kid, the same ones Heather had then used to build castles. Had Mom kept them all this time for Heather's kids, if she ever had them?

My throat felt tight, a mix of emotion caught there.

"I told myself that once the estate was closed that reality would sink in, and I could accept the truth and move on. But I can't. I can't believe that you're gone."

Under the blocks was a stack of Little Golden Books. The oldest went back to my mother's childhood. I picked up *The Poky Little Puppy*. It had been her favorite, the one she'd read to me when I was sick. I'd nearly forgotten about that. I'd preferred some of the newer-at-the-time books, like *The Monster at the End of This Book*. I'd begged her to read the others, but she'd insisted. What I wouldn't give to hear her read *The Poky Little Puppy* to me now. She'd also made me gargle salt water for a sore throat, which I'd hated.

"You were always so stubborn and set in your ways. I thought you were too stubborn to die," I said. "It's ridiculous, I know. It wasn't a logical thought. What did I expect—that you'd punch the grim reaper in the face?" I chuckled. "Maybe I did."

I flipped through the books, finding more familiar titles —*The Three Little Kittens, Scuffy the Tugboat, The Little Red Hen*. I didn't remember Scuffy at all. Much to my mother's chagrin, I'd preferred the Jon Scieszka's silly take on the little red hen in *The Stinky Cheeseman*. That book was *not* in the box.

"It was so unlike you to go to Aruba. Or to go on any vacation at all. Then I missed your call the day before you were supposed to fly home. If we're being honest, I saw the phone ring. I was in the middle of an argument with Scott, so I didn't answer. I should have answered."

"They told me you were caught in the tide. I couldn't accept that you could drown. I still can't. Your voicemail said you wanted me to come over when you got back, that it was important. But you never came home."

What would she have said? What did she need me to know?

Did she want me to know that she was giving her house to a cat?

I'd never get to find out. And I was stuck regretting that I hadn't answered the phone.

A piece of paper poked out between two golden spines. I plucked the paper out of the box.

Upon contact, a wave of intense emotions hit. Fear, anger, confusion. The air felt too hot, like I needed to rip my clothes off and jump into an ice bath.

I dropped the paper and stumbled back.

The sensations stopped. My body went numb. My mind blanked.

Had someone done something to me? I looked around, but I was still alone.

Had it been the paper?

It was crisp white, and based on the not-at-all aged look of it, relatively new. I could see writing through it, flowing script like my mother's handwriting, but I couldn't make out what it said.

Tentatively, I reached for it with my foot, and flipped it up against one of the boxes with the toe of my shoe. The note fell down, writing side up.

It was definitely my mother's handwriting.

August Ninth, Eight O'Clock
  Red Fox

August ninth—the day she should have flown home from Aruba. Could this have been from a different year? Some kind of meeting as dated as the books the note had been pressed between? No. It couldn't be.

The feelings I'd felt when I'd touched the note—they weren't mine. They belonged to my mother. I'd felt a connection, an immediate sense of her *right now*.

And even though I knew it made no sense, and I had no proof whatsoever, I felt with certainty that she was alive.

CHAPTER 14

I drove straight to my mother's house, on a quiet cul-de-sac, two hours away in Lingonberry. The gate was chained shut, so I parked along the curb. I hadn't been here since Christmas two years ago, and now the place was hardly recognizable. The grass was brown and knee-high. Vines grew up over the windows behind the shaggy hedge.

I could practically hear my mother snapping her fingers at me with that disappointed look on her face when I, at ten years old, had dared to suggest she hire a yard service. Instead, we'd spent the weekends that she was actually around pulling weeds, cutting the grass, and trimming the bushes. Then inside, we'd scrub every surface in the house until it was spotless, and we'd meal prep for the week ahead. The only help she'd allowed was a nanny for me. When she was working, as she usually was, she'd expected me to maintain that same impossibly high standard.

She'd turn over in her grave if she saw this.

What if I'd made a mistake? The sureness I'd felt at the storage unit had completely eroded on the drive.

If she were really alive, she would never stand for the yard to look like this. If she were really alive, she would have contacted me by now. Maybe it was only irrational hope that had brought me here, not some sort of supernatural sense of knowing.

This was stupid. I was being stupid.

Even though there was no logical reason to stay, I got out of the car. What could it hurt to look around a little bit?

An image of Bueford Gross, Attorney at Law popped into my head. He waggled a sausage-shaped finger at me. *Stay away from the property and the cat, or doomy doom will rain down onto you.*

If I was caught here, I would forfeit my right to the boxes in the storage unit. That part I remembered fairly clearly. I could possibly end up in legal trouble, too. I hadn't actually read the fine print when I'd agreed to stay away. Who knows what I agreed to? Not me.

I'd driven all the way here. I had to at least take a peek. I just wouldn't get caught, and everything would be peachy.

I went around the side of the stone wall to the pair of trees I used to climb to get over the wall. Their dense leaves offered cover from sight.

The trees had grown in parallel as saplings on opposite sides of the wall, entwining their trunks and limbs as soon as they could reach each other. From there on, they were one. It was the perfect friends-to-lovers story, in tree form.

Climbing was *not* as easy now as it had been when I was fifteen. The bark dug into my palms, and my legs flailed a bit. Still, I managed to heave myself up and over.

With a grunt and a shot of pain up my right leg, I landed on my feet in the side yard. I waded through the tall grass around to the back of the house.

One of the windows was broken.

Voices came from within.

I crept closer and tried to make out what was being said.

It wasn't voic*es*, just one voice, singular. It was deep, sultry, and female. Who was the mystery woman? Why had she broken in? And why was she talking to herself?

"I can't ignore Georgio's calls forever," she said. "He was the one who sent me here."

There was a pause. She had to be on the phone.

"He'll send someone else," she said. Her voice grew louder. "He'll make me disappear like he did Scott."

Scott? My Scott? If anyone was to blame for his sudden withdrawal from society, it was me, not whoever this Georgio guy was. But the fact that this woman thought Georgio would do such a thing didn't sit well with me. Who had Scott been involved with? What had they been up to? And what did it have to do with my mother's house?

The woman walked past the dining room. Her hair was pulled tight against her skull, lifted into the kind of ponytail that was prone to produce migraines. She wore head-to-toe leather.

I recognized her.

My stomach turned into a rock. I flattened myself against the outer wall and was for once thankful I no longer had breath I needed to hold. I licked my lips and flexed my fingers. Everything would be fine. I just had to think—stay still, listen, and think.

She was the woman from my bedroom, the woman who was sleeping with Scott—Sam. I should have hated her, but I didn't. I should have the urge to rip that ponytail right off of her head, but I didn't even want to. She could have Scott for all I cared. Not that she would want him now.

Something soft touched my shoulder.

I whipped my head toward the broken window.

Between the broken glass, a fluffy paw reached out. The

extended furry golden appendage attached to a furry golden head, with sharp eyes looking right at me.

"Ahh."

I slammed my hands over my mouth.

It was only a cat. Why had I let it startle me enough to make noise? That was stupid.

I made a run for it, glancing back only once over my shoulder.

The cat's tail was a little too bushy, like it had gotten stuck in an electrical outlet. Its ears seemed too long, too wide for a cat. A tiny tiara sat propped between its ears.

And on its face, it had a spot shaped like an eyebrow.

It wasn't just a cat.

It was Noodles McDoodles Butterbelly.

I couldn't focus on the cat. I had to get out of there.

I scaled the tree, flopped down over the other side, and hurried back to my car as quickly as I could. I glanced back a couple of times in case Scott's girlfriend was following me, or for any sign she'd spotted me. Then I drove away as fast as possible.

Nothing made any sense.

Had Noodles slipped into my car and come along for the ride? He had to have, right? There was no other reasonable explanation. Also, where did a cat get a tiara?

I pulled over at a convenience store and grabbed my phone to call Wendy. But as soon as I unlocked the device, a text from Wendy popped up on the screen.

I'm going to be late for the storage unit.
> *Uncle Ralph shot a nail into his hand and fell off the roof.*
> *At the hospital.*
> *Doctor says he'll be fine. :)*

I took a moment to compose my thoughts before texting back:

No worries. Hope he's okay. Hugs.

I had forgotten that she had offered to help me make space at the storage unit so we could stash Scott there. There were too many balls in the air, and I was poised to drop them all.

Deflated, I sank down in my seat. I needed to talk out the whole stalker cat business with someone, because I couldn't wrap my head around it. Or at the very least, I needed some time to think. Fortunately, the two-hour drive back to Piccadilly meant lots of quiet reflection time. I got back on the road and drove the rest of the way back to the city.

By the time I arrived, I knew what my next move would be. There were answers awaiting me, just not answers to the questions I'd been focusing on. It was time to woman up and ask.

I called Andrew.

He answered on the second ring. "You've reached Andrew Jensen, Chemist with Bioenergonomic. How may I help you?"

He sounded so business-like. It threw me.

"Chemist? I thought your job was alchemist? You just cut off the *al* during the day? You're just *al* at night? Incognito alter ego." I cringed at my own words. I tried to shake it off and started again with a more appropriate greeting. "Hi, it's Rosemary DeLaCrux. From the other night at the sports bar." Then more softly I added, "And from the graveyard. You dug me up."

"I know who you are, Rosemary."

Why did he have to sound so patient and reasonable?

"Oh good. That'll make things easier. I didn't want to

presume. For all I know, you may have brought fifty women named Rosemary back from the dead." My words died off in an awkward, pathetic chuckle.

"Only you," he said. "And you weren't dead. You were *mostly* dead."

"Right. That's totally different, I'm sure."

"Different enough," he said. "To answer your first question, I'm both chemist and alchemist. What can I do for you?"

"Right. Well, I was hoping we could try the chatting thing again. This time I won't run away. Probably."

"If you do, I promise not to be offended."

I could hear the smile in his words, which put a smile on my face in return. "It's a date."

Date? Why did I just say that? Because he was devilishly handsome and charming, and I was clearly desperate even though I was supposed to be swearing off men forever.

I cleared my throat. "I mean, whenever you're free would be lovely."

"How about now?"

"Now?"

"Yes, Rosemary. I'm free now."

"All right. Me, too."

"You pick the place. Somewhere you'll be comfortable."

Because last time when he'd chosen, I'd bolted. He wasn't just handsome and charming. He was considerate of my feelings. No wonder I was practically salivating. The Rosie-wants-to-lick-him bar was apparently sadly low. But the truth was, men didn't typically make it to middle age without serious baggage. The same had been true of the dating pool at thirty—not that I was interested in dating.

And I was supposed to be focusing on our meeting place. Where would I like to see Andrew? Where would I feel comfortable? Somewhere quiet but not so secluded it'd be easy to throw me into a serial killer van.

POTIONS AND PAJAMAS

"The park," I said. "The one on Lambert Street."

"I'll be there in twenty minutes," Andrew said.

"See you then."

We said polite goodbyes, and I was grateful that at least I hadn't butchered that part of the conversation as I had the rest.

I arrived at the park first, and sat on the only bench that was both unoccupied and had a decent view of the lot. I probably should have specified where to find me, but since I hadn't, this position would help me flag him down when he arrived.

The overhead lights clicked on in anticipation of nightfall even though the spring days were long and there was still plenty of sunlight left. Tall grass lined the mowed area along the jogging path. The field beyond danced with the wind, purple flowers waving. A mother rabbit paused at the edge of the field, watching across the park from the safety of the high grass. Beside her sat a tiny brown butt with a fluffy white tail. The rest of the rabbit was hidden in the grass.

I tried to enjoy the scenery, but my attention was set on the parking lot. After I spent a few minutes anxiously staring at the unmoving cars, Andrew arrived.

I didn't see his vehicle pull in, leading me to believe he'd walked here, or more likely ridden in an invisible chariot. But he walked through the lot either way with the kind of confidence that suggested he owned the place—or like a guy who rode a freaking chariot.

His white t-shirt and rugged jeans looked as natural on him as his lumberjack getup and suit did. Was he coming from his chemistry job, leaving the office in casual wear in the early evening? Or did he wear the suit in the lab, switching his business jacket for a practical white lab coat?

He locked gazes with me as he approached.

I was caught, trapped in that gaze. A wave of heat struck

me, spreading out from my core and straight up the back of my neck. A voice in the back of my head told me to run. We weren't even talking yet, and he had me off kilter.

"May I?" he asked, gesturing to the bench.

"Yep. Go for it."

He took a seat beside me, leaving as much space between us as possible. It felt too close and too far at the same time.

"How are you?" he asked.

"Weird," I said.

"You have been eating, right? Plenty of red meat?"

"Yes. I should have asked sooner what would happen if I didn't. I had a close call in the morning with a cat."

"I apologize," he said.

He was apologizing *to me?*

"Don't." I looked over where the rabbits had been, looking anywhere but at Andrew. "I'm the one who thought Noodles would make a good snack."

"Noodles?"

"The name of the cat," I said.

"Oh."

Even though I wasn't looking at him, I could hear his smile. I cautioned a glance just to be sure, because apparently I couldn't help myself.

Behind that full beard, a small smile curved across his fuller lips.

It wasn't fair, really. He was too sexy for his own good, really for my good. If I was going to be able to stick to my no-men plan, it would be a lot easier if I didn't look at those particular lips on this particular man.

"As you acclimate to your condition, you should gain control over the hunger." Andrew said. "Mature revenants don't need physical food."

"Mature. That's a PC way of calling me old," I said. Good, let him think I'm geriatric. It's easier that way.

"That was not at all my intention," he said. "You're newly turned, a baby revenant if you will."

"Oh." I wasn't sure that being considered a baby was any better or worse than the geriatric thing.

"And for the record, I would never explicitly or implicitly call you old," Andrew said. "I'm at least two decades your senior. And if I were to be so bold, I'd say you're in your prime."

"Yeah, okay." I let the sarcasm of my tone fill the space between us. It was a big fat pillow, keeping the distance. "I'm comfortable in my skin, yes. But prime is not a word I would use. And you can't really think you're twenty years older than me. Though I do appreciate that if you're going to lie to me that you're a flattering liar."

"I'm sixty-four."

I laughed, finally looking at him once more. By the distinguished lines around his eyes, and the sprinkle of gray, I'd put him around forty-five. "Sixty-four? No way. I don't believe it."

He reached for his pocket and banged his knuckles on the bench. And weirdly, I knew it had to have hurt because a jolt of pain hit me straight in my knuckles. Empathy was the worst. He didn't seem bothered.

He pulled out his wallet and flashed me his driver's license. Huh. He was sixty-four.

"I thought fake IDs were for teenagers," I said.

"And those of us trying to sneak our way into nursing homes." He crossed his fingers. "Though I should have added another decade or two. Maybe on the next one."

We shared a soft laugh, and it wasn't all that weird at all. It was actually kinda nice.

He was really sixty-four. He was some kind of super-hearing, life-saving hero. I was tied to him in a way I didn't understand at all. And he was *really* charming. What had I gotten myself into?

"I'd like some of whatever fountain of youth potion you've given yourself," I said.

"The one I gave you is likely to do just that," he said. "But I didn't drink a potion. Slow aging is a byproduct of my alchemy."

My aging would slow? If that was actually true, I wasn't actually sure I liked the idea all that much. What did that mean for Wendy and Heather? Would it be strange for them? Would it be strange for me?

What else did it mean to be a revenant? I wanted to—needed to—ask. But first, I had to ask about the other part of what he'd said. "Tell me about the alchemy. What exactly is that supposed to mean?"

He scratched his beard and tilted his head up toward the tree limbs above us. I watched his movements, the way his bicep bulged and his shirt tightened around it. I watched the flex of his forearm, and the way he moved his fingers.

"My mother's a witch," he said, glancing back at me. "I wasn't born with her gifts, but I grew up knowing that magic existed. By the time I could read, I began dabbling in the only form of magic possible for someone like me."

"Naturally," I said, in awe of his story. "And the magic for non-witches is alchemy?"

He nodded. "There are a few other specialties, but I make potions."

"Like what you poured into my almost-dead mouth."

It wasn't really a question, but he answered me like it was. He said, "Yes."

"And what you did to make the people at the bar freeze."

"That, too."

"What else can you do with your potions?" I asked.

"Many things," he said.

I waited for him to elaborate. He didn't. So I decided to move on for now.

"And your father? You mentioned you inherited sonic hearing from him. Let me guess what else—he can see through walls, and he can fly."

"Nothing like that," he said. "Though he does make a mean frittata. He's the one who raised me, and he inspired my love of science and figuring out how things work."

"Your mom wasn't around?"

"No."

"I'm sorry." I hadn't expected that. Between growing up with a single mom and raising a daughter as a single mom myself, my default assumption was always that moms are involved. You know what they say about assumptions.

Now that I thought about it, it was interesting that the photo I saw of him in his apartment was with him and an older woman, not a man.

He shrugged. "Don't be sorry. My father was everything when I was little. I never felt I'd missed out. How about you? Are you close with your parents?"

"My mom raised me alone," I said. "She died recently."

"I'm sorry," he said.

The tightness in his eyes said he knew the same pain, though he didn't express that with words, just as I hadn't told him about my father. Did that mean his mother had died? Was that why she wasn't around for him growing up?

"Thanks," I said. We took a moment to look at each other, and I couldn't believe how silly I had been. There was no reason to run away from Andrew. We could be friends, *should* be friends. He was easy to talk to, and he was funny, and I liked him.

I said, "The thing is...I'm having trouble believing my mom's really dead. I thought it was simple denial. But then I sensed something when I picked up this piece of paper that was hers. Maybe that's a revenant thing?" I looked to him with cautious hope. "I felt sure, if only for a moment, that she's alive."

"Some revenants gain different levels of telepathy," he said. "It's certainly possible that what you sensed is true."

I didn't realize how much I'd needed him to say that until he did. She could be alive. She was alive, and I'd figure out where she was and how I could help her, because even if she wasn't dead, something was definitely wrong.

"They also typically have no reflection," Andrew said. "Though they do show up on film."

I nodded. "Confirmed."

"Some are particularly strong physically, or develop other enhanced senses."

"Mmmm." I frowned, trying to think of anything enhanced that I could do. "I don't think that's me. Unless you count tearing into a steak like nobody's business."

He smiled. "Give it time."

"Right, I'm still a baby."

He nodded.

And then I remembered Scott. Too bad I couldn't forget. I said, "And we can accidentally make more of our kind, like a werewolf scratch or zombie bite."

Andrew tensed beside me. That easy feeling between us was gone in a second. Heat carried up my neck.

"What happened?" he asked.

I cleared my throat, thought about bolting for the parking lot, then squeezed my fists on the edge of the bench. "Well…I may have…bitten someone. In self-defense."

Andrew was quiet, too quiet. When he spoke, his voice carried a weight that it hadn't before. "Whoever this person is, he or she is not a revenant."

"Of course he is…." I said, wishing I could convince myself.

"He's a zombie," Andrew said.

"That's different?"

"Very different."

"Zombies can get better though, right? Gain nice happy powers and live nice happy lives?"

"I'm sorry, Rosemary."

He turned his body toward me, putting our knees only an inch apart. His expression was gentle, kind. He was trying to let me down easily, soften the blow. This was bad —really bad.

I eyed the parking lot once more. If I bolted now, I wouldn't have to hear him out. If I didn't hear whatever the bad news was, it wasn't true, right?

He said, "Wherever this zombie is, he's a danger to everyone around him."

"Like I am."

"Not like you at all. Zombies retain no humanity, no sense of right or wrong, no remorse. I'm sorry to be the bearer of bad news, but it's imperative to exter—"

Nope. Not hearing this.

"I have to go." I bolted up and hurried for my car.

Andrew rose from his seat and put his hands in his pockets. "I can help you—"

"No, thanks. Bye!" I ran to the car, and drove out of there as quickly as I could. Scott was a zombie, and I'd made him that way. No way could all of this be true. He had to get better. I'd prove Andrew wrong, and the last thing I needed was him tagging along to "help."

When I reached my house, I parked and raced up the front walk, hands shaking. My hands were so sweaty, I could hardly grip the keys or doorknob.

I stepped inside.

"Scott?" I called out, as if he could answer.

I ran down into the basement. The air was cripplingly cold. I lost my stride and tripped on the last step.

A dark figure lurked over Scott.

I waved my arms in the air and ran at it. "Ahhhh!"

Gooseflesh shot up all over my skin.

The figure faded to nothing.

I reached a hand out toward Scott. He wasn't moving. He was ghostly pale. His skin was icebox cold. I tried shaking his shoulder. His arm fell limp. His head lolled forward.

He didn't snore. He didn't move.

An icy feeling carried from my nose to my toes, one that had nothing to do with the room's unnatural cold. It was Scott I was feeling, his body a shell, housing nothing, not even a zombie husk of his former self.

Everything that he was, even the desire to eat my brain, was gone.

Scott was dead.

Not undead, but *dead* dead.

CHAPTER 15

*P*anic would have been a smart response. Sadness would have been appropriate too. Instead, I felt removed from the situation, like this was someone else's life, someone else's problem. Maybe, probably, loss would hit me later. Or maybe I'd already mourned our relationship enough over the course of our engagement. Maybe this finality would eventually be a relief.

I called Wendy. It went to voicemail. In a calm, even tone, I said, "It's me. I need you to come over ASAP." The smart thing to do was not to give any details that could be used against me later by the police. Apparently even though my empathy was gone, my sense of self-preservation was very much alive and kicking. "It's important. We'll talk in person."

Still surprised by my sense of calm, I hung up.

"You should have just left me, you know?" I told Scott's still corpse. "Instead of trying to kill me. Then we'd both still be alive."

Scott of course didn't and couldn't respond.

I opened the freezer and hefted him in. It was easier than

I'd expected, like somehow him being one-hundred-percent dead made him physically lighter.

I went upstairs, poured myself a glass of wine, and told myself this was all for the best and that Scott's death was somehow not my fault. The more wine I drank, the more I expected to believe it. But after a glass and a half, I wasn't even a little bit buzzed. And I still knew, with certainty, that I had killed Scott.

At least the wine tasted all right, unlike all non-meat foods, on my revenant tongue. I poured myself a little more and heated up some frozen cheeseburgers in the microwave. As I ate, I leaned against the counter, and stared out the kitchen window into the darkness. How long ago had the sun set?

I caught movement along the fence—human shaped movement.

Someone was here, creeping around in the backyard. Was it the reaper coming back to finish the job?

My phone rang. It was Wendy. I snapped the blinds shut, tipped back the rest of my glass of wine, and answered.

"Hey, where are you?" I asked. "Did you get my message?"

"Yeah. I'm here. What's with the fuzz?"

"What?"

"A police car is blocking your driveway. What's the plan? Okay, how about I'll casually turn around in Mr. Mulvery's driveway. You make a run for it, jump the back fence. I'll pick you up on the street behind here. You can hide out at my place as long as you need to. It's going to be okay."

"Jump the fence? That won't look suspicious at all," I said. "I don't know why they're here. Maybe they just have some questions they need to ask…about someone else. Like um…."

The flimsy alternate scenario died in my throat. I had nothing. But the police couldn't know I was stashing a dead man in my freezer, right? Unless someone had peeked through the broken window. A neighbor?

Or maybe Scott's girlfriend had called the police after she'd seen me attack him. Maybe she was trying to get that Georgio guy in trouble, the one she thought had made Scott disappear. Maybe the hospital had called them, after I'd dumped Scott on them. Maybe the police were only here to ask normal questions, and nothing to do with murder.

"Are the emergency lights on the patrol cars?" I asked Wendy. "No one has knocked."

"No lights. Do you think they have a warrant? Do you think they're going to break the door down?"

Oh my, what if they broke the door down?

"I don't know. I can't run, though. Scott's in the freezer, Wendy. He's *dead* dead. In no universe does running make this situation better."

Unless they actually came inside...and checked the freezer.

Maybe it *was* better to run.

At least I'd eaten something. No matter what was about to go down, the last thing I needed to do was go feral on a police officer.

"You should go home," I told Wendy. "I'm sorry. I shouldn't have dragged you into this."

"No, Rose, wait—"

I hung up the phone. I had to face this thing head-on. Alone. I opened the window and leaned out enough to see what was going on.

Two police officers were in the backyard, one with a dog, sniffing by the basement door.

"Hey," I called. "What are you doing back there?"

One of the officers approached, while the other followed a German Shepherd around as the dog sniffed every inch of the grass.

"Good evening, ma'am. I'm Officer Ramirez, this is O'Charles. We're responding to a request for a wellness check," the officer said. "Mr. Tochee hasn't reported to work at Pizza Palace in a week."

Pizza Palace? I didn't know Scott had been working at Pizza Palace. I'd thought he worked in a swanky office, or more recently perhaps as a criminal, given the whole Georgio thing.

"What's your name, please, ma'am?" he asked.

"Rosemary DeLaCrux," I said.

"This is Scott Tochee's residence, is it not?" the office asked. "This is his address on file."

Awkwardly hanging out the window I debated my next words.

"Shh," Wendy hustled around the back yard waving her arms. "Don't say anything without a lawyer present."

"Good evening," Ramirez said. "What's your business here, Ms.—"

"What's *your* business here?" Wendy asked.

A lump formed in my throat.

"Everything's fine," I said to Wendy. My voice sounded steady in my ears, much steadier than I felt. Then to the officer I added, "Scott doesn't live here anymore."

The officer's brows shot up and he wrote down something in his paper pad. "Pizza Palace said Mr. Tochee lived alone. Do either of you live here with him?"

"Clearly whoever told you that has no idea what they were talking about," Wendy said.

The dog barked by the back door, clawed at it. The officers shared a look.

Pulsing carried through my ears.

"Ms. DeLaCrux?" Ramirez said. He seemed to be waiting for me to answer a question, but I hadn't heard one asked.

"Yes?" I said.

"Where is Mr. Tochee?" he asked.

Wendy practically buzzed with energy beside him. With saucer eyes, she kept glancing at the far fence. Was she still thinking we should run for it? I really hoped she didn't run for it.

"Scott leaves for weeks at a time," I said. "For work."

It was true. Or at least he'd said it was for work. I doubted pizza delivery men were sent on swanky business trips for the company.

Ramirez furrowed his brows. Likely, he was thinking the same thing I was. His scowl deepened when he looked at Wendy. "What's your name, ma'am?"

"Wendy Ariti."

"It seems you have something to say about that, Ms. Ariti."

Wendy shot me a quick glance then returned her attention to the officer. "Scott's probably with another woman."

"Which is fine, because we're not together anymore," I said.

"It was probably happening from the beginning," Wendy said. "The man can't keep it in his pants. You know, one time, he just whipped them off when I stopped by to visit my friend Rosie, here."

What?

"He's probably ankles deep in some side piece this very moment," Wendy said.

"Mr. Tochee is having an affair?" the officer asked.

I felt all the blood drain from my face. My head swirled with dizziness. She was giving them motive. Once they went in and found Scott's body, they'd think jealousy was why I'd killed him. It wasn't. All of this was a simple accident, one I couldn't easily explain. No one would believe I was a revenant until they locked me up for murder and I ate the entire prison.

"Multiple, over many years," Wendy said. "He's a dog.

This one time we were camping at the lake and Scott dropped his drawers and swung his noodle around like a helicopter blade. He was trying to impress a woman, though she shielded her eyes and ran away. It was not a pretty sight."

What camping trip?

"Hit his whirlydo right on the branch of a tree, got splinters," Wendy said. "Poison oak, too. I bet that rash was just awful."

"Are you all right, Mrs. DeLaCrux?" the officer asked.

I didn't answer because I wasn't all right. I wasn't all right at all.

"It's not cheating," I said eventually. My protests sounded pathetic. "We're not together anymore."

"His car is in the driveway, ma'am," Ramirez said.

The dog whined and scratched the door.

"We're going to need to enter the basement," O'Charles said.

I was screwed.

"He's not here," Wendy said.

It was distant. My whole life was distant. I wasn't me, and this was all happening to someone else. Someone else was going to jail for the murder. Someone else was going to marry the kind of man who whipped his dongle out on a camping trip.

I climbed inside the window, walked down the stairs and unlocked the basement door.

Someone else's life was over.

Mine had already ended, right? The day I'd been buried alive.

The officers came inside.

The dog pulled hard on its leash, dragging O'Charles to the rectangle on the floor where the freezer was supposed to be.

But the freezer, and my dead fiancé inside it, was gone.

CHAPTER 16

*D*arkness threatened the corners of my vision. A pulsing sensation flooded my ears.

O'Charles and his trusty hound went upstairs. Ramirez dug around in old boxes in the basement.

Wendy asked me a billion frantic questions without speaking a word, and using only the expression on her face. If I had to guess, she was trying to convey something along the lines of *what happened to the freezer, what if they find evidence against you, isn't that a cadaver dog,* and *are we as so flipping screwed as I think we are?*

Where *was* the freezer? Someone had to have taken it, but how? Why?

I was dizzyingly clueless.

Had it been Scott's girlfriend? If she'd found him, she would have called the police. She wouldn't have taken his body…right?

Then there was the reaper. The reaper was the only one who had known that Scott was dead, given it had been the one who'd killed him. Though I hadn't figured out *why*. Also, if the reaper had wanted Scott's body, it could have taken his body from the start, instead of leaving him for me to deal with.

Maybe someone had taken Scott to use as some kind of leverage. Blackmail was a solid motive, but no one had made any demands. Also, who would want to blackmail me?

"There's no sign of him," one of the officers said as she trotted back down the steps.

"Duh," Wendy said. "We told you he was gone."

"His drawers appear full. The vehicle registered in his name is in the driveway," the officer said.

"A man can't have a lot of clothes? Scott loves fashion. Is that a crime?" Wendy put her hands on her hips.

"He doesn't like to leave his car at the airport," I said. "He calls a service."

"Who would want to park at the airport?" Wendy nodded. "There are never any spots, and then you get all those additional fees."

"It looks like he still lives here," Ramirez said.

"He doesn't," I said, firmly.

"We'll pack the rest of his things for him," Wendy said. "When he gets back from his trip, everything will be ready for him to take to his new place."

"Hmm," Ramirez frowned.

"What happened to your freezer?" O'Charles asked.

"It broke a few months back," I said. "I got rid of it."

"These wet marks look a lot fresher than a few months," he said.

"It sat broken for a while, dripping on the floor," Wendy said. "Is that a crime? Leaky freezer?"

"No," Ramirez said with a flat tone and a sharp glance at his partner. "If you think of anything else that might help, or you hear from him, give us a call."

"Of course, thank you," I said.

"Unlikely," Wendy said.

With that, the officers left.

We hurried up the stairs and peered through the living room window until their car was gone from sight.

Then I turned to Wendy and elbowed her. "What was that?"

"What?"

"I told you to go, and instead you stayed and gave them motive."

"First, you're crazy if you think I'd leave you in your moment of greatest need. Second, motive? What motive? I gave them a story they can follow up on—find the mystery women that Scott's sleeping with."

Moment of greatest need. I snorted. "Scott's not sleeping with anyone anymore."

"Except the fishes."

I narrowed my eyes at her and took in her stoic expression. "Did you dump the freezer in the lake?"

"No, I just always wanted to say that." Wendy crossed her arms over her chest. "Wait. You think I moved the freezer? I thought you must have gotten it into the storage unit. I was so worried when you opened that door and the dog ran down."

"Same. And no, I have no idea what's going on. Who steals a freezer out of someone's basement without breaking the locks?"

"Who steals a dead body?"

I sank down onto the sofa. Wendy plopped down into the cushions beside me.

"If it wasn't you, and it wasn't me, then who?" I asked, more to the universe than to Wendy, because really, who?

She smacked my knee. "What about your guardian alchemist?"

"Guardian alchemist?" I shot her a look, because really, this again?

"Humor me. You're going to die, knight-in-shining-armor Andrew shows up and magically saves your life. Then he freezes time, again with magic. And you're about to get caught with a dead dude in your basement, and someone has *magically* saved you."

"I don't know that it was magic, or that whoever took Scott is trying to save me."

"Okay, back up," Wendy said. "Start from the beginning. What happened with Scott? Last I heard, he was trying to eat your brains."

"A reaper killed him. I think."

"A reaper. Okay. Like the grim reaper?"

I shrugged. "It's a shadowy black man shape that's apparently stalking me for being mostly dead, or cheating death, or something. It's not my only stalker, either. I'm pretty sure with everything else going on, I neglected to tell you about what happened at the lawyer's office."

"Okay…." She waited patiently for me to continue.

"My mom left me a storage unit," I said.

Wendy nodded. "Right, where we were going to stash Scott."

"Yeah. And she left the house and everything else to a cat."

"A cat?"

Something tapped against the window. I sat up slowly and peeked out, expecting to see Noodles. Speak of the devil and he appears, and all that. But it was only the branches of the bushes swaying in the wind.

"Your mother hated cats," Wendy said.

"I know."

"And you think this cat who stole your inheritance is stalking you?"

"He is. I've been seeing him everywhere."

"How do you know it's the same cat?"

"He has his name engraved on his pearl collar."

"No freaking way."

"Yep. Noodles McDoodles Butterbelly."

Wendy clasped her hand over her mouth to try and hold back a laugh. "If your mother had a cat—which of course she never would—she would never ever name it Noodles. It'd be something more like François or Benicio."

I chuckled. "Right?"

"Leonidas Thaddeus DeLaCrux. I'll tell you what, you find the guy whose last name is Butterbelly, and you find the trickster who pulled this off."

We shared a small laugh. It was nice. I needed it.

"But for real, I am so sorry you've had to go through all of this." She wrapped her arms around me and pulled me into a hug.

My morality meter was on the fritz, apparently, or maybe it was crushed beneath my revenant heel. But Scott was dead. The emotional torment that came with him was dead, too—over and done. I felt lighter, and I knew that was wrong on so many levels.

"I'm okay," I said, because weirdly, I was.

Wendy let me go. "Are you sure it's not shock?"

"I don't think so," I said.

She nodded. "You tell me how you're feeling."

"I feel…nothing. No, not nothing. Relief that Scott's gone? Does that make me a terrible person?"

"No, of course not. Absolutely not."

Her denial was immediate and adamant. She said, "Let's do a little exercise."

I wasn't in the mood for a run, or even a walk. "Can we drink wine and vegetate instead?"

The corner of her lips quirked up. "Close your eyes and imagine the worst person you can. Ready? Say who on three. One. Two. Three."

"Hitler," I said.

At the same time she said, "Scott."

A smile pulled at my cheeks. I told her, "That is a terrible thing to say about a dead man."

"It is," she said. "And it's also true."

"Did Scott really flash you? And that camping story…."

"Ha, thank goodness *no*. I made all of that up. But remember when he threw a fit at Panera that there was too much bread in his bread bowl?"

"That happened more than once," I said.

"Like, guy, seriously stop ordering bread bowls. It doesn't take a degree in rocket science."

"Or when he grabbed that waitress's backside and said he fell."

"Also at Panera. Do they call the staff waitresses there? Or are they more bread and salad artisans?"

"I don't know." I shook my head and pulled my legs up onto the sofa. "I also don't know what I ever saw in him. I was stupid."

"You were optimistic. You saw the best in him, because that's what you do, Rose. You're a good person. Unlike Scott. If we find him, I say we bury him in the hole he dug for you. That is poetic justice if I ever heard it."

"I shouldn't have kept him in the basement. I should have called nine-one-one as soon as I hurt him."

"No. Then he would have zombified the hospital, and it'd be an epidemic of flesh-eating undead. No offense."

"But I did end up taking him to the hospital," I said. "And I left him there. What if that actually happened?"

"We'd have heard about it on the news. Or seen it in the streets. I'm sure it's fine. Everything's totally fine."

"What if it's not?"

"Then we go back to your sexy wizard friend. Really, whatever part of this isn't Scott's own fault is *his* fault. He's your sire. He's responsible for your vampiric tendencies."

"He's responsible for saving me," I said. "The rest isn't his fault. It's mine."

"Tomato, tom-*ah*-to."

"I'd really like to not go bother Andrew with this."

"Would you rather unleash zombies on the city?" Wendy raised a brow. When I frowned and didn't answer, she said, "That's what I thought. Get your coat. It's wizard time."

"Alchemist," I said. "He's not a wizard."

"What's the difference?"

"I have no idea."

CHAPTER 17

Shoulders sagging, I leaned against the elevator wall, wishing I hadn't gone along with this.

"He's probably not home," I said.

Wendy twisted her lips, hiding a mirthful grin. "We won't know until we knock on his door."

"He's probably the one who took the freezer. I'm sure he disposed of it responsibly," I lied. "And if there was a zombie herd, we'd have…heard."

"Homonyms are fun."

"I want to go home," I said.

"Suck it up, buttercup."

"You're enjoying this, aren't you?"

"Maybe a smidge."

The elevator doors opened, and Wendy pulled me out by my wrist. "Which door?"

I could just not answer her, but then she'd probably knock on all of them until we found him. So I pointed to the correct apartment. "That one."

"It should be you who knocks."

I sighed. "Fine."

I knocked on the door.

A moment later, Andrew answered.

Shirtless.

If he was a lumberjack with his flannel on, he was a god without. Just the right amount of dark hair decorated his bronze chest. If it were possible, his shoulders appeared even broader naked than with a shirt covering them.

He lifted the towel in his hands to the hair on his head, stretching his abs and flexing his arms. A droplet of water slipped down his neck from his wet beard. I watched it trail down his chest, down the valleys between his sculpted abs.

His jeans weren't zipped. Just a little tug and I could pull them off.

"Hi," he said.

I was busy trying not to drool.

Wendy leaned in toward me and whispered, "Great piggly wiggly."

"Isn't Piggly Wiggly a grocery chain?" Andrew asked.

"It is," Wendy said. "And it's great. Also, even if you have sonic hearing, you shouldn't listen in on people's private conversations. It's an abuse of super power."

"My ears have a mind of their own," he said. "But I'll try."

Wendy smiled. "Good."

"Would you like to come in?" he asked.

"Yes, we very much would," Wendy said.

I should have said no and gotten to asking the questions we had come here to ask, but I was blindsided and mute from pure shock. No one was allowed to look that good when they answered the door, or ever, really. Especially when I was supposed to be swearing off men. It wasn't fair play.

"We've clearly caught you at an inopportune time," I said.

"Not at all. It's perfect timing, actually. I just got home

from the gym and finished my shower. Give me a moment and I'll grab a shirt."

"Nah, you should be comfortable in your own home. No need to dress on our behalf," Wendy said.

Andrew chuckled and headed into his bedroom. I knew it was his bedroom because I'd been here before. I had woken *in his bed.* And I had bloodied my tooth on a fake apple that had been in a bowl on the counter I was standing beside.

Wendy grabbed my hand and whispered, "He is ridiculously hot. If nothing else, you have to admit that. And this place is nice. Clean for a bachelor."

I nodded. "I'm sure he can still hear you. And why do you assume he's not seeing someone? He could be married."

"I'm not married," he called out to us.

Wendy gave me two thumbs up and a way-too-enthusiastic expression of encouragement.

I shook my head at her.

Andrew rejoined us, wearing a black t-shirt to go with the jeans he had on. I found myself staring down at his bare feet. They were well-groomed and big, just like the rest of him. I could hear in my head what Wendy would tell me—*you know what they say about big feet.*

"Can I offer either of you something to drink?" Andrew asked.

"No thank you," I said.

"Water would be nice," Wendy said.

"Tap or sparkling?"

"Sparkling. Thanks."

He readied her a glass from the fridge, and Wendy and I shot looks back and forth. Wendy's expression said *check out that fine backside* and *why aren't you talking to him, silly woman?* Mine said *please stop before he sees us* and *if you want him so bad, you be the one to do something about it.*

He turned back and handed her the glass. "So what brings the two of you here?"

I appreciated the returned focus to our mission. Straightening my spine, I asked, "Did you take Scott?"

"Who is Scott?" Andrew said. "And no. I've never been much for kidnapping."

I paused, unable or maybe just unwilling to answer such a simple question.

Wendy looked at me, and when it was clear I wasn't answering, she said, "Scott's her dead ex-fiancé. He was a turd, and the world is better for his death."

"I'm so sorry for your loss," Andrew said.

"Don't be," I said. "I'm not. He's the one who buried me."

Andrew clenched his jaw.

"We also need to know if zombies can turn other people into zombies," Wendy said. "Like, are we in horror-movie trouble if Scott say, for example, rampaged at the hospital and bit a bunch of people?"

"The person you bit was your ex?" Andrew asked, his attention still on me. "Are you sure he's actually dead? Is it possible he wandered off?"

I glanced toward the door, eyeing my way of escape. It really would be for the best if I didn't run away this time, though. Something about Andrew kicked my nerves into hyperdrive.

"He's dead," I said.

"And stolen," Wendy said. "Along with the freezer Rose stashed him in."

I guessed we were laying everything out there now. Why not?

"Interesting," Andrew said. He rubbed his finger and thumb across his square jaw. "Zombies don't create more zombies, so aside from the possibility of Scott causing direct physical harm to someone at the hospital, you should be in the clear."

"Hypothetically," Wendy said.

She cleared her throat and shot me another look. I wasn't sure what this one was supposed to mean.

"Sure," Andrew said.

My stomach rumbled, audibly, drawing everyone's attention.

"There's an all-night restaurant a few blocks from here," Andrew said. "They always undercook their meat."

I couldn't think of anything that sounded better at the moment. One, I was getting out of the apartment. Two, food.

"Yes, please," I said.

We walked to a little hole-in-the-wall called Eats. I could feel Andrew's attention on me, even when I purposefully looked away from him.

"What are your intentions with my friend here?" Wendy asked Andrew.

I scoffed.

He raised his hands in defense. "Only a meal. No funny business, I promise."

Wendy thrust her phone in Andrew's face and snapped a picture. "Now I have your face in case you turn out to be a Scott."

The flash was bright, and he blinked.

"A Scott?" he asked.

"He's not a Scott," I said. There was nothing about Andrew that was anything close to being Scott-like. Maybe that's why I kept running. Maybe I wasn't used to men being kind and respectful of my boundaries, helpful without expectation of something in return. New was scary, even if that new made everything I'd put myself through with the men of my past seem foolish.

Wendy nodded. "As first and second impressions go, I agree."

"Is that a favorable comparison?" Andrew asked, eyes furrowed.

"Yes. Don't blow it." Wendy looked at her screen. "Sorry. I have to go."

I hadn't heard a ding or a ring. "Everything okay?"

"Mm-hmm," she said.

This was fake.

"Your car is at my place," I told her.

"That's all right, I can walk," she said.

"You're being weird," I said.

She shrugged. "Life's weird. Call me tomorrow. I want to hear everything."

"Everything about what?" I rubbed the center of my forehead, trying to smooth away the tension forming there. I wasn't sure I wanted to go home, certainly not alone, not after the day I'd had. I'd hoped we could go to her place after this. I'd expected her to offer, not to bail on me.

She walked away and gave a peace sign over her shoulder at me.

I sighed and turned to Andrew.

He had the hint of a grin on his lips. "Your friend is peculiar."

"Yes," I agreed.

"It's not too late to go if you want to, too," he said.

"Is that what *you* want?" I asked.

"Not at all."

"Good, me neither." Maybe I'd actually make it through a complete interaction with him without bolting. Mature, level-headed, like a forty-three-year-old woman *should* behave.

If I'd had breath to hold, I wouldn't bother.

CHAPTER 18

The waiter sat us in a cozy, dim corner under a collage wall of framed photographs of smiling people. I didn't recognize most of them, but then I spotted a comedian I'd watched choke, literally, on stage. I was fairly sure he'd died.

"Local celebrities?" I said.

Andrew pointed over my shoulder and above my head.

I turned and looked. A flickering red light sign read *In Memoriam.*

"Local *dead* celebrities," Andrew said.

"That's not morbid at all," I said dryly.

The waiter sidled up to our table. "I know, right? I think all of their deaths were food related. What can I get you? Can I start you off with some drinks?"

I practically choked on my own spit. Recovering, I flipped the very limited menu over in my hands.

Andrew said, "I'd like a Blue Moon and an order of buffalo wings."

The waiter nodded then turned to me. "For you, ma'am?"

"A glass of red wine, I'm not picky, and the biggest chunk of cow you have, still mooing."

The waiter gave me a weird look. "Uh…okay…but we don't serve wine. Just coffee, beer, and pop."

"Then I'll skip the drink," I said.

His eyebrows became one with his hairline as he scribbled a note on his order pad. "Just the barnyard animal then…okay. That'll be out shortly."

I checked out the wall of pictures some more as we waited. It was just the two of us back here, so instead of hearing other people talk, there was only flowy music playing. I expected the silence between us to be super awkward, but it was only mostly-awkward. Yay?

The waiter returned with Andrew's drink then disappeared once more. Andrew took a sip from his frosted mug and glanced up at me. "You make a fun date."

Date? Is that what this was? Heat coiled outward through my limbs, betraying the discomfort I felt about the possibility. And maybe, just maybe, a splinter of excitement.

"Acquaintance," I said, though we were more than that.

"Supernaturally connected dining companion," Andrew countered.

I raised my non-existent glass to that. "Agreed."

Andrew said, "How are you feeling?"

"That's a loaded question," I said, with a humorless chuckle.

"I can't imagine what you must be going through," he said. "If there's anything you'd like to discuss, I'm here for you. I'd like us to be friends."

Friends. His congenial smile offered no sense that he meant anything more. My neck felt like a vise grip clamped at the base. I rolled my shoulders and tried to release the tension.

"I could use a friend. If I'm being honest, I'm a bit lost," I said. I shot a look around the empty restaurant for prying ears. When I found none, I continued, "Thank you for not calling me out on running away every time we're together."

"No problem. I'm happy to not call you out, any time."

I smiled at him. He smiled at me.

This was too easy.

I was acutely aware that a power dynamic could exist between us, one that I would be on the wrong end of. Andrew was the one who had saved my life, the one who knew what kind of monster I was, the one who knew my secrets. Even though he held all the cards, I couldn't see him leveraging them. And I had no idea why not.

That's what men did. So why did I have this strange feeling that I could trust him?

It was his smile, those enviable lips. Those lips were the only thing about him that wasn't hard. At least I imagined they weren't hard. They looked absolutely pillowy, soft and supple, perfectly gentle for trailing soft kisses down my throat.

I cleared my throat and pretended I couldn't feel the heat rising up my neck and settling into my ears and cheeks.

The waiter dropped off our food. Andrew's wings appeared to be a reasonable, normal middle-of-the-night meal. Mine was a seared but dripping piece of meat dangling off the plate, a monstrosity. Maybe that's what the two of us were—him normal, me a monster. I took a look at him as he took his first bite. His eyes glittered as he looked at me. Even if I was a monster, he didn't seem to mind.

A part of me wanted to blurt out that I was done with men. I squeezed my lips together and fought the urge. Then, I said, "You know enough about me to land me in jail for the next fifty years to life."

"I'd still like to know more."

"More blackmail material?" I asked in a joking tone, but only half joking.

He furrowed his brows and looked at me with confusion. "Why on earth would I want to blackmail you?"

"I don't know," I said. "You tell me."

"Well," he set down his food. "I can say honestly that I have no desire to bring harm to you whatsoever. If you'd like information about me, I'm happy to provide, though I will not-so-secretly wish it's because you're interested in getting to know me rather than looking for blackmail to even some kind of score."

Now I felt silly for even half-thinking it was a possibility. Andrew was a good person. I needed to stop waiting for him to do something unkind, because he'd already proved more times than he should have needed to that he wasn't.

"I'd like to hear more about you," I said. "Because I'm interested in knowing you."

He smiled.

"I grew up in Piccadilly, an only child," he said. "For my sixth birthday, after I begged him relentlessly, my father bought me my first chemistry set."

"One of those ones where you make gummy toads and mix baking soda and vinegar volcanoes?"

"Something like that. Sadly there weren't any gummies," he said. "After the chemistry set, I was hooked and read every book I could from the library about science."

"You've always known who you are," I said. "That's awesome."

"I always knew that I enjoyed blowing up baking soda volcanos," he said. "I figured most of life out along the way."

"Just like the rest of us."

He shrugged.

"Show me more of your magic," I said, glancing around

again. "If that's appropriate, given the waiter could come back at any time."

"People who don't expect to see magic don't. The human brain interprets the world in the way it assumes the world should be. It's selective attention, which allows us to focus and tune out distraction," Andrew said. "It's an important tool to accomplishing anything."

"And a shame if we consider what interesting phenomenon we may have missed." I cut off a chunk of steak and popped it into my mouth.

"Not you, not anymore. Once you see, you can't unsee."

I swallowed hard. "Great. That's not ominous at all."

Andrew smiled. "Now you asked about my potions."

I nodded.

"I'd love to show you." He slipped a hand under the table, likely into his pocket.

How many potions did he keep in there? If it was more than one or two at a time, they'd quickly weigh him down. And I hadn't noticed any awkward pocket bulges. My cheeks heated at the thought. I wiggled forward to the edge of my seat and waited to see what he would do.

He lifted a tiny glass diamond over his drink. Inside the glass, emerald fluid sloshed. It was the ittiest bittiest bottle I'd ever seen, only about half the size of his thumb.

Excitement skittered up my spine. Here with Andrew, I was beginning to feel that maybe being a revenant wasn't a total curse. The rest of the world turned a blind eye to *magic*. But not me, not anymore.

His gray eyes sparkled silver in the flickering candlelight. "Ready?"

"Abso-freakin'-lutely."

He flicked the top off the bottle and poured the potion into his mug.

In a blink the glass, the beer it held, and the potion, completely disappeared.

"What a waste of a good beer," I laughed.

The waiter appeared by our tableside, not at all impressed or confused by what he must have witnessed. "Is there anything else I can get you?"

Andrew raised a brow at me.

"I think we're good, thanks," I said. I couldn't pull my eyes away from Andrew, or away from the space on the table where his mug had been. The only evidence of its existence was a wet ring on the wooden tabletop.

The waiter set the check on the table. I reached in my pocket to get some cash, but before I could get my money out, Andrew had already paid.

"You didn't have to do that," I said.

"I know," he said.

"I'm getting the next one," I said, realizing only after the words left my mouth that I wanted there to be a next time.

"I look forward to it." He grinned at me, pulling those gorgeous lips across a set of straight, white teeth.

I reached out where the cup had been, to see if I could feel it there. If it was invisible, I realized too late that I'd be knocking it onto his lap, but I also didn't feel the glass on my fingertips. Unsure, I cringed and tried to peer over the table. "Sorry. I wasn't thinking. Did I spill it on you?"

"I'm fine," he said, "and no. There's no spill."

I reached out again, tentatively to the space the mug had inhabited.

It wasn't invisible. It was *gone.*

"What exactly does that potion do?" I asked.

"This particular compound takes objects out of phase with what we experience," he said.

Whoa. "Is it gone forever?"

"It can be."

"Best not to spill it accidentally, huh? It would really suck to lose your favorite bracelet or your keys. Or your kid. Does the potion work on people?"

"It does," he said. "But there's a fix. So long as I don't accidentally pour the disappearing potion on myself."

He slipped another bottle out of his pocket. The contents of this one were green, too, but a lighter shade, more like spring grass than emerald.

He flicked off the lid and poured the potion over the ring on the table. I held my eyes open, afraid to blink and miss it.

The mug reappeared. The beer with it.

"You're not going to drink that, are you?" I asked. "Seems risky."

"I'm not," he said. "I'm about ready to leave if you are."

A pang of disappointment filled me.

"Yeah," I said, "okay."

"If you're interested, I'd love to show you something else. There's a place about a twenty-minute drive from here. I hope you'll find it illuminating."

Yes, please! I tried not to sound too eager as I said, "Sure, why not?"

CHAPTER 19

In the dead of night, outside city limits, I sat alone in my parked car debating if I should send Wendy a text. It was late, yes. But we'd just arrived at what looked like the perfect place to murder someone.

Andrew didn't seem like a bad guy, but it was better to be safe than sorry. I shot Wendy a quick text that said approximately where I was mile-wise just off of route four-oh-two. It was our system, and she'd berate me later if I didn't do it, even if I was sure she was asleep right now. I'd also driven in my own car, because you should never trust a man you don't know when out on a date. Always have an escape. And not that this was a date, but the rules still applied.

I climbed out and slipped my phone in my pocket.

"All set?" Andrew asked. His smile was easy, charming, and trustworthy.

"Uh-huh."

We set off into the dark night, through a darker forest. I followed him into the trees, with only one glance back over my shoulder.

"Where are you taking me?" I asked. "And what kind of *surprise* are you keeping in the middle of nowhere?"

"Just a little farther," he said.

"That's not a real answer," I said.

"When my father retired last year, he left for Scandinavia."

"That must be nice. I hear people there are some of the happiest on earth."

"His people are spread across the area. Our family is in Denmark mostly. When he left the states, he gifted his property to me," Andrew said.

"And it's out here in the woods somewhere?" I asked. While I was interested in finding out more about Andrew, I didn't understand how a trek into the woods to see his dad's house could be *illuminating*. "Is this where you do your alchemy? Out in the middle of nowhere in case something goes awry? So you don't explode the other people in your building?"

"I do, actually," he said. "But that's not why...*we're here*." He stopped walking, grabbed a lantern from the ground and lit it, illuminating a mountain range of metal.

A tiny shack sat in the center of stacked appliances and other machinery. Each mound appeared to contain the same types of things—one with refrigerators, some newer and decked out in stainless steel, some pea green and pink and as old as my grandma.

Even though I couldn't say exactly what I had been expecting, this was definitely not it.

"What's with all the stuff?" I asked.

"My father likes to fix things," he said. "These are parts stacks. Come on, this way."

We walked toward the shack that must have once been his dad's house, and was now Andrew's lab. Then we walked right past, to a field of old cars in high grass.

I crossed my arms, still confused. "In no uncertain terms, I'm going to need to know what exactly we're doing here."

"I thought we could test your abilities," Andrew said. "If you're interested."

"Test how quickly I can enter a list of numbers into a spreadsheet, or how strong my jewelry-crafting game is…or test how long it takes me to turn someone into a zombie?" I asked. "Those are my main skills."

He smiled. "You mentioned feeling certain that your mother was alive."

"Fluke," I said. "Not a skill. It was probably wishful thinking, and I'm over it." Or at least I was distracted, and hadn't thought about it.

"Some revenants possess the ability to psychically influence others."

"Mind control? Sadly not. I'm terrible at getting my way."

"Have you noticed yourself getting physically stronger?" he asked.

"Maybe. Not that I can think of." I tapped my lip and searched my brain. "Well, I did have an easier time doing some lifting than I'd expected." I really didn't want to think about Scott right now, or ever again if I could help it, but yeah, I hadn't struggled when I put him in the freezer. I definitely should have.

"The more you use your gifts, the stronger they will grow."

"Like physical strength," I said. "You think I have super powered muscles?"

"It's the most common revenant quality."

I added, "After the hunger."

"Okay, yes."

I looked around at the car graveyard once more, now through the lens of what Andrew had said. The tire on the ground by the toe of my shoe wasn't just a tire. It could be a discus. That axel lying in the grass was made to be a dumbbell.

"The more I lift, the stronger I'll become? I like the sound of that." It was like regular exercise, but more exciting. "Tell me I'll achieve results faster than at the gym, because being sore and sweaty and then gaining three pounds because I ate a single noodle is not fun."

"I'd bet my lab you'll see results before sunrise."

"That confident, are you?" I grinned at him. "All right then."

I approached the biggest tire I could, bent at the knees, and dug my fingers down along the rubber tread into the dirt. It must have belonged on a tractor or monster truck. No chance I could make this thing budge, but go big or go home, right? I hooked my fingers under the tire and lifted.

My thighs burned a little, and the weight pulled down hard on my shoulders, but I flipped the tire up with relative ease. Up on its tread, it stood a foot taller than me at its full height. I leaned it against a tree so it didn't fall back down on top of me and crush my organs.

"Whew," I said, and lifted my fists to the sky in victory.

"Nice work," Andrew said.

"Thanks."

A few years ago at a workout bootcamp, when I'd been twice as physically fit, I'd tried to do this same thing with a tire half this size, and I'd struggled. Andrew was right. Becoming a revenant had made me ridiculously strong. If I pushed myself, what else could I lift?

I looked around, skipping over anything smaller or even similar in size to the tire I had just lifted. The axel was out, the bumpers and spare doors, too. By the edge of the trees, I spotted a car frame, burned and degraded so far that it was only a shell.

I headed over, grabbed the front end, and braced my

squishy core. This car frame *had* to be heavier than the tire. One, two…I lifted with all my might. The strain pulled on my thighs, my back, my arms. It was a good stretch, a good burn. The frame lifted an inch, two inches, three inches from the ground.

Before I could blow out my back, I dropped the frame back down.

"I think that's progress already," I told Andrew.

Just like the candlelight in the restaurant, the lantern light flickered across his irises, turning his gray eyes silver. There was something more to it than a trick of light, or at least it felt that way, though I couldn't explain why.

"You can lift it higher," Andrew said.

I scoffed and lifted a brow at him. "You sound awfully sure. It's *heavy.* You want a go?"

"I am sure," he said. "And no. My strengths lie in other areas."

"Potions," I said.

"Exactly."

"Look at us, brains and brawn. You're not threatened by a woman having greater physical strength than you?" I asked, genuinely curious. In my experience, men always had to prove to themselves that they were stronger, that they were wealthier, that they were better at anything and everything aside from washing dishes and caring for children.

He took a step closer. "If my masculinity were so easily threatened, I'd deserve to have it crushed."

I felt my cheeks pull as I smiled at him. He smiled back. It was an unfairly gorgeous grin and did things to my insides.

Since I couldn't tell him how much I wanted to poke him in the lip and see what his mouth felt like, I went with a less creepy comment. "What's the deal with your eyes? They're all glowy and sparkly like silver glitter. Did you drink a see-in-the-dark potion?"

He chuckled softly. It was deep and genuine, and again my traitorous body responded to him. Heat swirled in my middle. Nerves all across my skin lit up, as if he could touch me at any moment, and it was imperative to be prepared or else miss the sensation.

"No potions," he said. "It's the wolf in me."

"No way. You're not serious, are you?" I stared at him, waiting for crinkles to form at the corner of his eyes, waiting for him to laugh and tell me he was joking.

He didn't.

"You're not joking. You're a werewolf." I couldn't believe the words even as they poured out of my mouth. "That's a thing? Do I have to worry you're going to bite me?"

"Wolf shifters exist. I'm not exactly one of them."

"Then what? Don't leave me hanging in suspense here." Also, no comment on the biting? That heat coiling in my middle spread its way up through my chest.

"My father is a wolf shifter," he said. "I inherited acute enhancements to my night vision and to my hearing. That's all. And it's not contagious, merely hereditary."

He still didn't say he wouldn't bite me. Why did I have to find that hot? This was serious, not sexy.

"So you don't get extra hairy on the full moon?" I asked.

"No."

"All right then."

I had to look away from him before he noticed how thoroughly I was blushing. I reached down and lifted the car frame again, three inches. The weight was intense, gravity doing her darndest to thwart me. But I could do more. I could lift more. I believed Andrew, and I believed in myself.

Ignoring the little voice in my head that was reason, I squeezed my fingers around the cold metal bar in my hands and straightened my legs. The car lifted up as I stood. I held the front end *three feet from the ground.*

"I did it," I gasped, shocked that it was true.

"Of course you did," Andrew said, not at all shocked by my accomplishment.

I dropped the car, then ran to lift another, this time one that wasn't hollowed out. It was harder. Much harder.

As I struggled, Andrew cocked his head to the side. "Do you hear that?"

Straining my everything, I answered, "Am I grunting? Did you hear my spine pop in two?"

"No," he said. "Never mind."

I lifted the sedan ever so slightly off the grass before letting go and rolling my shoulders.

"What did you hear?" I asked.

"There's a family of owls in a tree not too far from here. The chicks are being vocal."

"Aww. I wish I could hear, but I can't."

"We could get closer, but they'd probably stop. I guess we can cross enhanced hearing off the list."

I looked away from the lantern, to the darkness that was the forest. "No wolfman-like night vision. No enhanced taste. What's the opposite of enhanced? Inhibited? I'm going with diminished."

"Your strength is impressive, and not only physically." His eyes were pure silver, locking me in place. His stance was open. His tone was kind and confident, like this was simply the truth as he saw it, and he had no reservations about sharing it with me. "You have endured so much in such a short time, and you're still standing. You're fighting. You're a survivor, and I feel fortunate to be here to see you thrive."

I had never felt so seen. I was flattered, too. And speechless.

"I'm not ready to rule out psychic tendencies yet either," he continued. "Maybe you were right about your mother.

She could be still out there, and maybe as your gifts develop, you'll know more about where to find her."

I didn't know what to say to that, so I turned my attention back to my lifting. With as much focus as I could muster, I dove into my task. I lifted the sedan a foot up off the ground.

From there, I lifted another car, and then a truck. Andrew offered words of encouragement, and no deeper conversation. I was grateful.

I didn't realize how long we had been out in the woods until the sun began to rise.

"It's morning already," Andrew said.

"Looks like you won the bet you made against yourself," I said. "I am stronger than I was when we got here."

"I knew you would be."

I watched the silver fade from his eyes, turning back to the still-lovely gray. His daytime eyes weren't glittery; they were soft clouds in the spring sky.

Not quite ready for the night to end, I ran over to the largest object in the area—a heavy duty trailer.

"You must be feeling confident," Andrew said, looking up at the trailer with me.

"Actually, yes."

I moved around to the side and lifted the trailer quickly, because I knew deep down that I could do it.

Except I was too quick.

The trailer wasn't as heavy as I expected, not even close to the weight of the truck. I put too much force into it, and the trailer flipped up on its backside and tottered there.

It slipped out of my hands. I reached for it, my confidence morphing into uncertainty.

What if I couldn't catch it? What if I screwed up *again*?

My gaze went right to Andrew.

Time felt like it slowed, but all I could do was try to grab hold of the trailer, try to stop myself from killing someone else.

The trailer tipped, falling right toward Andrew.

"Andrew!" I couldn't hold on. I was too slow, too weak.

I raced toward him, to grab him and pull him out of harm's way.

Before I could even reach him, he sidestepped. The trailer crashed down against a tree, missing him. Thank goodness. And it remained perched there.

My legs were still in motion. As I slowed, I tripped on a root and tumbled forward.

Andrew was quick and sure in his movement. Instead of me saving him, he saved me, catching me before I fell flat on my face.

I landed flat against him instead, against his hard chest, enveloped in his pleasant warmth. He smelled like coffee and spice. I hadn't noticed that before, but I liked it.

His arms were gentle, unassuming, but strong. To my surprise and delight, he held onto me instead of pulling away. I knew I should pull back, that if ever there was a time to run, this was it. But I couldn't bring myself to do it. My legs wouldn't move. I dug my fingers into the fabric of his shirt instead, clinging to him.

He hadn't asked for this, or for me in his life, but I kept stumbling in, and maybe that wasn't such a terrible thing.

My nerves lit up under his touch, shooting off like fireworks under his large hands. Slowly, I tilted my chin up to see his face, nervous over what expression I might find there.

He tilted his chin down, almost brushing his beard against my cheek.

His lips were an inch from mine. I'd never wanted a man more in my life. I closed my eyes, my insides fluttering with anticipation.

Bang. The trailer that had been leaning on the tree crashed to the ground.

I flinched and pulled back, forcing my hands to let him go. Only then did my brain start working. I realized, to my horror, that I'd been about to kiss Andrew Jensen. He'd done the polite thing and caught me when I'd fallen into him. And then I'd almost taken advantage. I could still feel where his hands had been on my skin. His coffee scent still filled my brain.

I laughed it off.

"Sorry," I said. "Thanks. I am so clumsy. That was…let's forget that happened."

His brows quirked down. His expression was earnest, kind. "Rose—"

I took a step back, putting much needed space between us. He let me.

"I should go home now." I turned on my heel and briskly walked back toward my car. I was *not* running away. I was walking. And this time as I fled from Andrew, a big part of me wanted to stay.

CHAPTER 20

When I woke the next morning, I was surprised to find I'd actually slept. I was also surprised to find that my body was only mildly sore. After the night I'd had, the aches and pains should have been far worse. The bandage on my foot from my Scott bite had fallen off in the night, and weirdly there was no mark at all. I was completely healed.

The house was quiet. There was no zombie in my basement to feed.

Life was almost—dare I allow myself to think it and possibly jinx it—good?

Last night, I'd lifted cars.

Me.

After getting out of bed, I started my day with a hearty breakfast of meat. Surprise, surprise. Then, full and content, I sat down in front of my laptop to check my work email.

But if this was my fresh start—new powers, new life—did I really want to work my old job?

The office used to be my happy place. Forcing me to

work from home felt like a half measure. Why not simply lay me off? Rip off the bandage instead of stringing me along?

Thinking about it should have made me upset. It didn't. I felt fine.

Not having to work meant I could do something else, something for myself. What that would look like, I wasn't sure yet. I closed my laptop and popped some aspirin.

There was a text on my phone from Wendy that I'd missed: *How did it go last night?*

I wasn't sure what to say, so I dumped it all out at once.

Me: Weird. Helpful. Hot.
   Wendy: So, it went well.
   Me: I think so.
   Wendy: Good. You deserve all the good things. I'm expecting details.
   Me: How about tomorrow night at my place? Sleepover. Pajamas and The Princess Bride.
   Wendy: Yes! I'll bring the wine.

I gathered my keys, wallet, and biggest sunglasses, then headed out.

Floral scents filled the air. Birds chirped. The sun pelted extra bright rays as rogue raindrops drizzled down against my windshield. I rolled up my window and put the wipers on low.

It had been ages since I'd taken a "me day." But nothing I used to do felt quite right anymore. I drove past what used to be my favorite coffee place. I slowed down, but I didn't stop. The days of coffee and bagels were over. I was a red wine and red meat woman now, and those weren't served at Breakfast Bonanza.

There was one place, though, that always filled me with joy and inspiration, even if I hadn't given myself time to go in a while. And it had been a long while. I parked in the well-worn lot of the tiny strip mall.

Sandwiched between a Books Galore and an unnamed nail salon was Craftin' Like Crazy. The little bell above the door dinged as I stepped inside.

If you had asked me a week ago to describe what it felt like to be in Crafin' Like Crazy, I probably would have smiled and given a warm but vague answer from vague memories—bright, happy, clean. Maybe I'd even have used the wholly original descriptor—crafty.

But standing in the store in person, all of those memories became as sharp as if I'd been here only yesterday. The lighting wasn't just bright, but white, and not in that make-your-skin-blotchy way, but like the heavens shone their favor upon every hand-dipped piece of scrapbooking paper and every tube of jewel-infused oil paint on the shelves. The cedar and clay scents in the air were so familiar, I snuggled into them like a second jacket.

I headed straight for the back left corner of the shop and swept my fingers across bins of clips and chains and rings. I stopped on a bin with a single item inside—what looked like an antique pocket watch, only miniature. The gears were clear through its cracked glass front.

"A good choice." A young clerk with a tie dye apron sidled up next to me, a sweet smile on her face. The name embroidered over her right collarbone read *Emily*. "It came in a hodge podge box of costume jewelry from an estate sale. It doesn't work as a watch, but it's definitely got character."

"Swimming in character," I said, smiling back.

"I bet it would work well in a steampunk shadow box."

"Sure," I said, running my thumb over the cracked glass. But it wasn't meant to go in a box. This tiny clock belonged on a necklace. "I'm thinking jewelry."

"Love that," Emily said. "You could solder links on each

end and use some ethically engineered vegan leather cord to make a wrist watch and—"

"*Excuse me.*" A man at the front of the store snapped his fingers.

I hadn't realized there were any other customers in the shop.

Emily's smile fell. The excitement in her eyes dulled. In an even, yet markedly less chipper tone, she said, "I'll be with you in a moment, Mr. Needlemeyer."

I felt for her instantly. I'd worked my fair share in the service industry waiting tables in my youth. Some people got their jollies by taking out life's frustrations on those whose jobs involved any kind of service. The snapping was a clear red flag that Mr. Needlemeyer was the type.

A man walked to the edge of the aisle where we were standing. He looked to be somewhere between sixty-five and eighty-five. He wore a French beret, a tiny bowtie, and a button-down shirt. A worm of a black mustache crossed his lip and curled at the ends, almost like he'd used pipe cleaners to make it.

"How many minutes do you think I have left, girl?" Mr. Needlemeyer scowled at Emily down the aisle.

A flush of red crept up her neck.

"Death is pulling on my hair," Mr. Needlemeyer said. "Every moment you waste fooling around is one you've stolen from my grandchildren seeing their sweet Gramps."

First, *sweet?*

Second, after being stalked by a reaper, I took talk of death super seriously. Even though I figured Mr. Needlemeyer wasn't being literal, I glanced around for any sign of the reaper. There was none.

Emily closed her eyes and rubbed the crease in the center of her forehead. She gave me a pained smile. "I'm sorry. I've forgotten what we were saying. Was there anything I can do for you before I—"

"I'm fine," I told her. "Really. Go ahead."

"Thanks." She hurried over to help him.

I followed a few steps behind Emily and stopped at the end of the aisle while the two approached the counter. I pretended not to pay attention and busied my hands in a basket full of charms. I watched their interaction, him barely suppressing a pleased grin as he berated Emily, and her turning red with discomfort.

Something came over me. Call it a sense of duty, maybe, or a middle-aged disregard for keeping my nose in my own business.

Mr. Needlemeyer headed for the door. I cut him off before he could escape.

"Get out of my way," he said. His mustache twitched, and the end dropped two inches on one side. The glue had come loose apparently, on what was definitely a pipe cleaner homage to facial hair.

"You should apologize for your rude behavior," I told him.

He laughed without humor. "Not going to happen."

I wished someone would have stood up for me any of the times a customer had grabbed my butt. I wished someone had been there to tell me that it wasn't my fault when Scott said that it was. I couldn't go back and change the past, but in this moment, I could be that someone for Emily.

I squared my shoulders and tried to make myself look taller, because even though I was younger and likely physically stronger than Mr. Needlemeyer, he still had a foot on me in height. And quite a bit of anger.

"You can't treat people like that," I told him.

He laughed and glanced back at Emily. "Who is going to stop me, you?"

"Yeah, me." I put my fists on my hips, narrowed my eyes,

and tried to burrow into his skull with my resolve. "You *will* apologize."

"I'm sorry," he said.

I blinked. "What?"

"I apologize."

His expression was blank. He wasn't joking?

I cleared my throat. Was this actually working? Was calling him out all it took to discourage this jerk from his jerky ways? He had to be messing with me. Right? I said, "Not to me. Apologize to the clerk."

He turned on his heel, facing Emily. "I'm sorry."

It seemed it was working. I had no idea why, but yay for good things. On a roll, I told him, "You can do better than that. Put some feeling into it. Look her in the eye."

He whipped back around to me. "You want feeling? Try sciatica."

He brushed my shoulder and started for the door.

"Wait. Don't go," I called after him.

He didn't stop.

I got between him and the door again.

"You're pushing your luck, missy. Get out of my way or I'll break your nose." He shook his fist at me.

Okay, now it was on.

"Not so fast," I said. I leaned in closer, smelling the sardines on his breath. I looked into his eyes, staring, until something clicked in my brain. It wasn't that I'd taken this too far. It was that I hadn't taken it far enough. I could feel something flexing in my brain, like my muscles had when I'd lifted the cars. I could *make* him do this. I licked my lips. "Verbally prostrate yourself to the clerk. Then never come back."

His jaw clenched then loosened. He went back to the counter.

Emily's shoulders slumped. "Yes, Mr. Needlemeyer? Is there something else I can help you with?"

"I don't have grandchildren. I don't have children or a wife either. I'm angry at life for the loneliness I brought upon myself for being unkind my entire life. I apologize and I shouldn't take it out on you."

Emily's jaw dropped. Literally.

Mine did, too.

Mr. Needlemeyer turned to me. "Happy? If I don't get something to eat my blood sugar is going to drop and then I'll show you mean."

I nodded. "Mm-hmm."

He grumbled and walked away.

It worked.

I couldn't believe it actually freaking worked.

Emily turned to me. "What did you say to him?"

I shrugged, playing it off super cool. "Nothing he didn't need to hear."

I gathered my finds, paid, and went on my way feeling awfully pleased with myself. I was a powerful revenant, and I could use those powers for good. But how much of what had happened was because of my power? Was it all because of my undead, magical influence? Or was part of Mr. Needlemeyer's confession due to my physically blocking the door? Or could it have been his own deep-down regret over his actions?

Before I could proclaim myself a mind-control master, more testing was required.

My stomach growled.

Also required—lunch. I went through a drive through and downed a triple cheeseburger, no bun. Then I drove around a bit before settling on my next target. Controlling Mr. Needlemeyer was more or less an accident. This would be a purposeful attack. Manipulation was my weapon, and I would use it on those who deserved it. Why not try and make my life a little better during the process?

As I strolled into the building, I headed straight to my boss's office. The scent of cheese hit me as I stepped into the doorway. Colby Jackson looked up from his computer screen. Recognition flashed over his face.

"Mrs. Cruise, what are you doing here?" He checked his watch. "You aren't supposed to be in the office."

"It's Ms. DeLaCruz. Or Rosemary. Or Rose. I've never been Mrs. Cruise," I told him. "And *I* decide what I'm supposed to do now. Not you."

He threw his head back and laughed, rich and hearty, like slow cooker chili to go with the rotten cheddar he seemed to keep in his pockets. Tears welled in the corners of his eyes and he tilted his chair back.

I shifted my weight.

He said, "You're funny."

That was not how this was supposed to go. I narrowed my eyes at him and summoned my greatest force of will.

"Look at me," I demanded. "I'm not joking."

He wiped the tears from his eyes, but didn't bother wiping that smug grin from his face as he tented his fingers on his desk and looked right at me. "I see you. I don't understand what you're trying to do here, but I see you. You need to leave before you lose what little employment you have left."

Oh no, what had I been thinking? Did I really think I could waltz in here and get what I wanted? Apparently, but why? Now that he was staring at me, I wasn't so sure what I'd hoped to accomplish anyway.

Did I really want my job back the way it had been? No. I didn't think I did. I'd been comfortable in the stability, but I wasn't fulfilled here in any way, not like I was when I was out all night flipping cars with Andrew, or spending time with

Wendy or Heather. If I could actually manipulate anyone—something I was seriously doubting at the moment—why would I bother making that someone Colby freaking Jackson? Why not use my influence to obtain the job of my dreams?

Again, that implied a real ability to control people, which I clearly did not have. But why not take this opportunity, this life reset, to go for my dreams? What's the worst that could happen?

If I lost everything, Wendy would take me in. I could always find some kind of work if I had to. I wasn't too good to flip burgers if push came to shove.

"Mrs. Cruise?" Colby was still staring at me, now with his hand hovering over his phone. "Last chance to go before this escalates. Don't make me call security."

I plastered on a plastic grin and turned to go.

Step one—figure out what my dream life actually looked like.

Step two—figure out how to make it happen.

Step three—live the dream.

Only three steps, a small number. With superpowers in my arsenal, three little steps couldn't be too hard…right?

CHAPTER 21

My sticker and felt-tip pen collections lay sprawled across the coffee table, organized just so. The pens fanned out in ombre order. The stickers were arranged by size, with the smallest closest to me.

I looked over my work, pleased with the result. Then I looked down at the empty two-page spread in my spiral notebook.

My first task upon returning home had been to slip on comfy pajamas, because living my best life definitely included wearing pajamas as often as possible. My second task was supposed to be writing out two lists—what I wanted in life, and what I didn't.

The list part was harder to start than anticipated.

Since my supplies were definitely already in order, I didn't have any excuse left to procrastinate. Except maybe retrieving a glass of wine. It seemed I'd figured out two things to add to my Want list already—wine and pajamas. Yay me. I celebrated by pouring a glass of wine, and then settling back down and recording those two items on the left page. I went with a lavender pen—my favorite—and decorated the margins of the page with complementary stickers.

There, that wasn't so bad.

I stared at my work, pleased with the result. Then I added another item to the Want list—*steak*. Once the words started flowing, it got easier to write more.

For the No Thanks list, I opted for a shade of orange that reminded me of changing Heather's diapers when she was a baby.

On the purple page, I wrote, and I wrote, and I wrote until it was full. The orange remained significantly barer, with frowning stickers and only three items listed—*interacting with Colby Jackson, running for any reason,* and *men*.

Maybe it was my choices in color that had led me to focus on the positive, or maybe I was simply more excited to look forward than to ruminate. I chose to believe the latter.

My phone dinged in my pocket. I slid it out and found a text.

Hi, it's Andrew. Wendy left your number on my counter the other night.

I shook my head and debated for a minute what to say.

Me: Of course she did.
    Andrew: How are you doing after last night?

With the almost-kiss?

Me: Peachy.
    Andrew: Good. I was worried you'd be sore.

Because we hadn't kissed and I'd wanted to? And because now I was wondering why I wasn't going all-in, taking everything I wanted in life? My fingers hovered over the screen. It took me a moment to realize what he was talking about. He thought I could be injured because of the lifting.

Me: All good.
   Me: What are you doing right now? Are you busy?
   Andrew: Leaving work.

I didn't have any plans until tomorrow night, which would be wine and movies with Wendy. Tonight was wide open and brimming with possibility.

Me: Want to come over?
   Me: We can order takeout.

Three little dots flicked across the screen. I squeezed my eyes shut, nervous about what he'd say.

Me: Talk revenant stuff.
   Andrew: Text me your address.

I sent it, then looked over my living room as someone else would see it. The stickers and pens had to be cleaned up. Oh, and so did I. I clicked a picture of myself with my phone, then checked the state of me.

A single nose hair peeked out of my right nostril. In good but weird news, my chipped tooth no longer appeared to be chipped. I was fairly certain teeth weren't supposed to fix themselves. My complexion was reminiscent of that of an uncooked turkey, while the dark circles around my eyes belonged to a raccoon. This was bad. Really bad.

It was easy to forget about my appearance when I couldn't see myself in the mirror. I shouldn't care. But there on my lavender list was clear evidence that I did. It said, *look hot.* Apparently I also wanted: *my mother's approval*—too late—and *an easier rapport with Heather,* to own *a bazillion dollars,* for *chocolate to taste like it was supposed to again,* and *more time to make jewelry.*

And *Andrew.*

The final line at the bottom was his name, with no additional points. It didn't say revenant training with Andrew. Just Andrew. How did that get in there?

I snapped the notebook shut and raced to clean the living room and myself up. I used the camera on my phone as a guide to do what I could to fix my face. Then I wasted some time debating what was an appropriate outfit for casual hanging out around the house. Part of me wanted to stick to the pajamas, while another part suggested a classy, sexy dress. I went with the yoga pants that made my butt look good and hid my belly a bit and a loose, stain-free t-shirt.

The doorbell rang, and before I could rethink my choices, I hurried down and opened the door.

Andrew was there with a paper bag in hand.

"Hey, I stopped by the little deli on third. They have the best pastrami. If you're not in the mood, we can still order something."

"No, pastrami sounds great," I said. "Please come in."

"This is a nice spot," Andrew said. "The neighborhood feels more like a small town than the middle of the city."

"Thank you," I said, leading Andrew to the kitchen. "I bought it back when my daughter was little, so she'd have a yard to play in."

He pulled a loaf of bread out of his bag, along with a package of meat and one of cheese. I pulled out plates and condiments.

"I didn't know you had a daughter," he said.

Oh. With an anxious chuckle, I said, "I guess we know even less about each other than I thought."

What else did we not know about each other that we definitely should? For all I knew, Andrew could be in a long-term, committed relationship and I could have read all of our interactions wrong this whole time.

"There's an easy fix for that." Andrew leaned on the counter. "Tell me about her."

"Well, her name is Heather. She's twenty. She's a painter, and a talented one at that. She's warm, independent, and so smart. She's confident and driven. She's everything I wish I could have been at her age, and I'm so proud of her."

"She sounds great. Does she live with you?"

I laughed. "No. That's one way the two of us *are* alike. She was itching to fly from home as soon as she could."

"I bet you have more in common than you think," Andrew said.

"The curly hair," I said, with a nod. "But hers is black instead of dirty-blond like mine."

"We're still getting to know each other here, but I think you're warm and smart and independent."

"Thank you." I cleared my throat. "Speaking of getting to know each other...do *you* have any kids? A girlfriend?"

"No, Rosemary," he said with a small smile. "No wife. No girlfriend or fiancée either. No conflict of interest to interfere with what I hope could happen between us."

"Good." I chewed my lip. "And what do you think could happen between us?"

"Right now, dinner," he said, offering me a plate.

I took a bite of my sandwich to give myself a moment to think. The pastrami was definitely good. The soft bread didn't even taste too ashy, which was a nice surprise.

The silver was back in Andrew's irises, swirling there as he looked at me. His expression was open yet somehow also intense.

I swallowed. "And kids?"

"No kids. I've focused on my career and my alchemy. I never considered starting a family of my own."

"I see," I said.

"Do you? I believe it's my father's wolf side that made me hate casual dating."

"Didn't want to turn your girlfriends into werewolves?" I asked, jokingly.

"I couldn't do that if I wanted to," he said in all seriousness. "Shifters have one person, a mate, they are meant to be with. I've never committed beyond casual encounters because I couldn't connect. I didn't feel it."

"You've never been in love," I said. "And I thought you didn't shift?"

"I can't shift," he agreed. "And I never looked at someone and felt the primal bond before, the one that meant I'd found my person."

"Uh huh," I said, nodding. Then I shoved a chunk of sandwich into my mouth because I could sense the *but* on his lips. I could see it in his eyes and feel it lingering in the air between us. It felt heavier than any proclamation of love or devotion I'd ever been handed, and I'd been engaged *three times*.

If he said the words, this—whatever it was between us—was real.

It was time to run. Time to shut him up. But I couldn't make myself do it. I was terrified, hands sweating. But I needed to hear.

"Then I sensed you in the graveyard, your pulse faint, your cries muted by the dirt," he said. "And I felt it."

A lump formed in my throat. No, that wasn't a nervous lump. It was a chunk of pastrami on sourdough, and it was stuck.

I pounded on my chest and tried to cough it out.

Mild panic squeezed my lungs.

I didn't need to breathe, so why did it matter if I was choking? Heat rose up my cheeks.

Andrew walked around behind me and wrapped his arms around me, his hands together under my ribs. "I'm going to dislodge it, okay? You are going to be fine."

I didn't want him to hold me. I didn't want him to help me.

I shook my head no. I was not fine. I pounded on my chest again with my fist, this time so hard I was sure there would be a bruise.

A chunk of half-chewed food flew out of my mouth and onto the counter.

Sweet relief.

Andrew began to pull away.

I put my hands over his, holding him still. I leaned back against his hard chest, and I closed my eyes. It was easier to be brave when I wasn't looking at him. It was easier to accept his touch, his closeness, and his words. It was easier to accept that this was what I wanted, that he was what I wanted even though I'd thought I was better off without men.

"I'm terrible at choosing men," I whispered. "I like you, and it's terrifying."

"I like you, too."

"I don't know if I can be your destined forever woman," I said. "It's too much pressure right now for me."

"I'm not asking you for anything. You don't owe me the same feelings. You don't owe me anything at all, Rosemary."

"I owe you my life," I said.

"I had the opportunity to help you when you needed it, nothing more," he said.

Except it was more. I knew deep down that it was so much more, or at least it could be. *We* could be.

"I'm a mess," I said.

"You're a force of nature."

I turned around in his embrace and leaned my head against his chest. His skin was warm, his muscles hard. I could hear his heart beating like a drum. The rhythm soothed my nerves.

This was what we could be—not just fun and excitement, but comfort. I could see the two of us going to Lingonberry for Heather's next gallery opening. Instead of me lingering too much and smothering her until she pushed me away, Andrew and I would visit, then leave. We'd spend the rest of the night out at a dive bar, the two of us. And I wouldn't regret that I'd pushed too hard because I'd be happily doing my own thing with Andrew.

I looked up to where he was staring down at me, and I knew our dynamic wasn't going to only be about comfort either.

The air turned hot, an electric charge carrying up my skin. Nerves and excitement mingled in my chest.

If I let this happen, it would be *hot.*

I ran a hand through his beard. "No promises about what comes next."

His voice was rough. "I'm good with that."

I pulled on his neck and lifted up to my tip-toes. His Adam's apple bobbed in his throat.

I brushed my lips over his. They were even softer than I'd expected, gentle at first, then less so. His beard scratched my chin, a delicious bite to counter the sweetness of his mouth. He let me lead. I deepened the kiss, ran my hands up his shirt, over the muscles of his abs and twined my fingers in the hair of his chest.

His strong hands found my hips, pinning me against the edge of the counter. Reason and uncertainty transformed to possibility. As soon as he scraped his teeth gently against my bottom lip, all thoughts beyond need and sensation poofed away.

CHAPTER 22

When I woke to morning light, I stretched and rolled over in bed expecting to find Andrew beside me. He wasn't there, so I checked downstairs. He wasn't there either, but he'd left a note along with a small vial of purple liquid.

Sorry I couldn't stay. I have a meeting at the office. I had a great time, and can't wait to see you again.

The vial is a gift I'd intended to give you last night. It may help with your taste bud problem.

~A

He'd intended to give me a gift last night. There were definitely things I'd expected to happen last night that hadn't, too. I'd invited him over to talk about revenant issues, like my shoddy attempt at mind controlling my boss. But, I didn't regret not talking more. I couldn't regret a thing about last night because it had been mind-blowingly amazing.

Every future scenario I could imagine with Andrew in it now included out-of-this-world-amazing sex. We'd go to the woods to work on strength training, only instead of lifting cars, we'd strip naked and ravish each other. Or I'd stop by his apartment to talk about my mind control powers, and we'd end up naked in the kitchen, maybe on the countertops, and then definitely on the sofa by the big windows.

I popped open the lid of the bottle he'd left me and downed the contents. Only after the metallic yet floral taste coated my tongue did I realize neither the note nor the bottle explicitly said I should drink the liquid. What else could taste bud juice be good for though, right?

With a smile plastered to my face, I showered, got dressed, and decided to pick up right where yesterday went wrong.

At the office, I spotted Colby Jackson at the water cooler laughing with his bro squad. They completely ignored me as I approached.

I grabbed Colby's tie, and pulled.

He followed me, hands up in defense as I dragged him into his office.

"Whoa," he said. Then over his shoulder to his bros, "I don't know who this broad is, but who am I to say no to a woman who knows what she wants?"

Disgusting. The only touching I would consider was a knee to his balls.

I slammed the door shut behind us, and got right up in his face.

"Mrs. Cruise?" His stupid smile dropped. "I thought I told you yesterday not to come back here…What's going on? You seem…different."

"I *am* different," I told him.

It wasn't just the awesome night I'd had with Andrew, even though it was a contributing factor. I was confident. I knew what I wanted. And I was going to take it.

"You will give back what you took from me," I commanded.

His pupils dilated. "Whatever you want, it's yours."

This was going better than I'd expected, much easier than yesterday.

He reached inside his jacket pocket, pulled out a pen, and offered it to me. I picked it up and flipped it over. At the end, a tiny plastic muscle man bounced back and forth on his metal spring. A red bikini top was drawn on in marker. That part wasn't supposed to be there.

Wendy had given it to me. I thought I'd lost it. When I said I wanted what he'd taken from me, I meant my office hours and physical office. I didn't think he'd actually stolen from me.

"You stole my pen?" I asked.

"Yes."

"And drew on it? *Why?*"

"I like stealing things. I also took your sticky notes and your kitty cat mug."

I opened my mouth, shook my head, and took a moment to consider what to say next. "You have a problem."

"I have lots of problems."

I grinned with satisfaction. "Clearly. I'm not here for the pen." Though I would gladly take it home with me. "You have to restore my hours."

"Done."

"And my benefits."

"Of course."

This was so easy, too easy. I'd gotten my mojo back. What else could I get out of him? "Give me your parking spot."

"It's yours."

"Who's the boss, now, turd?" I cackled, not believing I'd actually said that out loud.

"You are?"

My smile pulled so hard on my cheeks I had to be freaking glowing like the sun.

If I wasn't careful, all of this power was going to go to my head. Pleased with the way this meeting was going, I realized something. It wasn't retrieving my job that had me giddy, it was the power and ease with which I'd reclaimed it.

I didn't actually want this job. It was not on my lavender list.

"And if I decide I don't want to work those extra hours?" I asked.

"Don't work them."

"I want the benefits," I told him.

"Of course."

I smiled down at my pen, the little man dancing back and forth on his spring.

"Give me your office. I might use it once in a while," I said. "But probably not."

"It's yours."

I booped him in between the eyes with my man pen. And I left.

The bro squad watched me go, whispering to each other. One whistled. I didn't care what they thought. It was me who ruled the office, me who could put any one of them in his place with only a few words of suggestion.

Maybe I would. Maybe I wouldn't, because at this point not a one of them was worth my time.

Of course I knew it wouldn't be possible for me to keep my medical and 401k going forever. At some point, someone above Colby Jackson would realize I didn't actually work for the company anymore. Or maybe Colby himself would regrow his backbone and cut me off. None of that mattered at the moment.

The important point was that *I* was in control of my life. I was my boss. And I could figure the rest out, because that's what bosses did. I'd take my Want list and put those desires into motion. I'd figure out how to make jewelry crafting a real job. Why not?

As I exited the building, I spotted a familiar shabby man in a familiar shabby suit walking down the sidewalk. He carried a briefcase in one hand, and a cup of coffee in the other. His attention was cast down at his feet as he walked.

Where did I know him from?

It hit me like a brick to the gut. He was the lawyer who had bequeathed all of my mother's possessions to a cat. If I was half the boss I felt like, I couldn't let that stand. Maybe it was mind control, maybe just confidence, but I could get things done when I stood my ground. I was sure of it.

I tried to recall the lawyer's name as I chased him down.

"Hey! Hey, lawyer man."

He stopped, turned, and gave me a strange look. His eyes were hollow, sunken, and distant.

"Are you…okay?" I asked him, suddenly unsure about my plan.

"Mmm," he said. "Coffee clears my brain. I need more coffee."

I glanced at the cup in his hand. The contents sloshed out over the hole in the lid and down his hand.

"Maybe you should drink the coffee you have first," I told him.

"Right, yes." He looked at his briefcase, then to his coffee, like he wasn't sure which was his cup. But then he took a sip from the briefcase.

That was…not so great.

"Do you remember me?" I asked.

"Rosemary DeLaCrux," he said. "Yes, I remember you."

I narrowed my eyes and focused my will. Maybe his confusion would work in my favor. Maybe he was just that tired, and he'd spill his secrets with a little push. I could do this!

"Tell me what you know about my mother," I said.

His eye twitched. "Lenore DeLaCrux. Sixty-eight years of age. Lives at eight-oh-five Magnes Place."

That wasn't exactly what I was looking for, but okay. At least he knew who we were.

"*Lived,* you mean," I said. "I find myself doing the same, thinking and speaking of her as if she's still with us."

"No," he said, looking me dead in the eye. "Your mother is still alive."

CHAPTER 23

My mom was still alive? I'd sensed it, what felt like a lifetime ago, but I'd written that feeling off as wishful thinking. There had to be some kind of miscommunication here. Looking for that misunderstanding, I asked the lawyer, "What do you mean my mother is still alive?"

He blinked out of sync, first one eye then the other.

Was this guy having a stroke? Had I somehow broken him with my revenant willpower? I sure hoped not. And he *had* seemed a little broken before I'd said two words to him.

"I think you need to go to the hospital," I told him.

His eyes rolled back, and his voice dropped. "This one does not require assistance."

"Uh—" I looked both ways for a camera. This had to be a prank. But no one was standing around to watch.

The lawyer started walking again. I followed, staying by his side.

"Where are we going?" I asked.

"Lenore DeLaCrux. Sixty-eight years of age. Eight-oh-five Magnes Place," he said again. His voice had returned to its usual pitch.

"Are you lost?" I asked him. "Did you hit your head? Does what happened to you have something to do with my mom?"

He didn't answer. Instead he repeated, "Lenore DeLaCrux. Sixty-eight years of age. Lives at eight-oh-five Magnes Place."

"Yep," I said. "That's my mom."

He stopped and turned to me. His voice dropped again and his eyes rolled back. "This one does not require an escort."

"Okay." I raised my hands in defense, waited for him to continue on his way, and followed from a few paces back. I decided it was best not to say anything else, so as not to agitate him.

If he was this messed up, it probably didn't mean anything that he claimed my mom was alive. He was so far out of it, I would be a fool to believe anything that came out of his mouth. Yet the possibility bounced around in my head.

What if he was right?

He walked to his office building. Before opening the door, he dumped his coffee on his head. Then he went inside.

I cringed for him, then followed him in, because I couldn't leave him acting like that. This whole situation could easily be my fault, and I had to make sure he was okay before I left. Should I try again? Will him to be normal? Could that work?

I waited a beat, then opened the door and walked inside.

The woman at the reception desk had wide eyes as she stared at the closed elevator doors. Beside those doors was a placard that read Bueford Gross.

That's what his name was! How could I have forgotten?

"Hi," I said.

"Hello," she said, without looking at me. She shook her head, put on a genial smile and turned to greet me. "Mrs. DeLaCrux, what brings you in today?"

I pointed to the elevator.

"Oh, no," she said. "Did you happen across Mr. Gross on the street? I hope he didn't say anything to you. Did he say anything to you?"

"He did, actually," I told her. "I'm worried he may have hit his head. Has he been acting strangely?"

"Yes." She leaned forward conspiratorially. "He's been strange for days. His wife knows. I'm supposed to give her reports each day. They've been running tests, but I really shouldn't be telling you any of this. So, um, pretend I didn't."

"Sure," I said.

"And disregard anything he said to you, too, please," she said.

I gave her what I hoped was a reassuring nod, but there was absolutely no way I was going to ignore what he had told me. I said, "I hope everything works out."

"Me, too."

I gave her a small wave and left.

Selfishly, I was relieved that *I* hadn't broken Mr. Gross, but I felt a little bad about it because there was still something seriously wrong with him. Whatever it was, I hoped the doctors figured it out and he'd be okay.

I hurried back to my car and headed out. There was only one place I could go. I *had* to go see for myself.

As I drove to Lingonberry, I thought about all the reasons not to go.

I'd planned the funeral myself. I'd grieved her death. So why was I indulging in this fairytale? It would only lead to fresh hurt. I was supposed to be past the denial stage of grief by now.

If she were alive, and somehow all of this was some big misunderstanding, she was most likely off exploring the world. The last place she would be was home, or she would have noticed that all of her belongings, including the house itself, had been given away. No matter what, she would have called by now.

By simply showing up, I could endanger my right to the belongings I had inherited. My mother's keepsakes—the only thing I had left of her—could be gone. And if I didn't go? If I drove back home without at least walking through the house?

I couldn't turn back.

I had to see for myself.

I dialed up the radio to try and quiet my brain. The distraction helped a little, but the two-hour drive still dragged.

Eventually, I made it. I parked on the street and climbed the usual tree to reach the top of the privacy wall. With a prayer that I wouldn't sprain something, I hopped down and landed on my feet on the other side.

Cautious but determined, I made my way to the broken dining room window I had found last time. I couldn't hear any indication of anyone inside.

Reaching through the hole, careful not to touch any of the sharp edges, I wrapped the end of the curtain around my forearm. Then I bashed out the remaining broken glass.

The cracking was *loud.*

If anyone was inside, say quietly hanging out in a different room, they'd hear for sure. I flattened myself against the wall and held as still as possible. Seconds ticked by as I waited to see if anyone was coming.

No one did.

Using my sleeves to cover my palms, I hoisted myself up into the frame and fell gracelessly through the window.

Immediately it became apparent I had missed some of the glass. Small cuts stung along my palms and my right shin. The sharp pains were pushed to the back of my mind as I spotted the holes I'd caused in the curtain. Mom loved those curtains.

"Sorry, Mom."

I'd sat here on the dining room carpet a billion times before, reading in the blanket forts I'd built using this table. Each day Mom had let the fort stand, I'd find a treasure here —a new book, a journal, a fruit snack, or one of those pens with all the different colors to click down.

I hadn't thought about those forts in years, not since Heather was little and had built her own forts in our living room.

I walked through the kitchen where I'd baked cookies at Christmas with my mother, where I'd taught myself to cook just about everything else.

I headed upstairs to my old bedroom. The furniture was gone, but the midnight blue ceiling remained. Star-shaped lighter spots decorated the ceiling where glow-in-the-dark stars used to stick. They'd all fallen long ago.

I headed down to the end of the hall to my mom's room.

Her bed was made, but not in the crisply perfect way she liked it. Imprints and wrinkles messed up the duvet, as if something had been on top. A suitcase, maybe? I found it hard to believe that Mom wouldn't fix the blanket after. Not that it mattered.

I checked her closet, where most of her clothes still hung. And her suitcase sat in the corner.

Okay, now that was weird.

Did she buy a new suitcase for her Caribbean vacation? She'd used the same suitcase for as long as I could remember. And it was right here.

Maybe her belongings had been sent back after she'd

died, and the lawyer had put the suitcase away. That could also account for the bed.

But the broken window? It couldn't have been how Scott's girlfriend, Sam, had gotten in here. The hole had been too small before I'd broken the large shards of glass out. Had she broken in through the front door?

I went downstairs to check.

The door was locked, and not broken in any way.

Had Sam somehow gotten a key? No, that didn't make any sense. Maybe the lawyer had left the house unlocked before, and Sam had locked it up when she left.

Still, I didn't know why she had been here at all. She'd been on the phone and she'd said someone named Georgio had sent her, and then she'd implied Georgio had been the type to make people disappear. Maybe the pizza place Scott had worked for was a front for the mafia.

I chuckled at the ridiculousness of that idea. But it didn't stop a dull ache from forming in the center of my forehead. I wasn't finding any answers, only more questions.

I peeked up in the attic, then went down to the basement.

It was official, Mom was not in the house.

Of course she wasn't. Why had I even considered the possibility? Why had I gone on this silly fool's errand?

Because she was my mother. And I loved her.

I went out the door instead of the window, and made sure to lock it on my way out. I couldn't do the same with the front gate, so I headed around the perimeter until I spotted the garden shed.

A strange sensation clawed at the back of my neck and prickled up and down my arms. This was it, the last possible place I could find her here, and my insides twisted in anticipation.

"I hope you're here, Mom," I whispered.

Like a sudden downpour, a wave of emotions struck me

—desperation, anguish, exhaustion. They were Mom's emotions, I could swear it.

I hurried to the doors, which were locked with a padlock. This was the moment my strength training had been preparing me for. I could do this. I grabbed hold with both hands, anchored one foot securely on the ground, and put the other on the door for leverage. Then I pulled.

The lock snapped off with little resistance. I stumbled back, barely catching myself from falling.

I laughed, gave myself a little pat on the back, and reached for the door handle.

Thump.

I froze, sure I had heard something.

A second sound came from inside the shed, this time louder—*thump*.

I threw the doors open.

A set of glowing eyes greeted me. Perched on a stack of cardboard boxes sat Noodles McDoodles Butterbelly in his fluffy orange glory. The tiara was still perched on the top of his head, though how it stayed there I had no idea. Added to the pearls around his neck were a stack of gold chains. A jewel-encrusted dollar sign as large as his face hung over the center of his chest.

"How did you get in here, kitty?" I asked.

He stretched and adjusted himself, then slowly licked the length of his extended back leg.

"I feel a little sorry for you, having to carry around all that mess. Whoever dresses you up like that is a jerk."

"Purrrr meowww?"

A moan came from behind the boxes.

I stepped into the shed, moving past the cat.

There on the floor with her eyes shut, and far too thin, was my mother.

I dropped to my knees and touched her arm. She was warm.

"Mom?"

She moaned again and moved her shoulders slightly. Her eyes remained closed. She was asleep, it seemed, and clearly malnourished, *but she was alive.*

CHAPTER 24

I scooped her up off the floor. I could feel the warmth of her body, the beating of her heart, so loud, so strong compared to the still quiet of my own chest.

My head spun. I could hardly believe that this was really happening. I raced us up and over the wall. I put her in my car and drove her straight to the hospital.

Time seemed to speed by. Doctors asked questions, but I had few if any answers. When everything quieted down and there was nothing immediate left to do, I called Heather.

She didn't answer, so I left her a voicemail. Then I texted, too, for good measure.

I found Granny. She's alive. We're at the hospital in Lingonberry.
Love you.

Then I inched my chair up against the hospital bed. I took my mom's hand in mine and stared at her hollow cheeks, her sunken eyes. She looked like death, more like me than she ever had.

"I'm here," I told her. "We'll figure this out."

My words felt empty, as emotions swirled inside of me. I wished it was only relief that I felt and joy, but I couldn't shake the worry or the regret. How could I have let this happen? How could I have waited so long to find her? How had I not known?

Hours passed. My eyelids grew heavy and I drifted off to sleep.

The sound of shuffling feet woke me. It could have been five minutes or an hour since I'd dozed off. I couldn't tell.

I scrubbed a hand over my face.

"Hey, Mom."

Instantly awake, I looked up to the doorway and found Heather standing there. Her expression was as stiff as her spine, and she held a large tote bag tightly in her arms. I rose to my feet, ushered her in, and hugged her.

"What happened?" she asked. "Where did you find her?"

"In her shed," I said.

"How? Why were you there? I thought you said a cat owns the house."

"He does," I said.

"And Scott? Why isn't he here with you?"

"Scott's…gone."

"Oh, Mom," she gave me a pitying look.

"Don't worry. I'm better off. I realize that now."

"Better before the wedding than after," she said.

"That's true."

"And if we're being honest here, he was terrible for you."

"I realize that now, too," I said.

"I brought this for you, for both of you." She held out the bag and twisted her lips.

I accepted and peeked inside. There were clothes, Heather's clothes.

"I knew you wouldn't leave her side, so I thought you

should have something to wear. I didn't have time to go by your place. I had to get here, you know?"

I patted her hand. "Thank you."

"There's also a granola bar and some quarters in there for the machines."

"It's perfect," I said.

She smiled at me and my heart was full. I just wished Mom was awake here with us. The two of them had always been close, even more so after Heather moved out of my house and to her apartment in Lingonberry. The two of them were the same in a lot of ways—independent and driven. They understood each other in a way I never quite understood either of them. And I was glad they had each other. I hoped they'd be able to share that kind of time together again.

"Any word yet? Do they know when she'll wake?" Heather asked.

"Not yet."

She nodded then checked the clock by the door. She frowned.

"You have work," I said.

"Yeah."

"It's okay if you need to go," I told her.

She swayed on her feet and sighed.

"I promise to let you know when she wakes up," I said.

Heather's frown deepened. "All right."

"I love you."

"I love you, too." With another hug for me, and one for my mom, Heather left.

A nurse came, checked the monitors, and left without sharing any news or answers. My hips, my back, and my butt all became a sore, numb blob of discomfort. I'd been sitting for far too long.

I stood and stretched. "I think Heather was on to something," I told Mom. "I'm going to see what the vending machines have to offer. I promise I'll be right back."

I turned to go, but a woman was standing in the doorway.

Her red hair was curled and up in a fifties-esque style, and her black and white polka-dot dress matched perfectly. This was the same woman who had shown up at my mother's storage unit warning me about reapers—Lily Fernsby, librarian.

In her hands were two cups of what looked like mint chocolate chip ice cream.

"It's you," I said. "Why are you here?"

"You never called. I got tired of waiting." She held out a cup of ice cream for me.

"No, thank you."

"It's delicious," she insisted.

"We are not friends. I don't know you." I gestured to our surroundings. "It's completely inappropriate to ambush a person in her mother's hospital room."

"If this were an ambush, I would not have brought ice cream." She set down the cup on the table beside me and took the seat on the edge of my mother's bed.

Her closeness to my mother set me off. I ground my teeth together. "If you insist on sitting, take the chair."

"Very well."

She moved and I took her spot on the bed. As I watched her take a bite of her ice cream, I contemplated why I had not simply thrown her out yet. I was too curious, it seemed, as to why she was here.

She closed her eyes, a contented smile coming over her face as if the ice cream on her tongue was simply divine. A *tap tap tap* sound alerted me to the fact that my foot was acting on its own accord, as if to stamp out a line of ants.

"Again," I said, "why are you here? Why are you stalking me?"

"I'm not," she said. "I'm monitoring, with interest, the reaper who is stalking you."

"It's gone," I told her.

She raised a brow and leaned forward. "Are you sure about that?"

I guessed I wasn't. I'd assumed so since it had killed Scott.

"What does it want?"

"It's a reaper," she said. "It doesn't *want* anything. It's waiting for your death."

"I'm not dying," I said.

"But you were supposed to," Lily said. "The last time we'd met I wasn't sure what kind of supernatural death defiance you had employed, but given the wizard and the zombie, I'm going with revenant."

"I don't know what you're—"

"Oh come now, there's no reason to lie," she said. "I've been watching, remember?"

"Stalking," I said again.

"Stalking *the reaper*," she said. "But that's not the point. The point is that I know your truth, so you might as well be honest with me."

I wasn't quite sure what to say to that. "If you already know everything, what do you want from me?"

"I was curious as to why you hadn't left the hospital yet," she said.

"My mother," I said.

"I see her."

"She was supposed to be dead, but she's not."

"And you're celebrating by hanging out in a hospital room?"

"You expect me to go out and celebrate when she can't open her eyes?"

"Absolutely," she said. "I expect you to celebrate together. Take her out of this sterile place. You're a revenant, right?"

I didn't answer.

"That's fine, you don't have to say. I know you are," she said. "You have a psychic connection to those who mean the most to you, even if you don't know how to control it, being an immature revenant and all."

I'd felt my mom in the shed, just like I'd felt sure she was alive when I touched that paper in her storage unit.

"Take your mom home. Involve her in your life." Lily nodded toward the ice cream she'd set on the side table. "Share some flavor."

If she'd thought I was a revenant, and therefore likely knew I couldn't enjoy ice cream, did she bring the ice cream for my mom? The sparkle in her eye said yes. But I was probably giving her too much credit.

"I don't think the doctors will agree with you on that," I said.

"You could make them." She smiled a knowing, not unfriendly grin. "They don't know anything about magical maladies anyway. You're better equipped to help. You don't have to believe me. Just ask your boyfriend."

Heat rose up into my ears. "I don't have a boyfriend."

Lily shrugged. "Sure." She finished her ice cream, rose from her seat, and tossed the trash in the bin by the door. "This has been fun. Don't forget to call me sometime."

I watched her go. *Could* I make the doctors do something they didn't want to? I turned to the ice cream on the table. Was it possible Lily was right, and it could help? What could it hurt to try?

Unsure, I lifted the spoon to my mother's lips and dotted ice cream against her mouth.

Her eyes remained closed, but her tongue darted out. She ran it across her lips and smiled. "Mint chocolate chip," she said. "My favorite."

CHAPTER 25

After a myriad of tests and an eternity of waiting, the doctors attributed my mother's mostly-out-of-it state to the fact that she was clearly malnourished. She hadn't spoken a word since the ice cream. We ran into insurance issues, mainly the fact that she didn't have any since she was considered legally deceased. Still, everyone was nice as they gently guided us out the door with recommendations of rest, plenty of food, and following up with a doctor.

I didn't fight it. I went through the motions leaving the hospital and driving home, not to her house, but to mine. Thursday evening had turned into Friday afternoon, almost twenty-four hours lost. I texted Heather to let her know what was going on. Then I carried my mom through the front door and set her in the big chair in the living room. I used pillows to prop her upright. She looked like she was asleep.

I wasn't certain, but I had a hunch that Lily knew what she was talking about. During our interactions so far, she seemed to. That meant the best way to pull my mom out of this daze, to bring her back to me in full, was to immerse her in living—to "share the flavor."

"How long has it been?" I asked my mom. "Nine years? Ten? It would have been nice to have you visit, and not taken a coma to get you here."

She sat unmoving in the chair with her eyes closed. She didn't respond. That was fine. We had all the time we could possibly need to get this right, because *she was alive.*

"I know why you didn't want to come, at least recently," I told her. "It was Scott. You didn't like seeing me dependent on a man, and you never liked him in particular. But don't worry, he's gone now."

See how clean my house is? See how independent I am? See how well I'm doing? Just like you taught me?

I squeezed my eyes shut and tried to calm my racing brain. What could I do that would actually help? Because clearly this wasn't it. She'd responded to the ice cream, so maybe other foods would help.

"I'm going to grab some snacks," I said. "Hang tight."

I scoured the cabinets for literal flavor, even if that wasn't what Lily had meant. Somewhat sad-looking, but still good, chunks of watermelon waited in the fridge behind Scott's ketchup. In the back of the cans shelf was a tin of anchovies Scott had kept for his pizza. I also found a bottle of Cinnaburn whiskey and a bag of sour popping candy so old it may or may not fizzle anymore.

I stacked all my finds on a plate and carried them back to the living room.

"You need flavor?" I said. "We can do flavor. Do you remember the fourth of July when Heather was six and she begged me to get her the candy with the fireworks on it and then you—"

My words died on my lips when I looked over to Mom. And to the cat sitting on her lap. The cat stared at her face, swaying its tail back and forth over her knees. The tiara on its head and the pearls around its neck made it clear that this was the same cat.

"Ca…t…*cat,*" Mom said, her eyes still closed.

"What's the story with you two?" I asked. "And how did you get in here, Noodles?"

Noodles flicked his ear and glanced lazily over his shoulder at me. "Mrrroww."

I set the plate of weird foods on the coffee table and took a seat on the sofa. "Is Noodles your cat, Mom? Did he win you over to the feline side with his furry charm?"

Noodles stretched his front paws on her shirt and knitted the fabric.

Mom frowned. He was getting more reaction out of her than I'd gotten so far.

"All right," I told Noodles. "You can stay with us for now, but you have to promise not to pee on any flowers. And you're going to have to stop scratching up Mom's shirt."

I made it all of two steps toward the cat before he jumped down from her lap and strutted his way out of the room. I took it as his agreement to my terms, and turned my attention back to Mom.

"Where were we?" I asked Mom.

Her eyes opened slightly, but they remained distant and unfocused.

"Right," I said. "I was telling you that I found popping candy. After you bought it for Heather that summer when I wouldn't, and she screamed and cried when she ate it, then it became her favorite. I think because it was you who bought it for her first."

She smiled softly. "Heather."

"She's wonderful, isn't she?" I said.

Mom's smile grew.

"She was as surprised as I was at your new fondness for

cats, or at least for that cat in particular," I said. "Would you like to try some food therapy?"

She didn't answer.

I poked a piece of watermelon onto the fork and touched it to her lips. She licked it.

"Sweet," she said.

"Yep. Watermelon is sweet. I have a variety of other choices for you to try, too. Would you like more watermelon first?"

She opened her mouth. I set the fruit on her tongue. She chewed and swallowed, her gaze rising to meet mine.

"Is it good?" I asked.

"Yes, good," she said.

This was working. It was actually working.

"After this, we can go up to Heather's old room. It's how she left it when she went off to college," I said. "When I found you, I went into my old room. Remember how much you hated the stars I'd stuck on the ceiling? You said they would leave gunk behind. They didn't. But you were right about staining. The star pattern is still there, which I'm sure you know. Why didn't you ever paint over it?"

She didn't say anything.

"How about anchovies? Want to chew on some slimy fish?"

She didn't say anything to that, either, so I opened the can, and tried not to inhale the smell. I stabbed a tiny fish with the fork and lifted it to mom's mouth.

"Did you ever use these in any recipes? I hear they add a lot of flavor to Italian sauces," I said.

I touched the fish to her lips. Her brows dropped and she pulled back.

"So no on that one, huh?" I chuckled. "It's a no for me, too."

She blinked, tilted her chin and looked at me. For the first time, it felt like she was here, all of her was here with me. She touched my wrist and parted her lips. She wanted to say something. What was she going to say?

"What is it, Mom? I'm here." I gave her a reassuring smile.

A crash came from behind me, in the direction of the kitchen.

I whipped around in my seat and glanced at the doorway.

Crash. Another one? That couldn't be good.

"Sorry, Mom. I'll be right back." I got up and headed into the kitchen.

Perched up on the floating kitchen shelf above the table, Noodles McDoodles Butterbelly sat by three of the decorative plates Heather had made for me.

My muscles tensed.

Two were missing, shattered on the floor.

My stomach dropped.

"You need to get your furry butt down from there *right now,*" I told the cat.

"Mrroww." Noodles batted the edge of one of the remaining plates. It jostled on its stand.

I put up my hands in defense. "Please, kitty. I'll give you whatever you want. Want a nice steak?"

It flexed its paw, inching the plate closer to the edge.

"We've got fish in the living room. Come down now and it's all yours." I took a tentative step forward.

Noodles nudged the plate right to the edge. It tottered there.

I ran for it.

My ankle twisted, and no question I was going down. I couldn't take my eyes off the plate—a fingerpainted cherry blossom tree on a cerulean sky. I turned and reached as I fell. I could catch it, I had to.

My shoulder hit a chair. My fingers met ceramic, and the plate slipped from my grasp.

I landed on my back, on top of sharp shards.

The plate landed on my chest—safe, unharmed.

I let out a sigh of relief, and a chuckle of temporary insanity. I kissed the pink flowers and hugged the plate to my chest. I'd done it. It was okay.

The other two plates crashed down beside my head, shattering against the tile floor.

I would kill that cat.

With a roar of frustration, I scrambled to my feet.

Noodles flipped over, feet flailing, and slipped from the shelf. He raced across the floor, back legs swinging wildly behind him. He righted himself and disappeared from sight.

Calm. I needed to find my calm. Nothing good could come from an angry revenant.

Red pressed in on the corners of my vision.

"Everything is fine," I said. "They're just things. I love the plates because I love Heather. Heather is still okay. *They are only plates.*"

I hid the only remaining keepsake in one of the lower cabinets so there was no way it could fall and break, not even if the cat grew fingers and the ability to open doors.

I imagined catching Noodles and punting his furry hide right out the second-story window. See how he liked being dropped.

I pushed aside the thought and returned to the living room where my mother waited. Her eyes were closed, her muscles were relaxed, and her chest rose and fell slowly. She was asleep.

A pang of sudden hunger clenched my stomach.

A knock came from the door.

I smoothed my shirt, told myself to be calm, and opened the door.

The sky was dark, the air wet with the aftermath of a sudden spring rain I hadn't even noticed. A uniformed police officer was standing there. He looked familiar. He'd been here before, on the wellness check for Scott.

"Hi," I said. "What can I do for you?"

The officer's nostrils flared. "Something bothered me the last time I was here, it's the same guilty look you have on your face right now."

My chest clenched. "What?"

I tried to smooth my features, to look as not guilty as possible.

"When we left, we left someone to watch you," he said.

I laughed nervously. "Why would you do that? I haven't done anything."

"You've had all manner of company following you around, Ms. DeLaCrux. But we never did catch you moving the body. How long before our first visit did you dispose of your fiancé? An hour? Two?"

I straightened my spine. "You're grasping at nothing. If you had any proof of anything, you would have arrested me."

He pulled the cuffs from his belt.

This was happening. I was going to get arrested.

I felt queasy. My stomach gurgled and whimpered and cried.

Without me, what would happen to my mom?

I looked the officer in the eye and said, "You're going to leave now. And leave me alone."

"I'm going to leave now," he said. "And leave you—"

He clenched his jaw and grabbed my wrist.

I pointed my intention at him as hard as I could, staring right through his dark eyes. "You were just leaving."

"I was just leaving." He let go of my wrist and turned to go.

I slammed the door behind him and leaned against it.

Relief and fear and a whole spectrum of emotions I couldn't quite process hit me all at once. I hugged my arms to my chest, and closed my eyes. Was it going to be enough? How long would he be gone before he or someone else like him came back?

Mom snored in the chair.

My stomach growled. How long had it been since I'd eaten? Too long, for sure.

I had to eat.

I ran into the kitchen, set up the stove, with my favorite cast iron on the burner. Then I carried Mom up the stairs and tucked her into Heather's old bed and came back downstairs. I was starting to feel a little better already. All I needed to do was have something to eat and everything would be all right.

The doorbell rang. And rang. And rang.

I thought about ignoring it, but I didn't. I'd just make this quick.

"Coming," I called.

When I opened it, Wendy was there, with wild eyes. She bent over at the waist, heaving for air. She held something, a jar maybe.

"What's wrong?" I asked.

"Everything's great," she said. "When did you get your tooth fixed? It looks good."

I hadn't gotten it fixed. It had fixed itself.

Wendy continued, "I've been thinking about the disappearing freezer, and do you think it's possible Andrew did it? It has to be him, right? Who else could get into the house without you knowing? It had to be the magic man. He probably even has potions to make things disappear, right?"

"He does, actually," I said.

She grabbed my arm.

My stomach growled.

I tried to pull back, she latched her elbow in mine.

"It's movie night. We should talk it all out. I was thinking if he did come into your house, even if it was to help you, and you didn't invite him, that's not so great, right? I mean, he said he didn't do it, but do we ten thousand percent believe him?"

My stomach twisted, saliva filled my mouth. I could practically taste the steak I was going to cook. I was famished.

Wendy was waiting for me to respond.

"No, that'd be not great," I said, pulling gently on her arm. "I don't need a man to fix my problems for me. I have to…I'm really hungry, Wendy." Did I say that last part out loud, or just in my head? I looked longingly toward the kitchen. My stomach was hollow, and it needed to be filled sooner rather than later.

"Except maybe you did?" she said. "And can this potion be used on garden weeds? Garbage? Kitchen spills?" Wendy asked. "Oh, what about muffin tops and crow's feet?"

She was saying something. I wasn't sure what exactly. All I could think about was the need to eat. I was starving.

This was bad. Really bad. I had to eat *now.*

I stumbled back, my head throbbing. I tried to warn her to get away from me, but I wasn't sure if I got the words out before everything went black.

And Wendy screamed.

CHAPTER 26

I woke on the living room floor with my shoulder sore, my cheek crusted to the carpet, and a throbbing pain radiating through my head. I rolled over onto my back. My vision swirled. I grabbed my forehead and tried to remember why I was on the floor.

A metallic scent filled the air, filled my nose, my mouth.

I shot up to a sitting position. My throat went dry.

Dark red liquid was splattered all over the room.

Blood.

Spots threatened at the edges of my sight. I gasped for breath I didn't need to take.

What had I done?

I tried to think. I tried to remember. The fire alarm went off in the kitchen, startling me. I ran to the kitchen and found a pan on the stove, smoke burning from overheated oil. The air was thick, metallic, suffocating. My stomach, already tight with worry, knotted so hard I could barely stand.

I had to eat.

I was starving.

I threw open the fridge, tore into a package, grabbed a handful of raw steak cubes, and shoved them into my mouth. The slimy texture was disgusting, but I couldn't stop. I opened another package and devoured the uncooked contents.

Hunger satiated, my focus returned to the events that had led me to this point.

I was heating a pan because I needed to eat.

Then Wendy had rung the doorbell.

Why had I answered before eating? I should have waited. What had I done to her? This had to be a misunderstanding, some kind of bad dream. Except when I pinched myself, it hurt, and I was still awake.

"Wendy!" I cried. "Wendy, where are you?"

I ran back toward the door.

The smoke detector blared incessantly. My head thrummed. I stopped where I'd blacked out, expecting to see her there with her sweet, lopsided smile. She'd be sipping a glass of red wine and starting up the movie we'd been planning to watch. I should have known she would be here. We'd made plans. I'd invited her.

Beeping, smoke, the pounding in my brain—the cacophony of sensations should have snapped me into action, but all I could do was stand there, stunned, and yell for my best friend.

"Wendy!"

Then it hit me. My mom was here, too. At least that realization was enough to spur me into motion. I ran upstairs and checked Heather's room. Mom was right where I'd left her, sleeping peacefully in bed. There wasn't even any smoke up here, thankfully. I approached slowly and put two fingers to the side of her neck. Her pulse was strong. She was all right.

With a sigh of relief, I searched the rest of the house.

Maybe Wendy was hiding in a closet after seeing me go all revenant monster. I checked all the rooms and closets, even the cabinets she was too small to fit inside. I found no sign of Wendy.

I opened the kitchen window, turned off the stove, then went outside and sat down on the porch steps. And I threw up.

Bile lingered there in my throat. Tears streamed down my cheeks.

I'd screwed up, really *really* badly, so epically terribly that there was no fix. If I could turn back time and just eat a freaking sandwich, I would. If I could go back and trade places with my best friend, so it was me whose blood was all over my living room, I'd do it in a heartbeat. Someone else's heartbeat, since I didn't have one.

I tried to swallow away the bile and the thickness in my throat. I tried to shake away the discomfort tingling across my skin. I tried to lie and trick myself into believing that everything was going to be okay.

But it wasn't.

I pulled my phone from my pocket and called Wendy. She didn't answer.

The first beams of morning light peeked out from behind my neighbor's trees. It was already morning? How long had I been asleep? How long had it been since Wendy had arrived, since I'd hurt her?

I dialed another number before I even realized what I was doing.

Andrew's voice was rough, scraping like the bark of a tree. "Hello?"

When everything else had gone to hell, apparently the one I went to now for help was Andrew. When had that happened? It snuck up on me, this feeling of safety I felt with him.

"Were you asleep?" I asked.

"Yeah."

"Sorry, I can—"

"Don't be, Rosemary. You sound…What can I do for you?"

I didn't even know where to start, so I started with tears. They weren't helpful. If anything, crying got in the way of focusing and figuring out a solution. There had to be a solution. *Wendy had to be okay.*

"I need help," I said between awkward sniffles. "In-person help."

"Are you at home?"

"Yes."

"I'll be right there."

"Thank you."

"Any time. Truly."

It was Wendy I would usually go to when everything went wrong. But it was Wendy who I'd attacked in my revenant craze. It was Wendy who was missing. I could count on Andrew though, too.

My stomach tensed up, bile crawling up my throat. I lurched to the side and dry heaved into the bushes.

Tiny hairs bristled on the back of my neck, a ping in the back of my head alerting me that I was the subject of someone's interest. I turned around, hoping that someone was Wendy.

It wasn't.

Noodles stood in the driveway, tiara perched between his bushy orange ears. He tilted his chin up, staring down his nose at me in judgment.

"Get out of here," I told him. "Before I eat you, too."

He raised a defiant leg, looked me right in the eye, and peed on my car tire.

I sighed. "Or you could do that."

He sauntered off to do whatever it was that jerk cats did

when they weren't tormenting people. As a general rule, I still liked cats. But with every interaction, Noodles McDoodles Butterbelly further secured himself as the exception to that rule.

Welling panic still coursed through my system, but as I sat on the steps waiting, I began to feel a disconnect. It wasn't possible for me to have killed Wendy. She couldn't be a zombie. She was too smart, too sweet, too *Wendy*. I loved her too much to hurt her. It couldn't be true.

I stared down at my hands. There was no blood, not on my palms, my fingers, not under my nails.

Any moment now I'd wake up. Any moment now, everything would be okay.

The sound of an engine pulled my attention. I looked up and watched Andrew's car pull into the driveway. I rose to my feet as he climbed out and approached.

His gaze was soft, kind. His brows were drawn together with worry.

I squeezed my fingers into fists and tried to hold it together, but when he looked at me like that, I unraveled. Fresh tears streamed down my cheeks.

He enveloped me in a gentle embrace. He was the strength I'd lost. He was the reassurance I needed.

A brick wall of exhaustion hit me, but Andrew held me. I fell apart. He held tight, brushed a tender kiss to the top of my forehead, and he picked up the pieces.

This was the love I'd searched my whole life for, the acceptance, the support.

Our relationship had barely had a chance to sprout, let alone blossom, yet I knew. Every other relationship I'd ever had paled in comparison to the fullness I felt in my heart. This was what love was supposed to feel like. The timing couldn't be worse, but maybe that didn't matter. Maybe it made the realization clearer.

I was in love with Andrew Jensen.

"I'm so glad you're here," I said, giving him one last squeeze before pulling back.

"Tell me what I can do," he said.

I took his hand and led him inside. The alarm was still beeping. Even with the window open, oily smoke clung to the air. Blood remained splattered all over the living room floor.

"I did this," I said, pointing to the splatter.

"What is it?" he asked, following the sound of the fire alarm to the kitchen.

Dumbfounded, I followed. "Blood. Wendy's, I think."

He pressed the blinking red button, stopping the blaring sound. Then he turned on the fan over the stove. He said, "It's not blood."

"Of course it is," I said. "What else could it be?"

"I'm not sure," he said. He stepped back into the living room and kneeled down on the carpet. He touched the red fluid, then rubbed it between his thumb and forefinger. "The color's wrong. So is the smell and the viscosity."

It wasn't blood.

"You're sure?"

"I'm sure." He gave me a kind smile, washed his hands, then led me away from the not-blood, to the kitchen table. "Tell me what happened."

"Wendy came by. I blacked out." My stomach howled and churned. I grabbed it, hoping to soothe the ache.

"You need to eat," Andrew said.

"Yeah." That was the problem, wasn't it? I'd let myself get too hungry while looking after my mother, and then I'd hurt Wendy, or at least scared her away. Then, after I'd eaten, I'd thrown it all back up. I didn't feel hungry now, but given the alternative, eating was definitely the right choice.

Andrew pulled a steak from the fridge and put it on the skillet.

I really needed to clean up the mess of not-blood by the door, but I was exhausted. It could wait.

The sizzle and scent of searing meat filled my lungs and soothed my twice-fried nerves. Saliva flooded my mouth so fast I had to press my lips together so I wouldn't drool everywhere.

After a quick sear on each side, Andrew offered me the steak. I devoured it ungracefully, unapologetically, like a starved monster. Only after I was done did my brain truly start to process everything properly. I hadn't even realized how fogged I'd been.

I ran for my phone and called Wendy. She didn't answer.

"What are you thinking?" Andrew asked.

"If it's not blood, what is it? I didn't hurt Wendy, I could have just scared her, right?" And given I'd gone into a revenant rage, she'd been smart to run.

"Sure."

"I need to go by her place and apologize. That's where she has to be." I only hoped I was apologizing for scaring her, and not for hurting her. *Please don't let me have hurt her.*

"Want company?"

"Yes, please."

"Wait," I said. "My mom—the one who is supposed to be dead—well, she's upstairs, alive."

"That's wonderful, Rosemary," Andrew said. "I'm happy for you."

"Thanks. It is great." I put my dishes in the sink and looked toward the stairs. "But she's also not herself. She's sleeping now, but when she's awake, she's in a…" I searched for the right word. "Daze? I guess? I don't know if it's safe to leave her alone. Do you have some kind of potion motion detector?"

"No," he said. "But we could call each other, leave my phone here, put it on speaker."

"Like a long-distance baby monitor," I said, beaming back at him. "Love it."

We went upstairs and set his phone on the nightstand beside her on the bed. Back in the hall, Andrew touched my wrist.

"She has a magical energy around her," he whispered.

I leaned closer and narrowed my eyes at him. "What does that mean? You think someone put a spell on her?"

"Possibly," he said. "Whoever or whatever happened to her, the effect remains."

"It doesn't have to be a person?"

"There could be an environmental factor at play," Andrew said.

"Do you have a cure?"

He shook his head. "The energy is weak, though. It seems to be naturally decaying. If anyone can, *you* will reach her. If you can't on your own, I will see what I can find. Maybe there's a counterspell."

"A cure." I nodded. "That's encouraging. Thanks."

"You're welcome. I'm here for you, Rosemary, whatever you need, whenever you need it."

Was Wendy right when she suggested it could have been Andrew who had taken the freezer along with Scott's corpse from my basement before the police could find it? He did have the means to make the freezer disappear. I'd seen it myself. And he'd just confessed his willingness to help me with anything.

But would he have entered my house, before I'd told him where I lived? I didn't think he would. Even if it was to help me, the idea of it felt icky. There had to be another explanation.

"I know I already asked you about the freezer," I said, "but if you didn't take it, I don't know who could have."

"I assure you it wasn't me," he said.

And yes, I ten thousand percent believed him.

I let Andrew's words float around in my head as I drove us by Wendy's house. Her car wasn't there. I tried the shelter after that. Then her favorite healthy pizza joint. She wasn't anywhere. Why wasn't she anywhere? Where had she gone?

Discouraged, I drove home. The front door was open. I slowed by the edge of the driveway without pulling in.

"We didn't leave the door open, did we?" I asked.

"No." Andrew's jaw ticked.

"An officer came by. I thought he wouldn't come back though. I revenant mind-controlled him not to. I'm pretty sure it worked. Maybe he broke it and came back?"

Andrew's eyes crinkled a bit at my choice of words, but the rest of him remained tense. "There's no patrol car."

"I thought my mom couldn't go anywhere without us knowing." I lifted my phone to my ear. She was still snoring on the other end.

"She's still inside," Andrew said with a certainty that suggested he knew from his wolf man half.

"Maybe Wendy came back." A glimmer of hope filled me.

"Maybe," Andrew said, in a tone that suggested he didn't think that was likely. *"Someone* is inside."

We pulled into the driveway. I parked the car. "We have to go in. Whoever is in there is in there with my mom."

Andrew nodded his agreement.

From the doorway, we spotted a blond man in a tan trench coat. He stood over the splatters of not-blood, a broody look on his face.

Without looking up, he pointed at Andrew.

"Andrew Jensen, son of Harriet Halifax, alchemic wizard in your own right, correct?"

"Yes," Andrew said. He turned to me so the other man

couldn't see his face. Andrew's gaze burned. His whole body tensed.

And he mouthed a single, private word to me.

Run.

CHAPTER 27

Part of me was certain that Andrew knew what he was talking about, that if he wanted me to run, I should run. Screw that. Whatever was going on, whoever this trench coat man was, this was my house and Andrew was my…something. The point was, I wasn't going anywhere.

"Who do you think you are, breaking into a private residence?" I put my hands on my hips, stood as tall as I could, and glared at the mystery man. "Leave now before I call the police."

Andrew positioned himself between me and the stranger.

The stranger sidestepped so we could see each other around Andrew. "I'm with the library," he said, with the kind of authority that suggested he thought his proclamation held serious weight.

Was this weirdo connected to that other weirdo, Lily?

"Well I don't have any outstanding loans, I assure you," I told him. "Now get out of my house."

"Did you have some sort of accident, Ms.…?" He gestured to the splattered fluid staining my entire living room.

The fluid that *was not blood*. I really needed to clean that up.

"Don't say anything else, Rose." Andrew shielded me from the librarian with his arm.

I didn't need protection.

This guy had broken into my house and hadn't even bothered to learn my name first? Why was Andrew so concerned? The librarian, and this situation, seemed like a joke.

A pair of glowing cuffs appeared in the stranger's hand. So quick I hardly caught the movement, the librarian whipped Andrew around, shoved him against the back of the sofa, and snapped the handcuffs to his wrists.

This wasn't a joke. It was deadly serious.

"Andrew Jensen, your magical signature has been detected on the body of a non-magical human, Scott Tochee."

Oh, poop.

My heart sank. This was *my* fault. It wasn't Andrew who had killed him. It was me. Where had they found the body?

"Andrew didn't do anything." I clenched my fists together and narrowed my eyes, pinging my intention deep into the stranger's skull. All I had to do was make him forget why he was here. All I had to do was mind magic him to go away and never come back.

"Don't." Andrew gave a quick shake of his head at me. His tone was firmer than I'd ever heard him be.

I froze.

He understood that I was trying to fix the situation but didn't want me to. *Why?*

The librarian roughly pulled Andrew upright.

"You can't do that," I said, a lot more pathetically than I'd intended. "You can't—"

"It's okay," Andrew said as the librarian nudged him toward the front door. "Remember, say nothing. *Do* nothing."

The librarian paused at the door, turned to me and narrowed his eyes. "It seems you're going to be essential to this case. We'll be in contact. Until then, don't leave town. We'll be watching."

I pressed my lips together, hating that I was actually listening to Andrew.

They stepped outside.

I couldn't just let them go, right? I could say nothing and not interfere but still follow them to the library. Given there was no car, they'd have to walk. There was no law that said a person couldn't go for a stroll.

Just outside my front door, the librarian swung his arm in a wide circle. On his hand was some kind of thin chain. It lit up a fluorescent blue color. A cool breeze blew into the doorway.

A shiver crossed my skin. I took a step closer and crossed my arms.

A shimmering silver oval appeared in front of the librarian. The surface rippled like a pond penetrated by a stone. The librarian stepped through the oval, pushing Andrew in front of him.

It was a doorway of some kind.

An open doorway.

Here goes nothing. I ran forward, using momentum to quash any hesitation.

One more step until I hit the silver surface. One more step until *something* happened. I closed my eyes, bracing for impact. Would I be transported to the public library downtown? What if there was some kind of magical key and since I didn't have one, I couldn't get—

Ouch.

I landed face first on the sidewalk. Bruises circled my wrists even though I had no idea how I'd managed that. Sore, hands scraped, I turned and looked back to see how I'd somehow missed the portal.

It was gone. Poof. I hadn't gone through it because it had disappeared.

Wendy was gone. Now Andrew was gone, too.

A ringing sound settled into my ears, drowning everything else out.

I'd screwed everything up, and there was no one left to help me fix it. I looked down at the scrapes and dents on my palms. My hands were shaking.

I slammed my fists into the grass. All of the frustration, the helplessness, the fury—everything boiled up inside of me. I couldn't take it. I was going to explode.

A wail burst from my chest, a yell that could have awakened a hibernating bear five miles away.

Let the neighbors hear me. Let them see the broken shell. Let them call the police.

When there was nothing left, I deflated and lay on my back. The grass was cold and damp. I didn't care.

I was devastated.

I was lost.

I had no idea what to do.

The sun stared down, blinding me. The warm rays were a pleasant counterpoint to the cold ground. I shouldn't have been lying in the grass. I shouldn't have taken even a fraction of a second to enjoy anything. I needed to act, to right the wrongs I'd committed, to do what I could to help the people I loved.

When the librarian had pulled out the cuffs, I should have spoken up. I should have told him without hesitation that Scott's death was my fault. Then Andrew would be here, free, instead of me.

My phone buzzed in my pocket. My first instinct was to

ignore it. But then, what if it was Andrew? Or Wendy? I pulled it out, and checked the screen.

Heather.

I answered. "Hi."

"Hi. Are you okay, Mom? You sound…."

"I'm not," I said. Tears rolled down my cheeks. "I'm very much not okay."

"Is it Granny? You're home, right? I'm on my way."

"Granny's all right," I said. "She's the same."

"Then what is it? Is it Scott? He hurt you again, didn't he? Told you somehow something was your fault when it was clearly his?"

"No," I said. "It's nothing like that."

"You know usually you're calling me nonstop, smothering me. But lately you're distant. I thought I wanted some space, but you're scaring me. This is worse, Mom."

"I'm sorry."

"It's okay. Just tell me what's going on with you. Let *me* be here for *you* for a change. Okay? I want that. Maybe we can find balance."

Despite the empty, exhausted feeling wrecking my system, I laughed. "I'd like that."

"Okay, so what's going on with you?"

I could keep Heather at arm's length now, like I always did. I hated to burden her, but I expected her to want to share everything with me. It wasn't fair. I could do better. She wanted me to do better, and it's what I wanted, too. She deserved the truth.

"Scott drugged me and buried me in a graveyard," I said.

"Oh my gosh. Are you hurt? Are you at the hospital?"

I cringed as I admitted the next part. "It happened the night I went to the lawyer's office."

Heather was quiet. The silence was deafening, and I

wanted to speak, to try and explain. But I held my tongue and waited.

"Over a week ago?" she asked. Her voice was soft, measured, hurt. "You almost died and when we talked, you didn't tell me?"

"I'm so sorry." A fresh wave of regret washed over me. "I should have told you. I've been screwing everything up. Everything's gone wrong, Heather. I'm so, so sorry."

"It's okay. I'm almost to your house now. Stay put, okay?"

"Yeah." Why was she almost here? Why wasn't she in Lingonberry in a class or working on her paintings? I didn't ask, because I was grateful. Whatever the reason she was in Piccadilly, I needed her.

We stayed on the phone, but we didn't say anything else. I could hear her there, breathing, driving. Then she pulled into the driveway and hurried over. I sat up and wiped the tears from my cheeks. I smiled at her.

"You're here."

"I'm here," she said, as she took a seat in the grass beside me.

"I'm sorry, Heather."

She shook her head and pulled me into a hug. "Don't be."

When she let me go, I pressed my knee gently to hers. "There's more I should tell you."

"I'm listening."

"I met a man."

She sucked her lips in.

"It's not like that, or it wasn't," I said. "He pulled me out of the ground and he fed me a potion. It saved my life, sort of. But I'm also a monster now."

Her gaze softened. "You're *not* a monster."

I raised my hand. "You haven't heard the whole story yet. It turns out that this potion was the only way to save my life, but it turned me into a revenant."

She narrowed her brows. "What's a revenant?"

"Like a sun-loving vampire," I said.

"Uh-huh."

She didn't believe me. "I have to eat meat all the time or I go into a ravenous rage. It's not pretty."

"Sounds like what happens to me on my period."

I smiled at her. "I wish it was like that. I bit Scott, which turned him into a zombie. And now he's dead. And my friend Andrew got arrested for his murder by a librarian. Also I went crazy on Wendy and I blacked out, and she's missing."

"This is a lot to process, Mom."

"I know."

"Is there any way you can prove to me that this is real and that you don't need to go to the hospital for some kind of mental break?" Heather asked, concern marring her features.

I took a moment to think. "I don't have a reflection."

"Let's see." She rose to her feet and offered me her hand.

I took it and we went inside. She paused at the splattered not-blood in the living room.

"I've been assured it's not blood," I told Heather.

"Great," she said, her voice tight.

I led her to the bathroom and stood in front of the mirror. She stood in the doorway behind me.

"See?" I glanced through myself in the mirror at her.

She waved her hand and watched, wide-eyed as her reflection did the same. She opened her mouth and shut it, then opened it again.

"Scott is a zombie…that's…for real?"

I nodded.

"And you…" She shook her head. "Freaky."

"Tell me about it," I said. I felt a little better just having her here. I felt better sharing with her.

"This changes everything," Heather said. "How are you handling it?"

"One disaster at a time. Now that you're here, maybe you can help with Granny. We're supposed to talk to her. Also she responded well to ice cream."

"Mint chocolate chip?"

"Yep."

"Do you have some?" Heather asked.

"No. And even though I really want to focus on helping her get back to herself, I have to find Wendy. I have to help Andrew."

"We'll divide and conquer," she said. "I'll stay with Granny. You find your friends."

"You're handling all of this surprisingly well," I said. "Me being a monster."

She shrugged. "I go to art school."

I chuckled. "All right. I'll pick up ice cream at the store while I'm out searching and trying to figure out a plan to deal with the library."

"I'll get the ice cream," Heather said. "And some of those fish shaped candies she loves."

"Thank you," I said.

"I love you, Mom. It's okay to ask me for help."

"In the future, I promise to," I said. And I meant it. I hugged her again.

My life had quickly spun out of my control. But there were things I could control. I would find Wendy. And Heather would help my mom heal. And then somehow, I'd figure out how to help Andrew, too.

I drove by Wendy's house again, and the shelter where she worked. I circled the park. Then I drove around downtown, because I wasn't sure where else to look.

On the sidewalk, I spotted a woman wearing a familiar head-to-toe black outfit.

That gait, that swinging ponytail, and that too-fit bubble butt made me somewhat sure that I knew who she was—

Scott's girlfriend. I parked and ran to follow her. I wasn't sure what exactly I wanted from her, but I needed some kind of answers, if for nothing else, for closure. Why had she been inside my mom's house? Why had she thought some guy named Georgio had killed Scott?

The closer I came, the surer I was that it was her.

She crossed the street and turned down the block.

I had to run faster or I wouldn't be able to catch up.

A horn blared. I whipped my head to the side, just in time to see a car about to hit me.

I shouldn't have stopped. I should have moved. Instead, I was caught in a moment of shock, paralyzed where I stood.

The car swerved. The wheels squealed.

And I was hit.

The impact was intense. It threw me down onto the street, twenty feet or more from where I'd stood. I rolled on the ground, everything hurting.

Worried, shocked voices carried through the street.

I lifted my head.

People were on their phones, snapping pictures, flashing lights.

The car was flipped over on its roof. Smoke filled the air. No one was helping the driver.

I forced myself to my feet and stumbled toward the overturned car. I ripped the door off.

"I'm so sorry," the driver said. "I…hit you. Didn't I? How are you alive?"

I wasn't alive, not really. Apparently I wasn't just strong, but fairly indestructible.

"Come on," I offered her my hand. "We need to get you out."

She unbuckled her belt and I helped her out of the car. She seemed all right.

Sirens filled the air. Phones flashed blindingly in my face.

This was not low profile. This was not how I was going to get my answers.

I ran in the direction I'd been heading, chasing after Scott's girlfriend. But I reached a crossroads, and I had no idea where she'd gone. I'd lost her.

A few more blocks and I put the accident and everyone who had seen what happened behind me. But there was no sign of Scott's girlfriend anywhere.

I leaned my forehead on the cold glass of one of the storefronts and let myself simply be for a moment.

When I opened my eyes and looked through the glass I was leaning on, I spotted a different familiar face inside—Lily Fernsby.

CHAPTER 28

This was Eats, the same restaurant I'd gone to with Andrew. And Lily was sitting at the same table where we had sat, under the In Memoriam wall. Her usually sleekly styled cherry red hair hung loose around her shoulders. She angrily chomped on a plate of cheese fries, looking as defeated as I felt.

I went inside and headed toward her, reveling in the kismet nature of our paths crossing. Unless she'd come here *because* I had before. I should have thought of that sooner. Before I could decide whether or not to turn back, she spotted me.

"What are *you* doing here?" she asked.

"I got hit by a car. Happened to see you as I fled the scene."

"You look good for someone who should be dead."

I snorted and slid in on the seat beside her.

She pushed the plate toward me. "Fry?"

"No thanks," I told her.

"Right, the whole revenant thing." She pulled her plate back and stared down at it like she wanted to punch it.

"What are you doing here?" I asked.

"Murdering a mountain of grease," she said. "Wishing it was my enemy's face."

I wasn't sure what to say to that, but I liked her so much more for it.

"If you go knife-happy on your potatoes, I won't mind," I told her.

"Noted." She smiled at me, a tired, commiserating smile. "I probably shouldn't tell you this, but it's your case the jerk stole from me."

"My case?"

"Remember I told you I was following your reaper?"

"I don't have a reaper. I'm alive. See me sitting here, upright, blinking and talking to you?"

"Sure," she said with a wave of her hand. "Let's skip the reiteration of you telling me you're not a revenant, even though we both know you are."

I pressed my lips together not because I was agreeing, but because I wanted to know what else she had to say. If anyone could explain what was going on with Andrew, it was Lily. And she seemed to be trying to, if I could just stay quiet and listen.

"Now that there's a corpse involved, I've been sidelined."

"By the guy who kidnapped Andrew," I guessed. I twisted my fingers together under the table and tried not to look too eager.

"*Great.* There's already been an arrest." She sighed and smashed the fry in her hand like she was putting out a cigarette.

"It's not an arrest if there isn't a law enforcement agency involved," I insisted.

"You don't know anything, do you?" She frowned at me. Then she cleared her throat. "That was uncalled for. I apologize. How's your mother?"

The change in subject threw me. "She's...um, unconscious."

"What have you tried so far? Have you taken her anywhere that would spark nostalgia?"

I sighed and rubbed the knot forming in the center of my forehead.

"I've been a bit preoccupied," I said a little harsher than I'd intended. "She's in good hands."

"Preoccupied with anything you want to talk about?" she asked, showing no signs of offense.

I really could use someone to talk to, someone with knowledge about the library and revenants, and all of the other magical weirdness I still hadn't come to fully grasp. "I can't trust you. We don't know each other, really. And what I do know about you is that you work for the people who took my friend away."

"Fair." She nodded. "If I was you, I wouldn't trust me either."

I scoffed. *"Then how do you expect me to trust you?"*

With a shrug she said, "Compel me."

"What?"

"You took your mom out of the hospital, so I know you can do it. Just look deep into my eyes and compel me not to betray you. What do you have to lose?"

Clearly Lily knew a lot about me already. Whether that knowledge came from her stalking me or from her know-it-all library I couldn't say for sure. But it didn't really matter either way. I had no idea what she was doing with that knowledge, but if she wanted me to compel her to be my confidant, there didn't seem to be any obvious downside for me.

"All right," I said, and leaned forward. "But I didn't mind-magic anyone to get my mom out of the hospital. She was discharged."

She wiped her fingers on her napkin and mirrored my posture, looking me square in the eye.

I narrowed my attention, burrowing into her skull. "You will not betray my confidence. You will not share—or use against me—anything I tell you."

"Agreed." She held out her hand, like she wanted to fist bump. Then she stuck out her pinky.

I took it with mine and we shook. It felt silly, completely unnecessary, and absolutely delightful.

"I haven't pinky sworn since grade school," I said with a chuckle. A weight had already lifted, knowing that Lily *couldn't* betray me. I would have felt guilty for forcibly compelling her into secrecy, except I hadn't made her. It had been her idea.

"It's been years for me as well," she said. "Now, let's dig in."

She leaned back, took a casual bite of her fry, and waited for me to spill my guts. I wanted to spill, but something still held me back. Even though I knew I could trust Lily, I didn't know her.

"You first," I said. "What's your story?"

She shrugged. "What do you want to know?"

"How did you get involved in the library?" I asked.

"My mother is a witch," Lily said. "When I was a kid, she tried to shield me from magic, wanted my life to be normal. Of course that wasn't possible when people chased us with pitchforks. And even if normal had been an option, all I ever wanted was to live up to her example."

Pitchforks? She couldn't mean that literally. Still, "You consider your mother not normal?"

"Anything but. She's a legend, a life witch who drew adoring crowds who wanted to worship her, or kill her. You likely know a bit about this already, given who your boyfriend's mother is."

"Harriet Halifax," I said, but the name meant nothing to me. I assumed she was the woman in the fishing picture with Andrew. I also knew she was a witch, not involved in raising him, and possibly deceased. Basically, I knew nothing about her.

Lily nodded.

"You know her?" I asked.

"Oh, I've met her." Her lips quirked. "Andrew didn't tell you about his mother, did he?"

"Not much," I admitted. Whatever she had to say, it was juicy. Maybe Andrew hadn't said more because his mother was a sore subject. Whatever it was, he should have the chance to tell me himself, after all of this was resolved. "It may be better to let him—"

"She was the worst of the worst, world-destroying level evil."

"Was?"

"She's dead. Thank goodness." Lily popped a fry into her mouth. "No offense to your boyfriend. For what it's worth I haven't seen him doing anything nefarious. And I'm proof the apple *can* fall far from the tree. It can plop itself down in a different time zone."

Andrew's mom was a bad person? I wanted to ask what she had done that made her so terrible, but I kept my mouth shut, because it really needed to be up to Andrew to tell me. Was it possible he didn't know what Lily knew about his mother?

Lily took my silence as an invitation to keep talking. "People always have strong feelings about my mother, because she basically performs miracles. Or she used to, at least."

I took a guess. "And you can't."

"No, growing up, all signs pointed to human. I had to

prove I wasn't weak, that I could handle myself in the magical world I was born into. So I joined the library."

I understood feeling the need to prove myself, of struggling to live up to my mother's example.

"All of that makes sense," I said. It shouldn't. I shouldn't believe that witches were real, or that any of this made sense. But, I was removed from the reality I'd spent forty-three years living. My new reality was the magical world Lily had grown up in. "What I'm still not understanding, though, is your library."

"Compendium of all knowledge," she said.

"And somehow also law enforcement?" I asked.

"Authority over all supernatural matters," Lily said.

"Says who?"

"Says the library," Lily said. "It's generally accepted in the community due to the fact that it's older than the planet. Say a new breed of weird pops up here, some hybrid flying vampire with laser eyes."

I needed to ignore disbelief for this conversation. This was Lily's magical world, and I was fairly sure she wasn't lying. "Okay…."

"The library knows what this monster can and will do. The library makes sure it doesn't blow up half of New Jersey."

"I can appreciate that," I said. "But Andrew didn't blow up anything. He didn't kill Scott. He hasn't done anything wrong."

"Like I said, I'm not privy to anything about your case anymore," she said with a sigh.

"You can fix this though, right?" I asked. "If I tell you all about it, you can tell me what to do to save him."

"Maybe I can help. I can't promise anything."

She couldn't make promises, but she also couldn't betray me.

"I'll take it," I said. "It all started when my mother drowned on vacation in the Caribbean. She died."

"I'm sorry for your loss." She gave me a quizzical look. "Do you have two mothers?"

"No. And thank you. It's been a tough year."

Lily was still clearly confused, and rightfully so, since she knew my mother was not in fact dead.

"Last week, I went to the lawyer's office to handle the final details and accept her estate, only to find out she'd left everything but a storage unit to a cat."

"The storage unit where we met," Lily said.

I nodded.

"Was—*is*—your mother one of those people who cherishes pets over all else? I mean, *you* are her *daughter*."

"I didn't think she was. She'd never liked cats."

Lily stared at me intensely. I could practically see the gears turning in her head as she popped another fry in her mouth.

"I couldn't make sense of it. Why would she do that? I was fairly certain she hadn't owned a cat."

"Sounds like manipulation by the cat's owner," Lily said. "Did she—*does she*—have a boyfriend?"

"Maybe," I said, squirming a little. "I don't know."

"Hmm."

"I went home from the lawyer's, needing to talk things out. My fiancé was there. He ran me a bath, poured me a glass of wine…."

"You can skip the intimacy details."

"We didn't." I shook my head, disgusted by the idea. Why was the suggestion of me sleeping with my ex-fiancé so repulsive? He had tried to kill me. But these feelings began long before that. How long had I felt this way? Ugh, emotions were difficult. "No. He buried me alive."

"Wow."

"Yeah." I scrubbed a hand over my face. "Andrew saved my life."

"Except not quite," Lily said. "He dug you up, but you were already mostly dead. Stop me if I'm wrong, but logic follows that the wizard transformed you into a revenant to prevent your otherwise inevitable demise."

"Yes."

"And it was *you* who…killed your fiancé."

I gulped. "Yes."

She scratched her chin. "I'll need to think on this."

"You can help, though, right? I don't know that I could handle prison, magical or otherwise, but…it should be me, not Andrew, who faces the consequences for my actions."

"That's very big of you," she said.

Was it, though? It felt like the least I could do.

"Well, I should probably get going to start working on this," Lily said. She rose from her seat and stretched.

"Wait." I grabbed her wrist. "Please. There's something else."

"What is it?"

"Two things really. One, the police. I won't be able to do anything to right my mistakes if I'm in prison."

"Once the library gets involved, the human police are out," Lily said. "They won't bother you again."

I wanted to ask more about how that worked, and what exactly she meant, but there was something much more pressing.

"The other thing—I blacked out and I fear I did something bad to my friend. Maybe I hurt her."

A heavy feeling settled on my shoulders. I needed to find Wendy. There were too many problems pulling me in too many directions.

"Did you bite her?" Lily asked.

"I don't remember. I don't think so. There wasn't any

blood." If I'd bitten her, there should have been blood. Probably. Hopefully. There definitely would have been blood. "But what if I scratched her?"

"Eh. She'll be fine so long as you didn't bite her." Her tone sounded less than certain.

"She's missing."

"Well, when you find her, check and see that she's not been killing people. If she's not on a murderous rampage, she'll be fine. It's fifty-fifty. No, more like seventy-thirty."

I hated to, but I had to ask. "Seventy-thirty what?"

"In favor of your friend not murdering people. I would make it a priority to find her, just to be safe."

"Great," I said, numb. "Super helpful. Thanks."

CHAPTER 29

I took a roundabout route back to my car, careful to avoid the location of my car accident, if you could even call it that. Decimation of a stranger's vehicle through my own distracted jaywalking was more apt. I hoped the driver was okay.

After a quick check-in with Heather—Mom was fine, still sleeping—I returned to my search for Wendy. Lily was working on the Andrew issue. And Wendy was out who-knew-where doing who-knew-what.

I tried calling her again for good measure. When she didn't answer, I left her another voicemail.

"Hey. Please call me. I'm so sorry."

I hung up the phone, rested my head against the wheel, and debated my next move. Where could she be?

My phone dinged in the cupholder. A text. The number was unfamiliar.

Mystery Number: *It's me. No reception, dead battery. Borrowed phone. I'm okay, don't worry. I'll come by tonight.*

I stared at the screen, started to type, then deleted. Was this Wendy? Andrew? A wrong number?

Another ding.

Mystery Number: *Bear trouble.*

Bear trouble meant Wendy. I relaxed in my seat, relieved. But then I remembered what Lily had said, about a thirty percent chance that I had transformed Wendy into a murderous monster.

Me: *Oh, thank goodness. What happened, where are you?*
Tell me you haven't murdered anyone.
Wendy?

I waited, waited, and there was no response. Just crickets. She probably hadn't murdered anyone or she would have led with that, or at least not said that she was fine. Murder wasn't fine, so she was fine. Probably. There was nothing to do but wait until she came over after she finished whatever she was up to.

If there was nothing to do to help Wendy, that made me want to jump back to helping Andrew. But I'd already done everything I could for him for now, too, given I had no idea where he'd been taken or even how to help him if I could find him. I'd talked to Lily and brainwashed her into assisting me, so I was by-proxy already working on the Andrew problem.

Which left my mom.

Or maybe the library. At this point, I knew the chances of the public library being connected at all to *the Library* were slim. I was grasping at straws for sure, and maybe looking for a reason not to go home.

But my mom would never get better if I didn't give her

the time. The time was now.

Mad at myself that I wasn't more excited about our second chance at mother-daughter bonding, I grumped all the way home.

It was nerves. It was fear. It was remorse.

What if we couldn't do better this time? What if I couldn't make her get better, and instead, she stayed in her coma-like state forever?

The house smelled like a savory mix of herbs—garlic and onions. It smelled like Sunday dinner when my mother used to make meatloaf. I passed the red mess on the carpet and admonished myself for still not having cleaned it up yet.

"Hey, Mom," Heather called. "I'm in the kitchen."

I set down my things and headed to the kitchen. Heather had on my apron. Her dark hair was pulled out of her face in a high ponytail as she scrubbed the counter. We used to cook together every day when she was growing up. She'd put her hair up just like that, the only time when I could see her whole, pretty face. I leaned on the doorframe.

"I'm making meatloaf," she said. "Granny's recipe. It's almost done."

"It smells good."

She smiled. "How was your hunt? Did you find Wendy?"

"Not yet," I said. "But she texted and said she's all right. She'll be by later."

"I'm so glad." Heather took off the apron and folded it neatly on the counter. "Granny's awake."

"Oh," I said.

Heather's phone dinged in her pocket—a text.

"She requested the meatloaf," Heather said.

"She talked to you?"

"A bit. She's tired and doesn't seem to remember what happened to her."

"It's still progress," I said.

Heather's phone dinged again.

"Do you need to get that?" I asked.

She glanced toward the front door and frowned. "No, I should be here."

"Heather, if you have something you need to do, I can be here for Granny. She's my mom. You should go if you need to."

"It's only there's this symposium, from my favorite local artist on his brand of color theory…Carlos can record it for me."

"Heather, you should go."

Her eyes lit up. "Are you sure?"

"Absolutely. We'll be fine."

"Okay, yes. Thanks."

"Thanks for coming over. I really appreciate it," I said.

"Anytime." She gave me a quick side hug and hurried out the door.

The timer on the oven went off, so I pulled out the meatloaf. Then I went upstairs and found Mom sitting up in bed.

"Where's Heather?" she said.

"She had to go," I told her. "But it's lovely to see you. Hello."

"It's not that I'm not pleased to see you, Rosemary."

"I know," I said. I reached down and scooped her up.

"What are you doing? You're going to *drop* me."

"No, I'm not. I'm quite strong, really. We're going downstairs."

"I know you're strong," she said, suddenly softer. "That doesn't mean we won't fall down the stairs."

"Mm-hmm," I said.

She was certainly acting like herself.

I set her down at the table and cut us each a slice of meatloaf. By the time I turned back to the table, she was asleep again.

"This is hard," I told her. "But I'm glad you're here, that you're alive."

I ate my meatloaf. She sat with her eyes closed.

This was not the heart-to-heart I'd hoped for. I could be at the library right now, searching for hidden cells and magical oddities.

"What do you think about a little road trip?" I asked her.

Since she didn't answer, I decided to take that as agreement. I finished eating, put away the rest of the food, and pulled out the old wheelchair that we had in the basement. I put it in the trunk of my car.

We drove to the library. I pointed out places on the way, telling her where I went to the doctor and where I bought my groceries. I talked to her just to talk, and hopefully some of it got through and meant something to her, too.

When we reached the library, I helped her into the wheelchair and pushed her up the ramp and through the automatic doors.

All public libraries had the same smell—old books, worn carpets, happy memories. We rolled through the aisles, me looking for magical doorways, her softly snoring. But the only magic in the library came from the books themselves.

On a shelf end I found a copy of *The Poky Little Puppy*. I picked it up, rubbing my thumb across the edge of the pages.

"Remember this one?" I asked her. "You always loved it."

We found a quiet corner. I opened the book, and I read.

I told her about the puppy who was slow to make it home and how that worked out in his favor, because he wasn't with his siblings. Only the last time does he miss out, which means more often than not he was rewarded for his bad behavior.

When I looked up, my mother's closed eyes were open, and sharp. Her attention was rapt, and on me.

"I remember this story," she said. "My mother read it to me when I was a girl."

"I didn't know that," I told her.

"That's why I read it to you."

"So I'd learn bad behavior is rewarded, like the puppy?"

"As Laurel Thatcher Ulrich said, well-behaved women seldom make history," she said. "Truly though, I wanted to share something with you that meant something to me."

I reached forward and hugged her. "I've missed you."

"I've missed you, too," she said. "Where are we? What day is this?"

"The library. Saturday. April twenty-eighth."

Confusion hung over her like a storm cloud. I could see it swirling in her doe eyes and in the clench of her jaw.

"You've been dead for eight months," I told her. "Or at least that's what I was told. They say you swam out to sea in the Caribbean and drowned."

"But I've never been to the Caribbean," she said. She rubbed her forehead. "I'm…I don't remember."

"It's okay. We'll figure it out." I squeezed her hand. And I believed it. We could figure it all out together. For now, she was awake, she was alive, and that was enough.

We returned the book and went back home.

When I got there, Wendy was in the living room, scrubbing the mess off the floor.

"Hey," she said. "Sorry about the mixed berry syrup."

CHAPTER 30

"You're all right." I dropped down on the floor beside Wendy and squeezed her in a big bear hug.

"I can't...you're...too strong." She wheezed.

"Oh, sorry." I let her go.

She beamed at me. I beamed back at her.

"I'm so glad you're here," I told her.

"Me, too. It has been *a day*." Her gaze lifted past me and her eyes widened. "Hello, Ms. DeLaCrux."

Right, my mom. In my excitement I'd almost forgotten she was sitting here in her wheelchair. I moved to the side so I could see both of them at the same time.

"Hello, Wendy," Mom said.

"You're not dead," Wendy said.

"No," my mom said.

"That's great. How are you feeling?" Wendy asked.

"Tired," my mom said.

"I imagine so. Coming back from the dead has to be exhausting." Wendy looked back at me and raised a brow.

"People don't come back from the dead," Mom said. "That's not what happened."

"What *did* happen?" Wendy asked.

"I'm not sure...." Mom looked down at her hands in her lap.

Wendy's face fell in regret for asking. She shouldn't feel bad for asking. It was the reasonable response when someone returned from the dead. I knew from experience.

"We're going to figure it out, though," I said, for all three of us to hear.

Mom made a non-committal sound.

I put the TV on and set Mom up in front of the news. "Let's get you caught up on current events. Maybe something will spark," I told her. "I'll make you some tea, and we can try again with the meatloaf."

"Thank you," she said.

Wendy followed me to the kitchen.

When we were alone, I asked, "What happened? What did I do to you?"

"You kind of...attacked me," she said, but in a rush added, "but I'm okay."

"It was the hunger," I said. "I screwed up, big time, by not eating preemptively. I'm so sorry. Are you sure you're not hurt? I didn't bite you?"

"I'm okay," she patted my hand, and pulled out the teapot. She started water and pulled down a cup.

She did seem okay. I popped a slice of meatloaf in the microwave. "What happened? And why did you bring over syrup? I thought for sure it was blood."

"You thought I brought over a jar of blood?" She wrinkled her nose.

"No, I thought it was *your* blood."

She shot me a sympathetic look. "Aww."

"And then you disappeared. What did I do to you? What does *I kind of attacked you* mean? Where did you go?"

"Okay, so Aunt Petunia made the syrup. It was supposed

to be a treat, to go with our ice cream, wine, and movie. I added ice cream to the plans."

"That makes sense. Sorry I broke the syrup jar."

"Everything's fine. Honestly though, you were scary. And *don't apologize.*"

I held my tongue.

"So when you slapped the syrup out of my hands, I got out of there, because I didn't want to end up like Scott. Not that you would have—"

"You must have been terrified. I really am sorry, Wendy."

She waved a hand. "It wasn't that bad. So I brought you these." She held out a bag.

I took it and looked inside. There was a bag of jerky and a wristwatch.

"I thought you could keep the meat in your pocket—pretend that doesn't sound like innuendo—and use the timer on the watch to make sure you don't go too long without eating."

"Is that jerky in your pocket or are you just happy to see me?" I smiled at her.

"Both."

We shared a chuckle. I couldn't believe how much of a relief it was that Wendy was all right. "Thank you for the watch, and the snack. It'll come in handy."

"Safety first."

"Rosie," Mom called, cutting Wendy's words short. "You're on the TV."

She had to be mistaken, right? *Please don't be about murder. Please be a mistake.* Wendy and I looked at each other and rushed back to the living room to see.

On the TV was the carnage from the car accident earlier in the day. Shaky hands shot cellphone footage of a woman ripping the door off an overturned car. It felt like that woman was someone else, even though I knew she was me.

"Whoa," Wendy said.

"You can't see her face," I said.

"You're wearing the same clothes, dear," Mom said.

I looked down at myself. Yes, yes I was wearing the same clothes.

I needed to change my outfit. I couldn't be this person. I didn't want this attention. I stared at the screen, unable to look away.

The reporters shared their thoughts. With the woman saying, "Do we know if the driver and the mystery woman are related? This reminds me of when you hear about a mother lifting a car off of her baby."

The man added, "I don't know, but I wouldn't want to get on her bad side."

The two laughed before moving on to a fluff piece about playgrounds.

My mom rose up from her wheelchair, surprisingly steady on her feet. She said, "You're not human anymore."

"What?" I laughed nervously, and looked everywhere, anywhere but at her. Where did that come from? "Look at you, you're standing."

"Don't change the subject, Rosemary," she said, stern as stone.

I hadn't felt so unlike myself, no, so much like my childhood self in forever. I hated it.

"I am a grown woman," I told her. "I'm forty-three. You don't get to talk down to me."

"I've been hard on you because it's what you needed," she said.

"No, Mom, it isn't. It wasn't. It never ever was."

She wobbled on her feet. I rushed over to help her down into her chair.

"I didn't need things, or harsh rules," I said. "I just needed a mom."

"I've always loved you. Everything I've done, I've done because I love you."

"I know," I told her.

Tears pricked at the corners of my eyes. Tears rolled down her cheeks.

The teapot whistled. I chuckled at the timing.

"I'm just going to—" Wendy hooked her thumb over her shoulder and scurried off into the kitchen.

"I didn't want you to grow up without the things you needed, like I did. I tried to be better than my parents were."

"I get it," I said. "I've done the same with Heather, and I smothered her."

"She loves you."

"And I love you."

We hugged.

"You're right," I told her. "I'm different. I'm a revenant."

"What does that mean?" she asked.

"I'm not quite dead, and I'm not quite alive either. I'm living in a weird, magical version of the world now. And I feel more at home in that weirdness, more myself than ever. I'm happy." Or I almost was. I could see how I could become happy. I finally felt like I was on the right track.

"Midlife can be magical," Mom said. "People expect women to treat change as bad. We're not young anymore, and somehow that is supposed to be a bad thing. But I never thought of it like that. Midlife can be a time to stop putting other people first, to finally become the best version of ourselves."

I expected disbelief. I didn't expect acceptance.

"Coming of age." Wendy said from the doorway to the room, a tray of tea in her arms.

"Let the twenty-somethings get all of the attention. Then no one is watching while we get to have all the fun," Mom said. "Personally, when I became an empty nester, it became a time of rediscovering who I was. The older I've gotten, the freer I've become, untethered from worry about what other people think. Free from having to be anything for anyone."

I was with her until the last bit. "I wanted you to be something for me."

"I'll try to do better," she said. "We have another chance, if you'll let me try."

"I'd like that," I said.

"I hate to change the subject," Wendy said, "But uh, can we talk about what happened on the TV?"

"I got hit," I said. "I was following Scott's girlfriend after Andrew got arrested. Boom, hit by a car. Then I ran into Lily from the library, who is going to help with Andrew who was arrested by the library, get this—for Scott's murder."

"Your Scott?" Mom asked.

Of course she had no idea what I was talking about. I wasn't sure Wendy did, either. They both looked at me with saucer eyes.

"Scott buried me alive," I said. "A wizard, Andrew, fed me a potion that saved my life."

Hearing the words out loud, they sounded a little less ridiculous than they had the last time I'd said them.

"Tell me you called the police on Scott," Mom said.

"Uh…he's gone," I said.

"He's dead," Wendy added.

Mom blinked twice then pursed her lips. "Oh."

"Yeah," I said.

"He was a cheater," Wendy said.

"The other woman was in your house," I said to my mom. "With the cat."

"I don't have a cat," Mom said, rubbing her forehead. She laced her fingers together in her lap and looked down.

"Do you know a woman named Sam?" I asked her.

"No," she said. "I don't think so."

"I say we check the area where you saw Sam," Wendy said. "See if we can find out something about this woman."

"I'm coming, too," Mom said, rising once more from her wheelchair.

I guessed if anything could help her be herself again and fill the gaps in her memory, Sam was our only lead.

"All right," I said, resigned. "I'll get the car."

CHAPTER 31

*E*ven though I could swear I'd just eaten, the little alarm on my wrist watch went off as I parked against the curb about a block from the site of my accident.

"I swear, I'm not even hungry," I told Wendy.

"Safety first," she said from the back seat.

"Safety first," I begrudgingly agreed. I ate a couple of pieces of jerky and did a quick look around. I had a lingering sense that someone might recognize me from the accident. It was silly, but I couldn't help feeling like I was being watched. I was wearing different clothes. It was getting dark. Still, I pulled the hood of my jacket up over my head for good measure.

"When you ran into the street, did you know you would survive being hit by a car?" Mom asked from the passenger seat.

"No," I said.

"So what's on the current list of superpowers?" Wendy asked. "Other than the super hunger, obviously."

"I wouldn't call them superpowers," I said. "But I can sometimes compel people to do things."

"Mind control is definitely a super power," Wendy said. "And you have super strength. And invincibility now, too?"

She was making me sound much more impressive than I truly was. "I'm not invincible."

"The front of that car you smashed would say otherwise," Wendy said.

"How are you handling all of this?" Mom asked, touching my hand. "Emotionally?"

"It's been a lot," I said. "You're alive, which is great. I'm not-ish, which is not so great."

"You're not jazzed about your superpowers at all?" Wendy asked.

"I still object to calling what's happened to me *superpowers*. It's been nothing but trouble so far," I said. Sure, I'd had fun with Andrew, lifting cars. And being able to force Lily to help me had been helpful. I amended, "Except maybe a few moments here and there. We should get going."

We all climbed out of the car, with Mom insisting she didn't need her wheelchair. If it turned out she was wrong, I could carry her, so I didn't argue.

"Sam was headed this way when I lost her," I said, pointing.

We walked a block, and looked around at the crossroads. Wendy hurried ahead checking down one of the side streets, then another.

"I know you're not going through the changes you expected," Mom said.

"That's an understatement. Do I get to grow old? Not that aging is all that great, but to not—" I frowned at her. "I don't want to be around longer than Heather."

"Perhaps you'll be healthier for longer, or perhaps not," she said. "None of us get to know how long we have. It's part of what makes life precious."

"And the moments together matter." I nodded my agreement. "And if I lose control and attack someone again?"

"The food is supposed to help, right?"

"Yeah," I said. "But what if something happens? What if I lose my pocket meat? I feel like a grenade with a faulty pin."

She made a face at the words *pocket meat*. "We all spend our lives getting to know ourselves. This is simply a new part of yourself you need to explore and learn to accept, perhaps even embrace."

If only it were that easy. After attacking Wendy, I didn't know how to trust myself. And now Andrew was gone.

"Over here." Wendy waved for us to follow.

At the end of the street, we spotted Pizza Palace.

"Didn't the cops say Scott worked at Pizza Palace?" Wendy asked.

"Yes they did," I said.

"I thought he had an office job like you, Rose," Mom said.

"So did I," I said.

We entered the pizza shop. With grimy floors, no seating, and no sign of a kitchen in sight, I wondered what the shop actually sold. It looked more like the kind of place Scott would have spit upon than one he would have worked in. But then again, apparently I hadn't known the real him at all.

There was a counter with plexiglass covering the front. A large man exited a back room and approached the plexiglass. He was at least six feet tall, and likely the same circumference around his waistband. His hair hung down over his face, making it difficult to discern if he had eyes under there.

"You three take a wrong turn?" he asked. "Nail salon's two doors down."

"No, we're exactly where we want to be," I said.

"Please tell me you don't actually make food in this place," Wendy said.

"The health violations alone…." Mom said.

The big guy turned around, as if to return to the back room.

"Wait," I said. "Please."

He stopped and looked back at us.

"We're looking for Sam. Can you help us?"

His jaw ticked with recognition. "What's it to you? You here to pay off your kid's debt or something? We don't take credit cards. Cash only."

Debt? What did that have to do with Scott's girlfriend?

"Are you a loan shark?" Wendy asked.

"No, no," the guy said with an increasingly devious smile. "Loan sharks work outside the law. I assure you any bonds given here are entirely aboveboard."

"He's a loan shark," Mom said.

Wendy nodded.

"Bail bondsman, totally legal," he said.

"No one working only in cash is doing something *totally legal*," Mom said.

"Strippers," Wendy argued. "Tiny businesses like that artisanal pretzel truck with the vegan options. Mmmm."

Mom shook her head.

Wendy shrugged. "It's true."

"We aren't here about any money owed, legal or otherwise," I said. "You clearly know her. And we mean her no harm."

He put his hands on the counter and leaned forward so his nose pressed against the plexiglass. Dark eyes flicked back and forth behind ratty bangs. Was he trying to get a closer look at us? He leaned back, seemingly having made his decision.

"Yeah, sure," he said, flipping his thumb to the side, gesturing to another door on our side of the plexiglass. "Sam's out back."

"Great, thanks." I smiled and hurried the way he'd suggested before he could change his mind.

"You can't go through that way," he said. "Go back the way you came in, circle the building."

I ignored him and pushed the back door open, Mom and Wendy at my heels.

"Hey," he called after me, followed by some curses.

As the door snapped shut behind us, I followed the sound of moaning, and a steady *thwack, thwack, thwack* rhythm.

My steps faltered. I'd expected Sam to be on a smoke break. Given the sounds, it seemed more like a sex break.

"Hello?" I called out ahead of us as I followed the sound behind a busted van.

What I found was a man pinned to the backside of the van, with his pants down. But the woman wasn't naked.

She let go of the man's collar. He crumpled to the ground, face bloodied.

"Oh," I said. *"Oh."*

Sam was the loan shark's enforcer. It was entirely possible I'd misread everything about her and her relationship to Scott up to now.

"Hi," I said. "You may not remember me, but—"

"Oh I remember you," she said with a wry grin. "What do you want?"

The man on the ground moaned some more, and tried to crawl away. Sam held him in place with a stomp on his ankle.

"This man needs medical assistance," Mom said.

"He's fine," Sam said, not taking her eyes off me. "Aren't you, Larry?"

The injured man nodded emphatically. "Pretend I'm not here, or you'll only make it worse for me."

"Larry doesn't just try to steal money from Mr. Georgio, he takes it from orphans, too," Sam said. "He doesn't deserve sympathy."

"Well, I mean—" The injured man wet his lips and tapped his fingers together like he was going to try and come up with some excuse, but he didn't say that she was wrong.

"Did Scott work with you?" I asked. "Here for the loan shark?"

"Don't let Mr. Georgio hear you call him that," she said. "As to matters of employment, I can't say."

"Can't or won't?" Wendy asked.

"Does it matter?" Sam smiled at her, a cruel smile.

I needed answers, and I knew how to get them. I burrowed my gaze into Sam's skull. "You *will* answer our questions."

Mom looked from me to Sam. She whispered, "Mind control."

Sam tilted her head to the side. "Yes, Scott and I were partners."

"Partners?" Wendy said. "Pssh."

"We weren't sleeping together if that's what you're implying," Sam said. "He wasn't my type, not that he didn't try." She shot me a look of pity.

I didn't even care about that. Not anymore. I asked, "Why did he try to kill me?"

"Why does anyone do anything?" Sam pushed her heel into Larry's ankle.

He mewled.

"Money," Sam said. "He picked you as a mark, a side job, because you were easy money. Or at least he thought you were. But he borrowed too much from Mr. Georgio, and he had to collect faster than intended. So he thought killing you would be the easy way to get money."

"He never cared about me at all," I said.

"Never say never," Sam said with a shrug.

"For the record," Wendy said. "Estates don't work like that. You don't get the money right away. And they weren't married. Scott wouldn't have gotten anything even if his plan had been successful."

"He was a stupid man," Mom said.

All of this was still too recent that it left a raw hole in my chest. It wasn't the betrayal that hurt the most anymore, it was the fact that I'd been stupid enough to trust him to begin with. I said, "But why were you at my mother's house? Scott didn't have any right to anything there. Even he had to know that."

"Your mother?" Sam asked. Her eye twitched.

"That would be me," Mom said.

"Even if Scott had any right to give everything I owned to your boss—"

"Which he didn't," Wendy said.

"I have no ownership over my mother's belongings," I said. "And I didn't when she was pronounced dead, either."

"I don't—" The woman's shoulder bounced up on one side. She shook her head.

"You weren't just at the house either," I said. "You were *inside.* Why? How?"

"I didn't, I can't…." she started pacing, then let out a scream. Then she dropped to the ground and started to convulse.

"Is she having a seizure?" Larry asked from his place on the ground.

"I don't know," Wendy said, "but if I were you, I'd run while you have the chance."

He scurried to his feet, pulled up his pants, and ran away.

Was this me? Was this what happened because I'd forced her to help us?

"I release you," I said, bile rising up my throat. Please don't let this be my fault. "You don't have to talk to me."

She stopped shaking, rose to her feet and walked back inside, mumbling under her breath.

"That was weird," Wendy said.

I tried to think. Did the officers do this? No. Lily? No.

But I did know one person who had behaved this way, and I hadn't controlled him at all.

"I've seen someone do the same thing before," I said. "It was the lawyer for the estate. It's like there's some kind of switch in both of their heads that makes them snap as soon as we start talking about Mom's house. Maybe it's a wizard's doing, like Andrew but evil. I don't think it's me."

"Wicked Witch of the West. Voldemort. Jafar. Ursula," Wendy said, ticking off her fingers. "When magic exists in a story, there's always a bad wizard or witch cackling and casting evil. And no way did you break her."

Messing with peoples' brains certainly wasn't kind magic. Which of course was a thing I had done with my own powers. That didn't make *me* the bad guy, did it?

"It's your house. Do you have any thoughts on what's going on with these people, Mom?" I turned to look at her.

She was leaning on the brick wall, staring down, looking pale. "Mom?" I hurried to her side and grabbed onto her arm for support.

"Do you need your wheelchair?" I asked. "I shouldn't have let you walk this long by yourself that was stupid."

"I'll get it," Wendy said.

Before she could get anywhere though, Mom said, "No. It's not that. It wasn't a person who did this…it was something else."

"What do you mean?" I asked.

"I don't know. It's right there, in my brain, but I can't reach it," she said.

"That's all right. Let's get you home."

"No. I'm fine, really," she said.

"Maybe we all could use a break," Wendy said. "It's late. Get some rest and pick up in the morning?"

It had been a heck of a day. My joints and muscles cried with exhaustion.

"That's a great idea," I said. With any luck, a good night of sleep would not only help jog Mom's memory, but help me get my head on straight, too. No amount of sleep could ease the worry I felt for Andrew, though. There was a hole in my heart that would only heal when I had him safely back.

THE NIGHT OFFERED no epiphanies on what I could do for Andrew or on anything else for that matter. I was fairly certain that *I* hadn't broken Bueford Gross or Sam, and I was eager to press Mom for more information. We decided it'd be best if we waited until after breakfast.

Wendy picked the restaurant, Eats, and we arrived before her. The hostess placed us at the same table I'd sat at both of the other times I'd been here, right under the In Memoriam wall. It was starting to feel like the universe was telling me something.

Wendy texted that she was running late, and to order without her, so we did.

Halfway through our meal, someone slipped into the booth beside me. It took me a second to realize that someone was *not* Wendy.

"Greetings," Lily said. "It seems this is our spot, huh? Club In Memoriam?"

I frowned.

"Mom this is Lily. Lily, Mom."

"I've been thinking about our wizard problem," Lily said.

"You know about what's happening to the people around me?" Mom asked.

Lily quirked her head to the side. "A different wizard problem. Your daughter's boyfriend."

"Andrew is not my—" I started, pinching the pain in the center of my forehead.

"We leave for the library at once," Lily said. "So long as you are fed well enough not to bite anyone."

My mom looked at me, unasked questions swirling behind her soft brown eyes.

"We should wait for Wendy," I said.

"Mmm, that's not a great idea," Lily said. "The appointment I've scheduled for us is *time sensitive*. Trust me when I tell you, *you do not* want to be late."

"What's the plan?" I asked. "How are we going to save Andrew?"

"Time's a wasting." Lily tapped a finger on the table and pursed her cherry-painted lips. "We have to go *now*."

"I don't trust her," Mom said.

"I compelled her not to betray me. We can trust her," I said. The tension twisting my insides disagreed.

My phone dinged. It was Wendy.

Bear trouble. Catch you for lunch?

I rubbed the knot in the center of my forehead.

"Let's go," I said. "I'm good."

I'd have to be. If this was my only chance to save Andrew, I had to take it.

CHAPTER 32

*L*ily headed not for the exit, but for the bathroom. Mom and I followed, hanging back by the door.

"Pit stop?" I asked.

"When weird strikes, people see what they expect to see. But it doesn't hurt to use discretion when possible," Lily said. She waved us into the bathroom with her, then bent down to check under each stall. When she was content that we were alone, she locked the door. "Plus, if anyone who matters is watching, well, it's for the best if they don't see me with this."

She pulled a thin chain out of a hidden pocket in her puffy skirt and wrapped it around her hand. It looked like the same kind of thing the grumpy trench coat man had used when he'd portaled Andrew away from my front porch.

Mom leaned against the sink, her skin a little pale.

"Are you all right, Mom?" I asked.

"I'll be fine," she said. "But whatever it is that we're doing in here, let's move it along."

"Given the exactness of the procedure required, I'm going the appropriate speed. Thank you very much," Lily said, her eyes glued to the chain on her hand.

Maybe Mom wasn't up for this after all. She had hardly had any recovery time at all after being unconscious for eight months, if that was even what had happened to her. We didn't know yet. Maybe whatever evil wizard had messed with Sam and the lawyer had messed with Mom, too.

I bit my lip and tried to push away the uncertainty that pricked in the back of my head. Worrying wouldn't help. Answers would.

Lily waved her hand in a circle. The chain lit up, and a portal formed.

"You first," Lily gave me a push, right into the shimmering surface of the oval.

In a cold, shivering instant, I was transported.

It was a strange, unnerving sensation that made my head spin and my breakfast nearly lurch back up my throat.

I landed in a white expanse that appeared to stretch infinitely in every direction. It was a hall of sorts, with a straight path. White shelves of white books lined the sides of the hall, creating a cross section of other seemingly endless walkways.

There was so much white, too much white.

Weirder, there were no sounds, no smell.

It was a void.

Lily appeared beside me.

"Sterile," I said. It felt more like a dream than a real place.

"It appears so," Lily said. "Though I would not suggest licking the floors."

"You think I would do that? Why would anyone ever do that?"

She shrugged and started walking. "Come on."

A sinking feeling settled in where queasiness had been, a rock in the center of my core.

"Where's my mom?" I asked, remaining in place.

POTIONS AND PAJAMAS

Lily paused, but didn't turn around. She rounded her shoulders. "Your mother is not coming."

"Why not? What did you do?"

"Nothing," she said. "Trust me when I tell you that you don't want her here. If this meeting goes sideways—not that I'm expecting it to—but if it does…."

Mom was wrong. I could trust Lily. I'd compelled her to not betray me. So, this had to be true. It was best that Mom had stayed behind. Something could have happened to her here, and not just if something went wrong in the meeting. If Mom was having trouble standing in the bathroom, she couldn't handle a portal and from what it looked like a forever walk to who knew what.

While I was able to admit to myself that it was probably for the best that she was safe in normal human reality, it would have been nice to have someone along who I could actually trust. And Lily didn't count.

Lily started walking once more.

"This doesn't look like any library I've ever been to," I said, taking everything in as I followed.

"Because it's not," Lily said. *"The Library* is knowledge itself, not simply a handful of stories lent out to the public."

I had to admit, *the Library* did have a lot of books. But it would be stupid to trust an organization that decides it has some right to police anyone it chooses without oversight. Maybe all of this white—white books, white floor, white everything—was to compensate for its true evilness.

"What's the plan?" I asked. "How are we going to break Andrew out?"

"Why do you assume I intend on breaking anything?" Lily said over her shoulder.

Why would I assume otherwise?

"Okay…" I said. "How do we *magic* him out? Or slip him out? Or *whatever* his butt out of here?"

"With the truth."

"What truth?"

Completely ignoring me, Lily approached one of the many, identical bookshelves. "Ah, here we are."

I scanned the too-white scenery. "What do you mean, *here we are?* Where's Andrew? You said we had a meeting, but there's no one here to meet."

Lily turned to me with a placating smirk on her face. The pink in her cheeks, the twinkle in her eyes—she appeared quite pleased with herself. *Why?*

She bent at the hip, like she was about to bow, then reached a hand out toward me and poked my nose. "Boop."

The white books, the white shelves, the white abyss—all of it disappeared. My eyes struggled to adjust to darkness. With the lack of light, other sensations returned. Dampness clung to the air. There were smells, too—metal, earth, cement maybe. I shivered at the sudden shift and folded my arms. I squeezed my eyes shut and then squinted as I spun around, looking for any grounding details to cling to.

Lily stood beside me, and I could make her out just fine. It wasn't dark in the new space we'd entered, but another void, this time gray instead of white.

"Where are we?" I asked.

Lily folded her arms behind her back. "Do you trust me?"

"No."

"Try to," she said. "Also be honest and don't get angry."

"I've been nothing but honest." I threw my hands up in frustration. "Get angry about what? The fact that you've dragged me who knows where for who knows what reason? Where is Andrew, Lily? *What did you do?*"

She winked at me. "Best of luck."

A thunking sound came from above me, traveling across the ceiling of the gray space. Light disappeared with each thunk, closing in on us from every direction.

"Lily?"

As the rest of the space went black, bright lights hit me from overhead. It was a spotlight, hot and blinding. I felt like I'd been caught doing something I shouldn't, like a fugitive on the run, cornered.

I cringed under the harshness of the light and shielded my eyes.

A deep voice boomed. "Rosemary DeLaCrux, you stand accused of murder. What say you?"

"This is how we get Andrew back?" I looked around wildly for Lily. I couldn't see her. She wasn't in the spotlight with me.

Be honest and don't get angry. Lily was bound to help me, wasn't she? My confidence wavered, big time.

"Don't I get a lawyer?" I asked, weakly.

"Speak," a second male voice said, this time from a different direction.

How many people were here? Were these the librarians? If I tried to run now, where would I wind up? Was there even a way to escape? Even though every fiber of my being screamed *run,* I had to stay.

Whether Lily was trying to help me or if she was only trying to help herself, I didn't know. But this was my chance to right my wrong. If someone was going to be punished for what I had done, it should be me. It wasn't fair. Andrew had saved my life. It was the least I could do to save his

This was what Lily had planned. This was how I'd save Andrew.

I forced myself to drop the arm that shielded my eyes. I forced myself to stand tall and strong. "You take my friend, accuse us both of murder, but where's the proof?"

With another thunk, spotlights shone down brighter beside me, and with another thunk, under that light, my freezer appeared.

The lid popped open on its own accord. Inside was a Scottcicle.

Okay, they had proof. Big time proof.

But this wasn't Andrew's fault. I summoned my voice, and belted out, "Scott Tochee's death had nothing to do with Andrew. It was me. It was all me."

"Explain."

I licked my lips. "Well, I got mad. I lashed out. Andrew wasn't even there."

"An admission of guilt," one voice said.

"It is truth," said another.

"She is guilty. A crime of passion," said another.

How many of these guys were there surrounding me in a circle?

"You did it, sure, but what made you mad?" Lily called out from somewhere in the darkness.

She was still here. And she was trying to help.

"Scott tried to kill me," I said.

Lily stepped out of the darkness, joining me in the harsh lights. She paced slowly, leisurely, with her hands laced together behind her back.

She had planned this all along, luring me here, knowing what would happen. Instead of correcting my assumption that this was a rescue mission, she hadn't warned or prepared me in any way for this ambush. And she expected me to trust her. Ha.

She wasn't my friend, even a little bit. This was about her, about proving her place here and fixing whatever work issues she'd been dealing with.

"How exactly did he try to kill you?" she asked. "Was it a heated debate that grew into a physical altercation? Did you see him coming for you, a knife in hand?"

"He buried me alive."

Silence reigned. My ears rang. My eyes burned as I

followed Lily's steps. I didn't blink. If I'd had breath to hold, I'd have held it.

"The events leading to Mr. Tochee's death did not begin with Mr. Jensen's potion. They began the day prior."

She was going to help Andrew after all, even if it meant throwing me under the bus. At least an innocent man wasn't going to suffer for my crimes. I could be strong for him. I could survive this, whatever came next.

"Ms. DeLaCrux, please tell the council what happened the evening of Wednesday, April eighteenth when you returned home, emotionally exhausted from the reading of your mother's will," Lily said.

"Scott was there when I got home," I said. "He immediately offered to pour me a glass of wine and start a bath for me. I thought he was trying to take care of me."

"But taking care of you wasn't his usual M.O. was it?" Lily asked.

"No," I said. "It was me who usually took care of him, which was why it meant so much to me."

"And this surprise gesture of empathy and caring," Lily said, "was it actually genuine? Or was it a devious ploy?"

"He must have drugged the wine," I said. "I never made it into the bath."

"This is the point where the man you trusted, your fiancé, dragged your unconscious body into the trunk of your car, drove you across town, and dumped you in a hole he'd preemptively dug for this very purpose. Correct?"

"I'm not entirely sure," I said, swallowing the lump in my throat. "I wasn't awake for any of that."

"The burial site was not in some remote recess of the middle of nowhere where the perpetrator of this heinous act could take his time digging. This was a public place, where he couldn't risk his fiancée waking while he readied the hole. All preparations were completed in advance, premeditated by a calculated, devious man with no reluctance or remorse about discarding the woman he was supposedly in love with."

Tightness gripped my chest.

"And the man who rescued you, was he a friend, an acquaintance?" Lily asked.

"No. I'd never met him."

"So, acting out of compassion, this stranger rescued you."

"Yes."

"Evidence at the scene proves Mr. Jensen hadn't come prepared for this situation in any way," Lily said. "He dug her out using his bare hands. The potion he used to save her left a magical signature in the graveyard, proving it was created in the moment, because it was the only way to assure Ms. DeLaCrux would survive. Does that sound like the act of a criminal to you? Or an act of compassion?"

Whispers carried through the shadows.

"Firstly, I submit to you, honorable council, that in an impossible situation, Andrew Jensen did the only thing a kindhearted person could. Second, as the only act of violence his revenant committed was against the man who had effectively murdered her, the act of ending the murderer's life was not actually murder in itself, but self-defense. And cosmic justice."

More whispers.

"Compelling argument," someone said. "But what happened the day of Scott Tochee's death? Are you claiming self-defense because he might try to kill her a second time? While it's an understandable fear, returning the next day also lacks urgency."

"How is this final act also not premeditated?" another asked.

Lily chewed her lip, turned to me with wide eyes. She hadn't thought this part through. She didn't know what to say.

I did.

"I didn't go home with the intent to kill Scott," I said. "I wanted answers. When I returned, he was with a woman."

Whispers came from the darkness.

Lily's concern lined her face. It sounded bad, I knew, but this was my truth.

"She was his business partner," I said. "I didn't know it at the time. Still, I didn't intend to kill him. It was an accident. We tussled. He choked me, in a second attempt to kill me. Only then did I bite him."

I should have felt sadness, remorse, too. But I didn't. Not anymore. I felt lighter after sharing what had happened. No matter what the council decided, I felt more at peace than I had since all of this began.

"Truth," said someone.

"The only one truly responsible for the death of Scott Tochee is Scott Tochee himself," Lily said.

The lights went out, returning the space to cool gray nothingness. The freezer disappeared along with the circle of judges. There was no one around but Lily and me.

"Where did they go?" I asked.

"They need to talk it all out," she said. "Our chances are good."

I laughed a humorless laugh. "Chances. You brought me here under false pretenses. We were supposed to be rescuing Andrew, and now it's possible we both end up in prison."

"You wanted to help. This is how we help."

"You should have told me. It should have been my decision. You're not supposed to be able to betray me like this. Not after I compelled you."

"Oh, that doesn't work on me," she said. "Only on humans."

What? She had to be lying. I didn't know what to say. "You led me to believe it had worked."

She shrugged. "I didn't explicitly say it did."

"You told me to do it! You told me to compel you."

"And it made you feel better. If you hadn't trusted me enough to tell me your story, I wouldn't have known where to start to help you with your cause. I couldn't have gathered the evidence we needed to exonerate Andrew. Plus, really, when I suggested you compel me, I never did say it would work."

"It. Was. Implied."

"Eh. All's well that ends well."

"All's well that ends well? What if this *doesn't* end well? Even if it does, the ends don't justify the means," I said, exasperated.

"We'll see."

My limbs surged with nervous, frustrated energy. I couldn't just stand here. I had to do something. So I paced.

Lily watched, her body language open, unbothered.

That only agitated me further.

"So it was your library who stole my freezer?" I asked with a sharp tone and a sharper glare.

"Yes. Though I wouldn't use the word *steal* to describe what the Library did. They confiscated evidence."

"Stole," I said. "They broke into my house and took something that didn't belong to them."

"Did they actually break anything?" She raised a brow, clearly already knowing the answer. When I didn't respond, she added, "When we're done here, so long as this goes in our favor, if you'd like I'm sure they'd be willing to return the corpse-filled freezer to your basement."

Ugh. "No thanks."

She nodded and plastered a smug grin on her face.

Her grin fell into a scowl in an instant as she looked over my shoulder. I turned to see what it was that she saw. Two men approached. One was Andrew. And he wasn't wearing handcuffs.

Hands trembling, relief washed over me. An elated burst of tears poured down my cheeks. I was grateful to Lily, to the universe. The man I loved was all right, and he was here, in front of me. Free. My heart was full.

I ran over and wrapped my arms around him. "We won?"

"It seems whatever you said convinced the council," he said. "It was reckless for you to come here."

"You think I'd abandon you?" I shook my head. "Never in a million years."

"Sweet reunion," the other man said, pulling me from the moment.

With blond hair and a tan trench coat, I recognized him. He was the one who had arrested Andrew. His presence also seemed to have put Lily on edge. Her shoulders went rigid and her scowl deepened as he smiled at her.

"You stole my case," she said.

"Stole is a nasty word," he said. "I was handed this case because of my proven competence."

"Oh, I'm competent," she snapped. "Remember what happened in Reno? I sure do. You wish you were half as competent as I am."

"Keep telling yourself that, sweetheart," the man said. Then he turned to me. "You're both cleared." He waved his hand, creating a portal.

Trench coat man and Lily shoved Andrew and me through.

CHAPTER 33

*A*ndrew reached for me. I braced for impact.

He twisted, putting himself first, and shielding me from whatever we were about to face.

Bright light struck first, daylight filtered through a wall of glass.

We landed on a soft surface, on Andrew's sofa. Well, he landed on the sofa, and I landed on top of him. He held me gently, his arms a cocoon of safety and warmth. He wasn't as soft as the sofa cushions would have been, but pleasantly firm.

With my hands on his chest, I lifted my head to get a look at his face.

His beard was a little longer than usual, a little wild. He didn't appear injured, or in distress, which hopefully meant he hadn't been treated poorly in the time the Library had held him captive. A comfortable warmth carried up my neck and settled in my cheeks. I'd succeeded. My Andrew was safe.

"Are you all right?" he asked.

I nodded, unable to speak just yet. My thoughts were jumbled as I tried to figure out just what I needed to say. I was ready to move forward. There were so many things I needed to ask him, because I was hoping we could move forward together.

"Are you?" I asked.

Silver sparks threaded through his gray irises. His pupils dilated. He inhaled slowly. I held tight and rode the rise of his chest. When he exhaled, we moved back down as one. His abs tensed beneath my soft belly. I resisted the urge to run my hands under his shirt.

"Better than okay." His full lips lifted up on one side.

A fresh shot of desire bloomed in my core. I wanted to lick those lips. I wanted to claim his mouth, his chest, his everything. I wanted his earthy coffee and man scent on my clothes, his skin on mine, and no barriers between us.

I'd spent my whole life giving, devoting myself to taking care of others. But with Andrew, nothing I did felt like an act of selflessness. I needed to save him, to taste him, to savor him. Not for him, but for me. My need for him was pure selfishness.

I hovered over him, lowering my lips an inch over his.

"Tell me what you want, Rosemary." His voice came out rough, delicious.

"You," I said. "Everything with you."

He'd told me that shifters had one person they were meant to be with. He'd told me I was his person. And as he claimed my mouth, I knew this kiss was a promise to give me exactly what I needed, not just now but always.

* * *

Sex was one thing, even out-of-this-world sex like we'd had

before. But making love was another. In the afterglow, wrapped in Andrew's sheets, I was finally ready to admit what this really was.

"I love you," I said.

He brushed his lips over my temple. "I love you, too, Rosemary."

"I haven't felt love like this before," I said.

"Everything with you is new for me, too."

"What does this mean?" I asked. "Do I move in here? Do you move into my house?"

"What do you want?"

"I really like your windows," I chuckled. "I bought my house for Heather, so she'd have a yard to play in when she was little. I don't really need that anymore. Seems I'm inviting myself to live here. Is that all right?"

"It's more than all right." He smiled. "You want me to ask?"

I nodded. I felt silly about wanting him to ask, but I really needed to hear the request.

"Rosemary," he said, 'will you please do me the pleasure of moving in with me?"

With mock seriousness, I said, "I'll have to think about it."

He wrapped his arms around me and tickled my sides. I squealed.

A phone rang. I couldn't say if it was mine or Andrew's.

Then another rang. It was both of us.

"I don't want to get that," he said.

"We should," I said. "I disappeared straight out of a bathroom last night, leaving my mom behind. She has to be worried. I should have thought of that and called her by now."

Andrew let me go. We climbed out of bed.

While he dressed, I found my phone in my pants where

I'd discarded them on the living room floor. I answered, "Hello?"

"Where have you been?" Wendy let out in a single breath. It was so rushed it came out like a single word.

"Hi, Wendy," I said. "I've been in the magical library saving Andrew. Did you meet up with my mom? Is she doing all right?"

"Yeah, I met up with her—*a week ago, Rose.* You've been missing an entire freaking week."

"What? That doesn't make sense. It was just one night."

"Well, whether it makes sense or not, it's true." Wendy huffed out a long breath. "Your mom's doing well. I've been watching out for her, but she doesn't need a babysitter anymore. I think I'm driving her a little crazy. She says she has to talk to you in person. Now."

"I'm on my way," I said. "Your house or mine?"

"Yours."

"Thanks, Wendy."

"Thank me by getting your butt back here quick," she said. "Wait. Your mom says we're coming to you. Also how did it go? Did you save Andrew? Tell me whatever you did worked."

"It did."

"Great. Are you at Andrew's?"

"I am."

"We'll be right there. See you soon."

"Bye."

I set my phone down, and first things first, put my clothes on. Andrew appeared in the doorway, looking like all kinds of delicious perfection in a pair of sweatpants and a t-shirt. A big part of me wished I could throw on some of his pajamas and spend the rest of the day in bed.

"Wendy and my mom are coming over," I said. "Sorry I didn't ask. They were insistent."

"Don't be. You can invite anyone you want over to your apartment whenever you want." A smile spread across his way-too-kissable-for-my-sanity lips.

"Noted." I realized then that time was running out for any talking the two of us needed to do while we were still alone. I needed to mention what Lily had said about his mom, so he could say or not say whatever he wanted on the subject before I heard anything else about her from anyone who was not him.

Before I could open my mouth to speak, he said, "What do you think the story is with those two librarians?"

"Lily and trench coat guy? History for sure. I know he stole her case—the case about us."

"You know her?" he asked.

"She's been stalking me. I thought I'd compelled her to help me, but apparently that doesn't actually work on non-humans."

"What kind of non-human is she?" Andrew asked.

"No idea. A tricky one. Maybe she's a prankster creature. Tell me fairies are real."

"Not that I know of," he said. "But I didn't know your ability to compel was limited, either. There's more I don't know than I do."

"Same as the rest of us," I said with a smile.

He smiled back.

"Speaking of Lily," I said before we could move on to anything else. "She mentioned your mom. I didn't pry, but I thought you should know she said some…unkind things."

"My mother had plenty of faults," he said. "She lived a long life, coveting the abilities of other witches. She hurt a lot of people. The library informed me a few months back that she had died in the course of trying to steal magic."

"I'm so sorry."

"Thanks. I try to hold onto the good memories, the few of them that exist."

"Like fishing?" I pointed to the picture.

"Yeah. We only went once about ten years ago. It was the last time I saw her."

I wanted to apologize again, but instead I hugged him.

The doorbell rang, followed by the insistent banging of a fist.

Andrew opened the door. Wendy and Mom burst in.

Wendy grabbed me and hugged me hard. Mom took the opportunity to walk around and scope everything out.

"In the time you've been missing, we were worried sick," Mom said.

"I know the feeling," I told her.

My stomach grumbled.

It twisted, suddenly starving.

"I've come to remember what happened to me," Mom said. "It began…"

She was losing me. I shook my head, knowing I needed to listen. But all I could focus on was the hunger.

"Food," I said.

Andrew opened the fridge. "There's nothing salvageable in here. Are you okay, Rosemary? I'm ordering carryout. You haven't eaten in a week."

I hadn't eaten in a week.

"Give her space," Andrew said. He used a firm but gentle grip on my upper arms, positioning himself in front of me so I had to look him in the eye. "Hey. Look at me, Rosemary. You can control this."

I had to eat.

Needed meat.

"You crave sustenance, energy," he said. "Take it from me, with your hands."

He put my hands on his cheeks.

I stared into his eyes, the gray clouds and silver sparks. I leaned into our connection to ground me.

"It's all right," he said. "Let me help you."

I didn't know what he meant. I didn't know how to take his energy.

I flexed my fingers and closed my eyes, trying to ignore the thrumming hunger.

A wash of cool energy flooded into me.

The uncontrollable hunger faded, and everything was back to normal. Except Andrew was pale.

My chest tightened. I took a step back. A ball of guilt formed in my stomach.

"I hurt you. This was supposed to be better, and I still hurt you."

"I'm fine," he said, "just a little tired. I'll be back to one-hundred-percent in no time, promise."

I looked into his dark circled eyes, and I believed him. Relief washed over me. I really could maintain control.

"This is you now?" Mom asked, her voice hesitant.

"I know," I snapped, too tired and emotional to be nice. "Hugely disappointing to see your only daughter turned out to be a monster."

"Never." She walked over to me and wrapped her arms around me. "You do not disappoint me, Rosie. You never have. I'm sorry you have to deal with this…change. It doesn't make you less. If anything, your strength shows."

I wanted to squeeze her so hard I'd burst, but given my unnatural strength, I settled for a soft embrace. I hadn't realized how much I'd needed that. After forty years, I'd finally gotten warmth and approval from my mother. All it took was both of us dying.

"I love you," she said.

"I love you, too."

We both cried.

Wendy came over and hugged us, too.

"You were saying something, Mom," I said. "When I turned all crazed."

"Right," she said. "I remembered what happened to me."

"You never went to Aruba," I said.

"Correct. I was painting the trim on the shed, and a man appeared in the yard. I have no idea how he got there."

"He probably climbed the tree by the wall," I said. "It's a natural ladder."

She raised a brow, likely questioning how many times I had used that same tree as a teenager. Then she continued, "He was particularly unremarkable in a shabby gray suit. And his voice…the man should sell tapes of himself talking to insomniacs."

"He puts you right to sleep?" Wendy chuckled.

"He told me his name…said he was a lawyer," Mom said.

"Bueford Gross?" I asked.

"Yes, that sounds right," she said.

"That's the lawyer who is handling your estate," I said.

"I didn't die," Mom said. "Everything is still mine. And if I had died, everything was meant to be yours."

"It went to a cat," I said.

"What is the deal with this cat?" Wendy asked.

Everyone appeared to be at a loss for words.

"More importantly, what happened after Mr. Gross introduced himself?" I asked.

"I heard a woman's voice. She was humming a song, like a lullaby. And that's it. I don't remember anything else until you found me, Rose."

Interesting. Had she been asleep for eight months? How could she survive that? What about the phone call? She'd called me from her trip to Aruba and left me a voicemail. It had definitely been her. I'd listened to the message a thousand times after she'd "died." So she'd made the call, but didn't remember it.

"When I last saw that lawyer," I said, "he was acting just like Sam did behind Pizza Palace once we mentioned you, Mom. It was like he was broken in the head. He wasn't like that the first time I met him."

"Was the singing woman Sam?" Wendy asked.

"I don't think so," Mom said. "And Mr. Gross seemed fine when I saw him. Perhaps something happened to him in between. A head injury."

"Two people with that severe of brain injuries? Seems too weird to be a coincidence," Wendy said.

"We could go to his office," I said.

"Confrontation?" Wendy rubbed her hands together. "Should we bring the police along to arrest this guy? I mean he made you seem dead and stole all of your money, Lenore. Did he somehow give it to himself by giving it to the cat?"

"Maybe," I said. "But one look at those financials and anyone could say he'd stolen the estate. Maybe the cat belongs to a friend of his, and they're in on it together. And it doesn't explain the voicemail from Aruba, or how you survived so long without any memory."

"Quite the conundrum," Wendy said. "There's only one way to solve this mystery."

"Food first," Mom said, nodding to me. "Then we can play detective."

Wendy rubbed her hands together. "I want to be the bad cop."

"Not to be unkind, dear," Mom said, "but Rosemary's easily the most intimidating of us."

"What about Andrew?" I asked.

Mom patted my hand. "It's nothing to be ashamed of. Own your strength."

I wasn't ashamed of being a forty-three-year-old woman. I was comfortable in my skin, in my roles as mother, friend, daughter, and lover. I was certain I knew what I wanted for myself, too. I wanted to make jewelry crafting into a job, and I wanted to be with Andrew. I embraced everything the world threw at me. The only thing I was holding back was the monster.

CHAPTER 34

We hit the closest drive-through on the way to the lawyer's office. With a full belly, I felt a lot more prepared for whatever exciting interaction would come next.

But when we arrived at Mr. Gross's office, his receptionist told us he wasn't there. Apparently he had to do something at the DeLaCrux estate and would not be back until super late.

So we went to Lingonberry.

Wendy drove, with Mom in the passenger seat. The two certainly seemed to have bonded over my week away. They sang along to the oldies station while Andrew and I sat in the back. A strange thought passed through my mind as I looked from his hand to mine held together on the seat between us. We had the same bruise on our wrists. I didn't even remember getting hurt there.

When we arrived, we parked in the driveway behind Mr. Gross, blocking him in. Wendy handed Mom her taser, and pulled Aunt Petunia's shotgun out of the trunk.

"Don't bring that," I told her.

"We have no idea what we're walking into," she said. "I'm not taking any chances."

I sighed.

"I don't have keys," Mom said.

"What do you think about trying the front door?" Andrew asked.

"Bad guys won't open the front door," Wendy said.

"They might," I said.

"Sure, they invite you in if it's part of their trap," Wendy said.

"Don't say that," Mom said. "You'll jinx us."

"We can go in through the dining room window," I said. "I broke it last time. Sorry, Mom."

"It's the least of my problems," she said with a sigh.

I shook my head and gestured for everyone to follow me to the side yard. As we climbed the tree, Mom mumbled under her breath about having the tree removed. As soon as I was safely on the other side, I smoothed my clothes back into place.

A strange sensation prickled at the back of my neck. Something was off here. I scanned the yard.

People lay in a circle in the grass around the house, all spaced out with their arms and legs spread. There were at least twenty of them, maybe more.

"They're doing grass angels," Wendy said. "Like snow angels, but with no snow. They aren't dead, are they?"

Their eyes were open. They all looked fine.

"They're all breathing," Andrew said.

It was super weird. They were awake, eyes open, staring up at the sun.

"Mrs. Crawford?" Mom leaned down and poked one lady in the cheek.

Mrs. Crawford didn't respond.

I glanced at the shotgun in Wendy's hands and chewed on

my lip. A taser was one thing, but guns made me nervous.

"That gun is a very bad idea," I said. "Whatever weirdness is going on here, someone could get hurt."

"I'll be careful," Wendy said.

She wasn't going to listen to reason, so I held my tongue.

"What do we do?" Mom asked.

"We go in," I said.

We stepped over the line of people, weirded out.

The back door was open, so we went inside. The dining room table was crooked. I didn't remember it being like that last time. The broken glass beneath the window remained.

"The energy here is off," Andrew said.

"You think?" Mom said. "What gave it away? The cult circle outside? Or the creepy lullaby?"

There was no song playing. I asked her, "What lullaby?"

"You don't hear that?" she asked.

I shook my head.

"I don't hear anything either," Wendy said.

"There's magic here," Andrew said.

The sounds of pounding feet, groans, and the thuds of crashing bodies pulled my attention to the yard behind us.

The people from the circle had woken up. They scrambled over each other and raced toward the house.

"They're trying to get in, close the door!" I shouted.

Some began climbing through open windows, others pushed open the back door.

"Don't shoot them," I said, pointing at Wendy.

We backed out of the dining room into the hall.

The yard people swarmed us, pressing in from the dining room, the living room, the kitchen.

An elderly woman in a house dress swung her walker at me. I put up my arms in defense. Wendy kicked the shins of two middle-aged men when they came close to her.

Mom cried out as a young man pulled her arm, wrestling

her toward the kitchen. Andrew punched him in the face, and he let Mom go.

"How dare you all break into my home," Mom said. "Go back to your own lives. What would your husband think of this behavior, Sherry?"

Mom knew her? Now that I was paying attention, I recognized some of the faces, too. These were her neighbors.

What was causing this? Who was the one pulling the strings? I tried to look past the swinging walker into the crowd. My ears began to pound, a rising sense of frustration coursing through my veins. How were we supposed to get answers if we let these people beat us to death?

"Close your eyes," Andrew yelled. "And hold your breath."

I slammed my eyes shut and hoped Wendy and Mom were doing the same. I had no idea what Andrew was doing, but I hoped it worked.

A floral scent wafted into my nose, like a honeysuckle smoke.

I waited a moment then opened my eyes. The horde wavered on their feet, eyelids growing heavy. Then they began to drop one at a time. A yellow smoke filled the air, slowly dissipating.

Wendy still had her eyes squeezed shut, her shotgun held tight to her chest.

"It's okay," I said and touched her shoulder.

She opened her eyes and looked around. Mom kicked the young man in the arm who had tried to pull her, even though he was already down.

"Sleeping gas," Andrew said.

"Great work," I told him.

"Let's not celebrate yet," Mom said.

The lawyer walked down the stairs clapping his hands.

"Thank you for returning here, to my center of power. This will make disposing of you all that much easier."

"Come get some," I said, putting myself between him and my family.

Wendy aimed the gun at him. Mom held her taser at the ready.

"With all of these other tools at my disposal? I think not," Mr. Gross said. He pointed to Mom.

She squeezed the trigger on the taser. It hit me. In a shock of electric pain, I fell to my knees. My muscles betrayed me. My nerves fired like crazy. My body convulsed.

Andrew ran forward.

Mr. Gross pointed at Wendy.

The gun went off.

Andrew collapsed beside me.

He was bleeding. His shoulder was bleeding. Wendy had shot him.

A fresh jolt of pain radiated out from my shoulder, followed by cold.

Andrew had been shot, not me. Why was my shoulder bleeding?

I remembered the twin bruises on our wrists. The bruises had first appeared when the librarian had handcuffed Andrew. Even back in the park, sitting together on the bench, he'd bumped his knuckles and I'd felt it in my hand. When he was hurt, I was hurt. How many other clues had there been in our time together that I'd simply overlooked?

Mr. Gross chuckled. "The interesting thing about revenants is they're nearly impossible to kill. I could hit you with a rocket launcher, and you'd likely survive. We could try and find out for sure, but there's no reason when you brought along your only weakness."

Andrew wasn't my weakness, he was my strength.

As the blood poured out of me, I tried to get up. I tried to do something, anything to save the people I loved. I couldn't move. I stared at Andrew, the man I loved, and I knew true fear. I could lose him.

Mr. Gross said, "Any harm that comes to your wizard comes to you as well."

Andrew reached into his pocket. He pulled two potions out. He reached for me, a pained but loving expression on his face. "Remember where I am."

It took a moment for me to understand.

And then he disappeared.

The second potion clattered to the floor beside me.

A cat curled around Mr. Gross's feet. Not just *a* cat —*the* cat.

A tiara perched in the center of the cat's head. Pearls dangled from its neck. In its mouth…was a knife.

Mr. Gross reached down and grabbed the knife from the cat's mouth and charged.

"Watch this spot, Mom, Wendy," I yelled, as I forced myself to my feet.

I held onto the potion like my life depended on it, because Andrew's did. He'd disappeared himself like the drink in the bar so I could fight, so we could use the monster inside of me without reserve.

I threw Mr. Gross to the ground and twisted his arm behind his back.

He cried out in pain and dropped the knife.

Wendy grabbed the cat.

It writhed in her arms, scratching and flailing.

Mr. Gross went limp. He began to snore. All of the neighbors who had charged us from outside did, too.

"That cat," Mom said. "That cat is the one singing the song."

Wendy said, "I don't think it's a cat."

Noodles McDoodles Butterbelly's ears grew taller. His tail filled out, growing bushier, like a squirrel's.

A hummed lullaby filled the air. I covered my ears. Maybe that was how it did it, how the not-cat controlled people.

"We need something magical to hold it," I said.

Mom held the taser to the not-a-cat's nose. "Stop singing right now."

If she tased Noodles, she'd end up tasing Wendy, too.

Noodles's fur darkened to a deep red. His cat nose grew longer. He wasn't a cat, but…a fox? The tiara dropped from his head and clattered onto the floor.

He opened his fox mouth and said, "I submit."

I didn't trust it for a second. Still, we had all the weapons. We'd caught the fox. If anyone knew what to do next, it was Andrew. We needed him. I needed him. I scrambled to find the exact spot where Andrew waited for me, trapped as nothing.

Sweat made the bottle slip in my fingers. The trembling in my hands didn't help.

I looked on the ground where two matching puddles of blood marked where we had been.

Please work. Please be all right.

I poured the potion on the floor and promised the universe anything if it would only give him back to me.

Andrew reappeared, lying still. He gasped for air, put a hand to his wounded shoulder and looked at me. "You did it."

"I did. I had to. You have to be okay. I can't lose you."

"I'm right here." He reached for me.

I grabbed his hand and squeezed. His eyes sharpened when he spotted the fox in Wendy's arms. "It's a kitsune. I've never seen one in the flesh before."

"Yes, I am kitsune," the fox said. "Exceedingly rare. Undeniably superior. Prostrate yourselves. Worship kitsune."

I laughed.

"No joke," the fox said.

"Didn't you say *you* were submitting to *us*?" Wendy asked.

The fox tilted its chin up.

"Paralyzing a woman and taking over her life, causing who knows how bad of brain damage to innocent people," I said. "I bet Lily could bring some magical cage, dump this thing in the library."

"No, no," the fox said. "Misunderstanding, clearly."

"The library is equipped to deal with the most treacherous of prisoners," I said.

"I can fix," the fox said. "Kitsune fix everything. No cage. This is home."

"How can you possibly intend to repair the damage you caused?" Wendy asked.

"Kitsune bound to home," the fox said. "Kitsune need this home. *Please.* Let kitsune try."

Wendy frowned. "I don't trust it."

"You don't trust anyone," I said.

"I trust *you*," Wendy said. "And I'm really sorry I shot you guys, by the way. Maybe we start by shooting the fox. That would make me feel better."

"No, no shoot," the fox said, shaking its head and flicking its tail wildly.

"Kitsune do bind themselves to a home. They enjoy causing trouble, but they are also bound to the person who owns the property. Once their nature is revealed, they're unable to control that person anymore or lie to them," Andrew said, holding his injured shoulder. "Essentially it's your magical servant now, Lenore. It's entirely up to you if we allow the kitsune to stay."

The fox flicked its tail faster as it stared wide-eyed at Mom.

"Where did you get the tiara?" she asked.

The kitsune bared its teeth, or no…was that a smile?

It said, "Online ordering. So sorry."

"Prove you've changed your ways. Start by fixing these people," Mom said.

The fox wiggled out of Wendy's arms. It pressed a paw to Mr. Gross's head.

He bolted upright. "What's…where am I? Who are you people?"

"Kitsune true to word," the fox said.

"Is that a talking fox?" Mr. Gross asked.

"You were just leaving," Wendy told him.

"Sounds good to me." He scrambled for the door.

The fox tilted its chin up.

I couldn't believe this was happening.

Mom pulled a small smile. "I've never been much for cats, but I am quite fond of foxes."

EPILOGUE

After a bazillion phone calls and half a bazillion in-person check-ins over the past few weeks, I wasn't sure it was possible for me to ever fully trust Noodles McDoodles Butterbelly. My mother, on the other hand, was perfectly content—excited, even—to live with the cat who was not a cat.

There had been no incidents to report, and from my time spying on Mom's neighbors, Mr. Gross, and Sam, I found no evidence that any lasting harm had been done to anyone. Andrew and Lily both assured me that Noodles couldn't betray my mom, many times. If anything, Mom seemed happier than I ever remembered seeing her. I wasn't sure how much that had to do with Noodles, and how much to do with having the family together to celebrate Heather's birthday.

Noodles perched himself on top of the fridge, wearing his tiara and lazily licking his extended back leg. His orange fur, his long tail, and his pointed ears all looked very cat-like, all completely innocent.

Mom and Heather huddled together over the stove,

taking turns tasting and adding components to the sauce they'd created.

"Come over here, Rosie," Mom said, waving a hand at me. "Taste this."

I joined them and stood between the two, grateful to be pulled back into the moment. Heather leaned her head on my shoulder and gave me a small squeeze.

"I can't appreciate the depths of flavor in sauce anymore," I told them.

"We know," Heather said.

"Have you tried since drinking the potion I gave you?" Andrew called from the dining room.

Right, the taste bud potion. I'd forgotten all about that. After I drank it, I'd kept on eating meat, and not given anything else a try.

Mom held out a fork with a meatball on it.

"Oh," I said, and gladly accepted. "Thank you."

The meat was moist and flavorful. "Is there pork in there, too?"

Heather nodded.

I gave two thumbs up, grabbed the wooden spoon and tasted the sauce, too. Garlic, tasty herbs I couldn't quite place, onion, tomato—*I could taste them all.*

"Is that carrot?" I asked.

"Yes," Heather said. "You can tell?"

"Two thumbs up to the sauce, too. I. Can. Taste. It." Then louder, I called to Andrew, *"I can taste!"*

"I'm so glad," he called back.

"That's wonderful," Mom said.

Heather agreed.

I moved to where I could see Heather's friend Carlos helping Andrew install the new dining room windows. I tried not to smile too hard and let Heather see how happy I was to see her and Carlos spending time together. I was going for chill mom, not overbearing mom vibes.

She narrowed her eyes at me and shook her head. "You can just say it. It's all over your face."

I pretended to zip my lips.

She chuckled.

I handed Mom the potion Andrew had made at my request. "It's petrification." I shot a look in Noodles's direction. "Just in case."

She rolled her eyes. "I'll be sure to keep it close, like all the other *just in case* items you've given me. But I'm sure I won't need it. Noodles is a lovely companion. She reads my stories to me. You know how hard it's been for me to read since the cataracts."

I nodded. Then it hit me, Mom had said *she*. "I thought Noodles was a boy?"

"No, she's female," Mom said. "Did you know kitsune can bring good luck? We've won the scratch offs five times already. Isn't that right, Noodles?"

"Mrrow." Noodles continued licking her leg, mostly ignoring us.

According to Lily, kitsune were both a blessing and a curse. Most infestations ended in misfortune before a family discovered the creature's true nature. Often the kitsune drove the owners from the home and claimed the property for themselves. Since people saw what they expected to see, that meant actually identifying a kitsune was almost impossible.

If a kitsune was actually caught, it brought good fortune to the family. All the books said so. Supposedly, the Library's books knew everything. We could use a little good fortune, so I tried to believe it to be true.

Turning my attention back to my daughter, I reached in

my pocket and pulled out a little lavender box. "Happy birthday, Heather."

"Oh yay, a gift. These are the boxes you're using for your store, right?"

"It's only an online shop," I said, "but yes."

"A thriving online shop," Andrew said from the other room.

I grinned. "It's going pretty well so far, but I'm still starting out. I need to build up more stock, figure out the whole marketing part."

"Carlos runs ads and social platforms as a side hustle," Heather said.

"I'd love to pick his brain," I said. "Hire him once I grow the business a bit."

"Well the box is lovely," Heather said. "And I'm sure you two would work well together."

"And all of this business talk certainly sounds like a real store," Mom said.

It was still hard to think of it that way, but she was right. "I guess it is."

I couldn't wrap my head around the fact that people were *actually paying me* for doing what I loved.

Heather opened the box and pulled out the necklace I'd made for her. The bead work was delicate and minimal and in the center was the miniature antique pocket watch I'd picked up a few weeks ago. Andrew had fixed it for me, so it worked.

"Oh my gosh, Mom. This is gorgeous," Heather said. She hugged me hard. "I love it. I love you. Thank you."

"I love you, too."

We shared a wonderful dinner, with wonderful conversation. Carlos offered me some tips to start "building my brand" as I built my business. Heather and Andrew chatted about chemistry in art. And when it was time to go, I didn't want to. But we all promised to get together more often, and I hoped we would.

When we got home, I boxed up my sales for the day, prepping each piece of jewelry to ship in the morning before breakfast with Wendy. Then I ventured back out of my office and paused by the huge window in the living room that overlooked the city. The lights of the skyline, and on the street below still stole my breath away—or the non-breathing equivalent of it. This was *our* apartment. This was *our* view. This was really my life, this perfect evening ending in the place with the perfect man.

How had I gotten so lucky?

And speaking of the perfect man, where was Andrew?

The sound of running water led me to the bathroom. In it, rose petals were scattered all over the tile. Andrew poured two glasses of red wine—a rich fruity blend that I'd recently discovered and was my absolute favorite—and offered me one.

"You're taking a romantic bath in here?" I asked.

"I thought you might like one," he told me. "We could share."

Silver threads spread through his gray eyes, a cue my body had quickly learned to respond to. Heat spread out from my core, lighting up my nerves in anticipation.

"Oh yes," I said. "I'd love to share."

I unbuttoned his shirt slowly, running my knuckles down his bare skin.

He stopped my hand on the last button, and lowered himself down on one knee.

I put my hands over my mouth. "Tell me you dropped something and you're going to pick it up. Tell me this is not what I think this is."

I'd given up on men and on happily-ever-afters, and then I'd met Andrew. Everything changed. I hadn't thought about marriage, only enjoying every moment we shared. I'd never loved a man so much. I wanted forever, and so did he. It was enough.

He pulled a ring out of his pocket and held it up to me.

A nervous giggle bubbled out of my chest. I was shaking. Was this for real?

"Rosemary Annetha DeLaCrux, will you do me the honor of becoming my wife?"

Yes, a billion times, yes.

"You want to marry me?" I asked, stunned, my heart full. "What if I'm not actually the marrying type?

His smile grew. "I want to spend the rest of my life with you, Rose. I want to give you everything, and spend my days and nights trying to be the man that you deserve. I want to bring you joy and companionship and pleasure. I want to fill your life with love."

"Wow," I said.

"If you don't want to get married, none of that changes," he said. "You are my world. And no matter what, I'll devote my life to you."

Hands still held over my mouth, tears of joy clouding my eyes, I said, "Yes."

* * *

WENDY

Rose was already seated when I arrived at Eats. She sat under a sign that read *In Memoriam,* on a wall covered in the portraits of what I assumed by context were dead people.

"This is a little morbid," I said, gesturing as I took the seat across from her.

"It's me, I guess. They always seat me here."

I shrugged. "Own it. A thousand percent."

My legs tapped on their own accord. I squeezed my fingers together under the table to give them something to do. All I could think about was the itchy spot on my shoulder. And it took all of my might not to tear the bandage off it and scratch the bejeezus out of it.

I had to tell Rose the truth about what had happened. She deserved to know.

Before I could summon the nerve, she picked up a menu, and I spotted a monster of a rock on her finger.

"You're engaged!" I squealed.

"I'm engaged!"

I grabbed her hands and we bounced in our seats together.

The need to scratch my shoulder intensified. I needed to try another salve, maybe add some lavender and aloe vera to the next batch.

"If it were any other man, I don't think I could have said yes. I mean, I figured after Scott, I was done."

"But Andrew is perfect for you," I said, because he was. I couldn't be happier for the two of them.

"I love him so hard, Wendy." She smiled so wide she practically beamed sunlight. "But we aren't supposed to be talking about me. You said you had something to tell me, and here I am hijacking our breakfast with my news."

My news. Right.

I needed to tell her that when she'd gone feral and knocked the berry syrup out of my hands a few weeks ago that she had bitten me. I'd been trying to tell her ever since. Over and over I'd tried, but I hadn't been able to get the words out.

There was supposedly no cure for a revenant bite.

I knew what that meant if it was true.

So far, I hadn't turned into a brain-hungry zombie. I refused to be a Scott.

"Wendy?" Rose looked at me with her big, doe eyes. "What did you want to tell me?"

She was so happy, I couldn't ruin it. I couldn't spoil her special news with my own dreadful reality. It could wait another day.

"Nothing," I said. "I just wanted to see you. I can't believe you're getting married!"

I *had* to find a cure, or my fate was sealed.

ABOUT THE AUTHOR

Sassy. Snarky. Supernaturally Sparkly.

Keyboard ninja, late-blooming bibliophile, proud geek, animal lover, eternal optimist, visual artist.

USA Today Bestselling Author Keira Blackwood writes exciting paranormal romance with all the snort laughs and all the feels.

www.keirablackwood.com

Printed in Dunstable, United Kingdom